NO REMORSE

Other Walker and Company Mysteries
by James D. Brewer

No Bottom
No Virtue
No Justice

NO REMORSE

A Masey Baldridge/Luke Williamson Mystery

JAMES D. BREWER

WALKER AND COMPANY
NEW YORK

First published in the United States of America in 1997 by Walker Publishing Company, Inc.

Published simultaneously in Canada by Thomas Allen & Son Canada, Limited, Markham, Ontario

Library of Congress Cataloging-in-Publication Data
Brewer, James D.
No remorse / James D. Brewer.
p.   cm.—(Masey Baldridge/Luke Williamson mystery)
ISBN 0-8027-3302-6 (hardcover)
1. River boats—Mississippi River—Fiction. 2. Mississippi River—Fiction. I. Title. II. Series: Brewer, James D. Masey Baldridge/Luke Williamson mystery.
PS3552.R418N63   1997
813′.54—dc21   97-4095
CIP
Printed in the United States of America
2 4 6 8 10 9 7 5 3 1

To Bethany and Shannon—
the joy of a father's heart,
the sparkle in his eyes,
the hope for the future.

NO REMORSE

1

Cairo, Illinois, Saturday, June 14, 1873

"THIS BOAT IS leaving in two minutes with or without Mr. Baldridge," Captain Luke Williamson called to his first mate, Jacob Lusk, who stood peering into town from atop the texas of the steamboat *Paragon*. From his vest pocket Williamson slipped a gold watch, its cover bearing an intricate etching of deer antlers, the symbol of an accomplished riverman. Opening the watch, he glanced down just as the minute hand moved closer to the twelve.

"This is getting ridiculous," he grumbled, as he scanned the steady flow of wagons and drays moving cargo about the landing. It was the third time since leaving New Orleans on Tuesday that he had threatened to leave Masey Baldridge behind, but in each instance Baldridge had come riding up just in time. But today would be different. He would just leave Baldridge's sorry ass in Cairo until the return stop. He could get his own room and board and pay to stable that worthless horse himself, Williamson figured. Again he checked his watch. One minute until five o'clock.

"Stand by that landing stage," Williamson ordered the deckhand near the bow.

You would think that a man receiving free room and board could at least make it back to the boat on time, he thought. Williamson had moved next to the deckhand and lifted his hand to order the stage raised when Jacob Lusk called down from the texas.

"Here he come, Cap'n!"

"Are you sure it's him?" Williamson asked.

"Oh, it's Mr. Baldridge, all right," Lusk said with laugh. "Whoooooo-hoooo," he yelled, removing his hat and waving it over his head.

"He's racing again, isn't he?" Williamson said.

"Yes sir, he sho' is," Lusk called out, "and I'd say he was leading by near 'bout two lengths."

The deckhand standing ready at the landing stage looked puzzled. "The stage, Cap'n? You want me to bring her up?" Williamson closed his watch and put it away, then jogged up the stairs to the boiler deck for a better view. "Cap'n?" the deckhand repeated. "The stage?"

"Oh, hell. Just leave it down," Williamson said, catching sight of a dust trail billowing up from right to left and bearing down on the landing. Teamsters frantically maneuvered their cargo wagons out of the street and pedestrians sought refuge on the wooden sidewalks that lined the storefronts as Baldridge came galloping toward the *Paragon* mounted on Nashville Harry, a onetime racehorse that Williamson had sold him in a moment of weakness for five dollars. A second horse in pursuit was falling behind.

When Baldridge passed a mercantile near the wharf, he reined up in a billowing cloud of dust and a barrage of profanity from nearby teamsters, who struggled to calm their nervous horses.

"He done whupped him another one," Lusk observed from

the railing above. "That's some fine horse Mr. Baldridge got there, Cap'n. Some fine horse."

Williamson struggled to contain his anger as he watched Baldridge. Not once in more than a dozen races the past spring at the Chickasaw Jockey Club in Memphis had that nag finished in the money. The dust settled enough for Williamson to see Baldridge's opponent ride up to him and hand him something. Then Baldridge turned and rode full speed for the *Paragon*. Slowing just enough to negotiate the landing stage, Baldridge trotted aboard and reined up near the capstan.

"Am I late?" Baldridge asked the deckhand, but Williamson answered him from the boiler deck.

"Goddamned right, you're late!"

Baldridge dismounted and handed his reins to a deckhand. "See to Harry for me, will you?"

"Yes, sir, Mr. Baldridge."

Baldridge lifted a small bag in the air and shook it at Williamson. "Had another one eatin' dust, Luke." He removed his hat, wiped his brow with his sleeve, and called to the deckhand leading Nashville Harry toward the stern. "Could you have someone bring me a drink? Whiskey."

"Yes, sir," the deckhand said.

Baldridge started up the stairs, his characteristic limp creating a familiar, rhythmic clomp.

As he emerged onto the boiler deck, Williamson stood, arms folded, jaw set, glaring at him.

"Man, it's hot today."

"Just what do you think you were doing down there?" Williamson asked.

"Racin'." Baldridge shook his bag of coins in front of the captain.

"Do you know what time it is?"

Baldridge looked puzzled. "No. Somewhere around five, I reckon."

"Somewhere around five."

"Yeah, I reckon."

"It's after five, Masey," Williamson said, gritting his teeth. "Did it ever occur to you that I've got a schedule to keep?"

"I'm sorry, Luke, I just—"

"I realize that you don't work on this boat. I realize that you don't work at all. But the rest of us do. And in the steamboat business, that means leaving on time."

"I was just havin' me a little race."

"The *Paragon* leaves at five o'clock. This is not the first time I've had to hold the boat while you took your own sweet time ashore."

"But I won," Baldridge said, leaning toward Williamson and again shaking the bag, his breath betraying his other afternoon's activity.

"You've been drinking, haven't you?"

"So?" Baldridge put his hands on his hips. "I ain't drunk." He again shook the bag in front of Williamson, his eyes dancing from the heat and the alcohol. "I won, didn't I?"

"I don't care if you won or not, I expect you to—"

"You don't care? You don't care? The hell you don't care!" He poked Williamson's chest. "I know what's wrong with you." He leaned back as if to bring Williamson into focus. "You're jealous."

"What?"

"You're jealous."

"That's ridiculous."

"No, it ain't. That's what's wrong with you," Baldridge declared. "You're just mad that I won on ol' Harry, and you never did."

"That has nothing to do with this boat leaving on time."

Baldridge began to laugh. "That's it. You're jealous, all right." He leaned foward and winked. "If you want to buy him back, Captain, I'll make you a real good deal." Williamson offered no reply as Baldridge continued to chuckle, bouncing the bag in his hand and listening to the coins clink. "I'd like to stay and talk, Luke, but I've got to get cleaned up for dinner. But I will gladly buy you a drink tonight."

"Just use some of that money to settle your own tab."

Baldridge walked down the deck toward his cabin, waving his hand in acknowledgment but not looking back.

Williamson watched him clomp down the deck and wondered how in the world this arrangement was ever going to work out, much less make any money. Just over a month ago he, Baldridge, and Salina Tyner had set up Big River Detective Agency, and thus far it had brought in a grand total of five dollars. That came when Baldridge got a missing persons case and managed to locate a Memphis store clerk's wife in half a day, catching her taking horizontal communion with a local minister. The whole sordid affair made the *Memphis Appeal*, but no new business resulted, and the net gain was one day's per diem and a general sense among people in Memphis that Baldridge had cruelly brought down a man of God. Thus far, all Williamson had to show for his time and effort in support of Big River Detective Agency was Baldridge's growing bar tab and the cost of free room and board for him on the *Paragon* and for Tyner aboard his other boat, the *Edward Smythe*. And there were the forage costs of that insatiable horse. . . . Something had to change, and Williamson determined to have a talk with Baldridge after dinner that night.

ABOUT 8:30 P.M., having completed his rounds, Williamson entered the grand hall through the stern door and took a seat at the captain's table. From the tripod of knife, fork, and spoon—stood on end and leaning together like a tepee in the classic steamboat table setting—the captain retrieved his spoon. Before he could place his napkin in his lap, one of the dining room stewards arrived with a cup of coffee, the menu, and a folded copy of the Cairo newspaper. Williamson thanked him and examined the menu.

"I'll have the saddle of venison, Mr. Griffin," he said, "and ask Anabel if she's got any black olives."

"Yes, sir, Cap'n," Steward Griffin replied. "Mashed potatoes as usual?"

Williamson nodded and handed him the menu. "And a piece of that lemon pie."

"Have it for you right away, sir."

"Uh, Griffin?"

"Yes, sir?"

"Have you seen Mr. Baldridge tonight?"

Griffin stood on his toes, leaning back and forth as he tried to see past the diners at the far end of the room, over one hundred feet away.

"I believe I see Mr. Baldridge up at the front table, Cap'n. Looks like he's into a pretty heavy five-man game."

Williamson unfolded the newspaper. "How about stepping down there and telling him I'd like to see him?"

"Yes, sir. I'll do that right away."

The smell of the dining room was enough to make anyone hungry, as Anabel McBree, his chief cook since beginning his packet business, offered her usual impeccable fare. The menu selections rivaled those of any first-class hotel in the country, and the *Paragon*'s reputation as a riverboat of elegance had spread to every port along the Mississippi River. Rich oriental carpet ran the length of the grand hall, and the walls on both sides revealed intricate wood- and ironwork. Four chandeliers, placed an equal distance apart, gave the room a warm glow, and a four-man string band played a soothing waltz. No one was dancing as yet, but it was still early, and rare was the night that the grand hall was not alive with music, dancing, and games until two or three o'clock in the morning.

Griffin arrived with a glass of red wine and placed it on the captain's table.

"I didn't order any wine."

The steward gestured toward a table some twenty feet away. "Compliments of the gentleman and the lady."

Williamson saw a nod of acknowledgment from a planter he had met when he came aboard at Vicksburg. The man's wife smiled. He waved back, then lifted the glass and took a sip. It was all part of the game. Show them a good time. Let them feel important. Keep them coming back. His late partner, Ed Smythe, killed in a steamboat wreck nine months earlier, had been so much better at humoring the passengers. But he was learning. He had to. No one else was around to handle it. Now, with the acquisition of a second boat, named after his late partner, he found himself bouncing back and forth between the two vessels, never feeling he was doing justice to either. And this detective business was not likely to help the situation. What was he thinking when he agreed to such a thing? He had made it clear to Baldridge and Tyner that his packet line came first. And while he was disappointed that no significant cases had come along, he was also relieved, for that meant one less draw upon his time. Still, he needed to get some things straight with Baldridge.

His dinner arrived, and he ate several bites before unfolding the June 13 edition of the Cairo newspaper. He turned immediately to the river news and read the water stage reported in St. Louis, then checked the listings for Keokuk and Davenport, Iowa, to anticipate changes. He consulted the weather report, read the latest gossip along the Cairo landing, then moved back to the front page of the paper. In the lower right corner he saw a headline that drew his attention: HUDSON VAN GEER—VICTIM OF A REPREHENSIBLE MURDER. Hudson Van Geer, president of the largest packet company in St. Louis, was one of Williamson's chief competitors. When Ed Smythe was killed in the wreck of their other boat, the *Mary Justice*, Williamson had been convinced that Van Geer and his ace pilot, Creed Haskins, were involved in the tragedy. He had confronted Van Geer and threatened him, only to discover that Van Geer had nothing to do with the wreck.

Stunned by the headline, Williamson read on.

> Hudson Van Geer, well-known gentleman of talent and position, was yesterday killed by his own son, Stewart Van Geer. The events surrounding the murder of this champion of river shipping are so appalling, so horrible, as to defy belief. Killed by his own son, by the young man to whom he gave the breath of life! Hudson Van Geer's blood had not yet pooled when his son walked up calmly to the police station and handed over his revolver, declaring, "I have killed my father. I wish to surrender myself to the law."

Williamson laid his fork on the edge of his plate, folded the paper in half, and read the remainder of the story. The coroner, upon arriving at the Van Geer home, had found Hudson Van Geer lying facedown in the parlor. His investigation concluded that the shipping tycoon had sustained four gunshot wounds, two to the chest, one to the arm shattering the bone, and another to the head—the latter being determined the proximate cause of death. Upon finishing the article Williamson resumed his meal, his mind wandering back to the details of the story. What would become of Van Geer Shipping Lines? Who would take Hudson Van Geer's position on the regulatory board that oversees operators from the St. Louis wharf? For all his faults, and he had plenty, Hudson Van Geer had been a tough business competitor. Williamson caught himself wondering if he might be able to get a piece of Van Geer's market, then felt bad about even entertaining such a thought at a time like this. Killed by his own son. What kind of man would gun down his own father?

"This better be important," Masey Baldridge said, pulling out a chair and plopping down next to Williamson. "I just lost on a full house, kings over nines, to a fella with aces over fives, and I'd really like to get back there and win my money back."

Williamson looked up from his paper, his mind still turning over the incidents of the Van Geer murder. "What?"

"What do you mean, what? Didn't you tell the steward you wanted to see me?"

"Oh, yeah," Williamson said, his thoughts returning to Baldridge.

Baldridge lifted the captain's wineglass. "What the hell you drinkin' here, anyway?" He took a sip. "Couldn't be this weak squeeze that's got you clouded up."

"No. I was just reading about a murder up in St. Louis."

"Murder? Did someone say murder?"

Williamson handed him the paper. "Hudson Van Geer. You remember, he runs the biggest packet line in—"

"Yeah. I heard something about that in the saloon back in Cairo. Something about his son shooting him."

"That's right."

Baldridge glanced over the story. "Damn. His own flesh and blood." He tossed the paper onto the table. "Can't hardly trust no one, can you? What was it you wanted to see me about?"

"I want to talk about the business, Masey."

With his right foot, Baldridge slid a chair from beneath the table and braced his left leg in it.

"Hell, Luke, I can't hardly give you no advice on the shippin' business."

"I'm talking about the detective business. We *are* supposed to be in the detective business, aren't we?"

"Damn straight." Baldridge grinned. "Found that cheatin' woman in less than six hours, didn't I?"

"Yes, you did."

"You should've seen that preacher's face when I caught 'em. Why, I bet he wished Jesus would come and get him right then and there."

"And that was good, Masey, but it only made five dollars. That's all the business we've had."

"So?"

"It's been over a month since we started."

"Takes time, Luke. You should know that. Sally and I took out advertisements in every major paper along the river, the *St. Louis Democrat*, the *New Orleans Picayune*, the *Memphis Appeal*."

"I know. I paid the bills."

"Something will come along. You'll see. Why, Sally Tyner's probably drumming up more business than we can handle down in Vicksburg."

"Yeah, but what kind of business?"

"She ain't whorin' no more, Luke."

"Maybe not. But that doesn't mean she'll find us detective business."

"Sally can be pretty damn convincing," Baldridge said with a smile. "You know Sally."

"Yeah, I know Sally. And I know you, too. And I know that I keep getting bills and more bills, and I'm not seeing anyone hiring you or Sally."

"You worry too much about money, Luke."

"Somebody has to. You're living high on the hog around here, and—"

"I'll pay my own way," Baldridge said, pulling his bad leg from the chair and rising awkwardly to his feet. He reached in his pocket and slapped a handful of gold coins on the table. "I've got my racin' money."

"Horse racing? Come on, Masey. How long do you think you can keep that up?"

"Until somebody figures out that Nashville Harry used to be a racehorse, that's how long. And I figure that's gonna take a while. Long as I don't race him in Memphis, I'll be all right. You see, what I do is, I get to talkin' to a fella in a saloon, and I lead the conversation around to horses, then to racing, and I can almost always find some fool that thinks the nag he's ridin' can beat my horse. Get him to drinkin', and he'll bet cash money on it. Hell, Luke, it's the easiest money I ever made. And I've got you to thank for it." He pointed his finger at Williamson. "You should have never given up on ol' Harry. He's a hell of a ride. Now, if you don't have anything else to talk about, I'm going back to my poker game."

Without waiting for Williamson's answer, Baldridge limped down the grand hall, stopping a steward and arranging the delivery of what was no doubt yet another bottle of whiskey. The captain's eyes fell upon the headline again, but instead of focusing on the horror of Hudson Van Geer's murder, his mind went to the possibility of buying, or perhaps leasing, one or two of his boats. The thought made him feel like a vulture, scarcely waiting for the corpse to chill. He picked up his fork and went to work on the lemon pie Steward Griffin had brought.

ON SUNDAY MORNING the *Paragon* had been docked at Captain Luke Williamson's St. Louis wharfboat for less than an hour when, at a quarter past nine, the captain heard a knock on his cabin door. His eyes did not wander from the profit-loss ledger that his clerk, Steven Tibedeau, had placed before him.

"Are you *sure* this is right?" Williamson asked.

"Yes, Captain. I checked it over twice myself," Tibedeau replied. "After payroll, fuel, and costs for accommodations, including the dining room, we cleared $1,500."

Again someone knocked at the door.

"Just a minute," Williamson shouted. He looked at Tibedeau intensely. "We're working our asses off, Steven. We ought to be doing better than this."

"We're running two boats now, Captain. Price of cordwood is going up. Expenses are bound to go up."

"Yes, but we ought to be taking in more for the freight we're hauling."

Tibedeau, a small-framed man, nervously tapped his fingers together. "Freight shipments are down, Captain. This dry weather has slowed the planters that usually move vegetables this time of year." He leaned over and pointed to the ledger. "But passenger income is about the same, maybe a little better."

"If you ask me," Williamson said, again eyeing the ledger, "it's the damn railroad. It's hurting all the packet lines. Everywhere you look someone's building a new rail line." He turned to face Tibedeau. "But they sure as hell aren't building any new rivers."

Again a knock at the door.

"Answer that, please."

Tibedeau pulled the tiny curtain aside from the window in the door.

"Message for the captain," one of the stewards called out.

Tibedeau opened the door, took an envelope, and passed it to Williamson.

"Captain, I wouldn't worry too much. I think business will pick up in the fall."

Williamson closed the ledger with his free hand and gave it back to Tibedeau. "It's a long time until fall." Examining the pale green envelope, he found his name, penned in ornate calligraphy, covering almost the full width of the front. He ran his fingers over the letters "HV" embossed on the upper right corner. Williamson opened the envelope to find a note on matching paper, folded in half, as well as a printed card. He read the card first.

The Van Geer family regretfully announces the funeral of longtime St. Louis resident Mr. Hudson Van Geer at Dean's Chapel on the corner of 9th Street and St. Charles, Sunday, June 15. The funeral procession will move to St. Vincent Cemetery, where Mr. Van Geer will be laid to rest. Visitation with the family will be from 1:00 until 3:00 P.M. at the chapel.

Tibedeau, who was inching closer and trying to catch a peek at the contents of the envelope, stood erect and glanced quickly toward the door as Williamson looked up.

"As much business as we've lost to that son of a bitch, I'm not about to go to his funeral," Williamson said, handing Tibedeau the card. "Here. You can post it on the board in the grand hall just in case anyone gives a damn."

Tibedeau read the card. "I heard about this. They say his son killed him."

"Probably hated the son of a bitch as much as the rest of us."

"Will there be anything else, Captain?"

"No. But I want you to find us more business down on the wharf between now and when we leave on Tuesday. Any sodbuster that even *looks* like he hasn't made up his mind on who's going to handle his shipment, I want you face-to-face with him. I want his business. Is that clear?"

"Yes, sir."

After Tibedeau left, Williamson placed the envelope on his writing table and opened the folded note.

Captain Williamson:

By now you most certainly have heard about the untimely death of my dear husband, Hudson Van Geer. You will, no doubt, be surprised that I am writ-

ing to you, knowing the stormy nature of your association with Hudson. Quite simply, Captain Williamson, I have nowhere else to turn amid this horrible
family crisis with my son, Stewart. I wish to retain the
services of your Big River Detective Agency in the
matter of my beloved son's arrest. Please, upon your
arrival in the city, come to see me at Dean's Chapel
during the announced visitation period. With every
hope that I may talk privately with you, I am, in your
debt,

— Helen Van Geer

Williamson had reread the letter twice before he realized it,
studying each sentence and trying to make sense of it all. Hudson Van Geer had built his shipping line on wartime contracts,
hauling troops and supplies for the U.S. government at premium
rates. Some had even suspected Van Geer of handling cargo for
the Confederacy whenever he could get away with it, though
nothing was ever proven. While Williamson was in the uniform
of the U.S. Navy, risking his life to protect Van Geer's boats
along the Mississippi, Van Geer was enlarging his fleet and
expanding his operation. By the end of the war he had the steamboat industry by the throat. Williamson's reward for protecting
the property of men like Van Geer was to have Van Geer do
everything possible to run him out of business when he and
Smythe started their own packet service in 1866. Men working
for Hudson Van Geer had stolen freight and hired away some of
Williamson's best crewmen; Van Geer pilots had even attempted to run him aground on more than one occasion. It was
little wonder that when Ed's boat went down near Natchez, Van
Geer would be Williamson's most likely suspect, and though he
was proven wrong, Williamson had never brought himself to
apologize. But despite Van Geer's pressure, and the loss of Edward and the *Mary Justice*, Williamson had persevered. And

over the past two years he had even managed to win over some of Van Geer Shipping Lines' most loyal customers. As he studied the message, he wondered what Helen Van Geer could possibly expect Big River to do about her murdering son.

The apple don't fall far from the tree, he thought.

He wadded the note and started to toss it in the trash, reconsidering at the last moment. Suppose he went to see her? On behalf of Big River, of course. How could it hurt? He could take Masey Baldridge with him—at least get him out of the ship's bar for a while—and he might even learn something about Van Geer's operation that he could use. It might not be bad business to pay his respects and at least talk with whoever was going to run Van Geer Shipping Lines now. Might head off trouble later. Williamson unfolded the note and placed it on the writing desk.

Damn shame about Van Geer. Damn shame it couldn't have happened sooner.

2

"HAVE I GOT a what?" Masey Baldridge asked, leaning against his cabin door and running his fingers through his hair as he struggled to wake up.

"A suit. A suit of clothes," Luke Williamson asked.

Baldridge scratched his head. "No, not exactly."

"What do you mean, 'not exactly'? Either you have or you haven't."

"I got me a pretty nice shirt," Baldridge said, pointing to a Saratoga trunk in the corner.

"A pretty nice shirt? That's not a suit."

"Well, I never said it was." Baldridge motioned the captain inside. "What's this all about? And shut that door behind you. The daylight is giving me a headache."

"We're going to a funeral."

A puzzled Baldridge rubbed his swollen eyes. "Who died?"

"Hudson Van Geer."

"Why go to his funeral? I thought you—"

"Business," Williamson said, handing over the note.

Baldridge limped to his bedside table, removed the cork

from a bottle, and poured a drink, his disappointment transparent as he managed to fill only about a half-inch in his shot glass before emptying the bottle. He shook it to retrieve the last drop, placed the bottle on the table, tossed down the drink, and read the note.

"She wants to hire us?"

"Looks like it, though I can't quite understand why. Stewart Van Geer confessed to the police. What could she possibly—"

"What the hell difference does it make?" Baldridge said. "I mean, after all, if she's paying good money—"

"That's what I figured. It wouldn't hurt to talk to her. We don't have to take the job."

A grin slowly emerged on Baldridge's face. He shook his head slowly. "No. No, that's not it."

"What do you mean?"

"You're not going just to talk to her. You hate these people. You told me so." Baldridge chuckled. "You're a cold man, Luke Williamson."

"Now listen—"

"No, I mean it. You're one cold bastard." He stared at Williamson. "It never takes long for the vultures to gather."

"What's that supposed to mean?"

"You're after his business, aren't you?"

"Look, the woman asked—"

"Hey, I don't give a shit. Ain't no skin off my back." He winked at Williamson. "But I'm right, ain't I?"

"Look, Masey, we'll go to the chapel and see what she wants. There's probably not a day's worth of work in the whole thing. I just thought—"

"Hold on, there." Baldridge lifted his hands. "I ain't arguing with you. I ain't got nothing else to do this afternoon. Hell, I might as well watch 'em drop somebody."

"And you call *me* cold?" Williamson opened the door. "I want to leave at twelve-thirty . . . *sharp*."

"Yeah, yeah. Twelve-thirty. But I've got to shave and get something to eat." Williamson started out the door. "And I ain't got no suit of clothes."

"Just put on something clean and meet me on the bow at twelve-thirty," Williamson said, closing the door behind him.

ME AND THE captain's gonna have us a talk, Baldridge mused.

Big River Detective Agency was supposed to be a partnership, the way he figured it, and the high-'n'-mighty Captain Luke Williamson was giving entirely too many orders. *Typical Yankee. Always has to try and run things.* He wished Sally Tyner were there. She was pushy, sure, and she got on his nerves, but she didn't strut around and give orders like Williamson did. He picked up the bottle again, remembered it was empty, and returned it rudely to the table. *I ain't takin' no goddamned orders. Twelve-thirty, my ass. I'll be there when I get good and ready.*

Baldridge was good and ready at twelve-thirty, but he took charge of Nashville Harry and hid near the stern until twelve-forty just for spite.

"You're late again," Williamson said, standing by his horse.

"Are we going or not?" Baldridge said, bypassing Williamson and leading his mount across the landing stage. "Don't make me wait for you all day."

TWO BLOCKS FROM Dean's Chapel on Olive Street a young boy had strung some rope between two sycamore trees and was making fast money by keeping an eye on the horses and carriages belonging to the mourners of the late Hudson Van Geer. Baldridge fumbled in his pocket for a coin just long enough for Williamson to pay the boy, and the two of them walked toward the chapel. The humid air teased with promise of a much-needed rain, as it had the day before, and the day before that, and the sun directly overhead cast a miserly shadow at their feet. Baldridge glanced at Williamson, walking tall and looking dignified in his freshly laundered dress uniform. The sleeves on his double-breasted, navy blue jacket were trimmed in maritime braid, and he wore his hat pulled low on his forehead, his mustache and sideburns neatly trimmed. Limping alongside the dignified captain, Baldridge felt self-conscious. His boots were worn and scratched where Williamson's sported a fresh polish, no doubt the additional duty of some steward. It's easy to look sharp, Baldridge reasoned, when you have folks cleaning your clothes and shining your shoes. Still, he felt awkward. His pants showed some hard wear, his hat was old and dusty, and his vest was missing the second button from the top. At least he had a clean shirt. Before the war he would have never let himself look so frayed. A successful farrier with a loving wife and a modest home east of Memphis, he was every bit as much a gentleman as Williamson. But the fever had taken his wife, the war had taken his home and business, a Yankee sharpshooter had taken his knee, and whiskey had taken the rest. For almost seven years after the war he had drifted from job to job. Then, while he was working for the Mid-South Insurance Company, he had saved the *Paragon* from destruction and earned Williamson's appreciation. Baldridge liked Luke Williamson in spite of his occasional gruff manner—liked him enough to form Big River Detective Agency—but he particularly liked the lifestyle of traveling on Williamson's boats and living like a man of means. He knew Williamson was right about finding work for the agency, though. The good captain was not about to subsidize the business indefinitely, and without money coming in, they'd be tits-up in a month, maybe less. Perhaps today was the day.

As they crossed the street, Williamson's shiny boots gathered a light layer of dust that made Baldridge feel somewhat better about his own. He envied Williamson's steady gait, for even on good days, when the pain was mild, the liquor kept it at bay, and Baldridge tried to steady his walk, he still moved like a cripple. It didn't help much when a half-dozen other mourners who passed them spoke only to Williamson.

"Good afternoon, Captain Williamson," a middle-aged woman said, her husband stopping to shake his hand at the foot of the steps into the chapel.

"Captain," the husband said. "Ervin Taylor."

"Mr. Taylor," Williamson responded.

"Shame about Hudson Van Geer," Taylor said. "Damn shame."

"Henry," his wife scolded, "it's Sunday."

"Well, it *is* a shame, Miranda."

"Is it crowded inside?" Williamson asked, as Taylor's wife eyed Baldridge curiously.

"Fifteen or twenty people. But it's early yet in the visitation. Good to see you, Captain."

"You, too."

The Taylors departed, and as Williamson and Baldridge climbed the steps, Baldridge spoke.

"How come you didn't introduce me?"

"I didn't know who the hell he was."

"He said his name was Taylor."

Williamson stepped in the open chapel door and removed his hat, a gesture that Baldridge quickly echoed.

"Masey, I see all kinds of people. He probably traveled with us sometime. I don't know the man from Adam."

An attendant handed the two men a page with some song lyrics printed on it and a paper fan bearing an image of Jesus on one side and "Dean's Chapel" on the other. Walking down the center aisle, they joined a line of a half-dozen people slowly filing past the casket. The family was seated on the left, perpendicular to the pews and just beyond the head of the casket. A woman in the last chair was gently sobbing as she spoke to one of the gentleman visitors, who placed his arm around her and patted her gently on the back before moving along. Baldridge figured her for Helen Van Geer. Seated beside her was a younger woman, visibly pregnant, and a man in perhaps his thirties.

Williamson filed past the casket first, stopping momentarily to view the late Hudson Van Geer, then offering condolences to the family members. Baldridge stepped up to the coffin and looked inside. Van Geer was dressed in an expensive black suit, a wine-colored cravat tied neatly below his pale chin, which sagged awkwardly against his chest. He was nearly bald in front, and the remaining hair on the sides of his head was neatly combed and dressed lightly with oil. His hands, one bearing a gemstone ring, were folded over his chest. Baldridge lingered longer than he realized, for the woman who had taken a place in the viewing line behind him cleared her throat loudly. He glanced back to find her arms folded, her expression a mixture of frustration and wonderment.

"If you please?" she said.

"Excuse me, ma'am," Baldridge said, standing erect and moving along to the first family member in the receiving line. He noticed that the young man was looking at him disapprovingly, but he extended his hand nevertheless.

"And you, sir, are—"

"Masey Baldridge."

"I'm Robert Van Geer. How is it that you knew my father?"

"I've traveled on Mr. Van Geer's boats."

"Is that right?" The man continued to eye him curiously even as he turned to take the hand of the pregnant woman. She introduced herself as Claire Van Geer, Hudson's daughter-in-law and Stewart Van Geer's wife, and then Baldridge greeted the older woman. Her hand trembled mildly, the black lace mitt she wore unable to disguise the chill in her palm.

"I understand," she said softly, "that you are here with Captain Williamson."

"That's right. My name is Baldridge. I'm his associate."

"I'm Helen Van Geer. I've asked the captain to wait in the anteroom where I might speak with him. Will you be joining us?"

"Yeah, I'll be there."

"I see." She examined his apparel with transparent disapproval, then turned, said something to her daughter-in-law, and moved into the anteroom, Baldridge following her. She turned and stared at him.

"The door, Mr. Baldridge. Would you please close it?"

Baldridge complied, leaning against the door to prevent interruption as Helen Van Geer spoke to Williamson.

"Captain, I very much appreciate you responding to my note. I realize that your relationship with my husband was . . . well, I know that the two of you—"

"It's all right, Mrs. Van Geer. Regardless of my personal feelings about him, what happened to your husband is a tragedy."

"It is indeed, Captain. It's a double tragedy, given what they are trying to do to my son, Stewart."

"I understand he confessed to killing Mr. Van Geer."

"My Stewart would never harm his father, Captain Williamson."

Baldridge straightened. "The newspaper said—"

"The newspapers are full of lies," she said firmly, her eyes darting to Baldridge.

"But Masey's right, isn't he?" Williamson said. "Your son did confess to the killing."

"So the police tell me. But something is terribly wrong, Captain. And that is why I need you"—she eyed Baldridge again, reluctantly acknowledging him—"and your associate."

"Why me? Your husband never had a—"

"My husband is hardly in a position to make decisions anymore," she said, her gaze returning to Williamson. "But if he could, he would have come to you."

Baldridge noted the surprise on the captain's face.

"Your husband hated me. He tried everything he could think of to run me out of business. He was—"

"That's true, Captain. But in his own way, he respected you. Hudson respected you as a man of action, and right now that is precisely what I need."

"What exactly do you want me to do?"

"When this horror began three days ago, I knew immediately I must find someone to help me. I learned of your Big River Detective Agency several weeks ago, actually, through something Hudson said."

"What was that?"

"It's not important."

"It's important to me."

"Well, Captain, if you must know, my late husband said you had lost your mind. He read about you forming your detective agency and, well, frankly, he said that such a ridiculous endeavor was doomed to failure."

"That's what I call respect," Baldridge said.

Helen Van Geer frowned. "Mr. Baldridge, the captain is a riverman. And given your dress and demeanor, I am relatively confident that *you* are not. Now, maybe my husband and Captain Williamson did not get along. Who could expect them to? They were competitors. But I know I can trust a riverman. And frankly, I don't know anyone else I can trust right now."

"What do you expect us to do?" Williamson said.

"I want you to find out who killed my husband."

"That shouldn't take long," Baldridge said. "They got him locked up in the jail down the street."

"Stewart did not kill his father. He is innocent. I will admit that Stewart has been acting strangely for some time. I've tried to get him to see a doctor, but he has refused. I have said all along he is ill. But a mother knows her own son, Mr. Baldridge, and Stewart is no killer. So . . . I want to hire your detective agency to prove it." From a small black bag attached to the waist of her mourning dress, Helen Van Geer produced an envelope identical to the one she had sent Williamson. She held it out to the captain. "Here is two hundred dollars to get you started," she said.

Williamson would not take the envelope. "Mrs. Van Geer—"

"There's plenty more where that came from," she added, waving it in front of him. "Money is not the issue. My son's life is at stake, and I'll not sit by helplessly and see him hanged."

When Williamson hesitated again, Baldridge stepped forward and grabbed the envelope from Mrs. Van Geer.

"We'll look into it, ma'am," Baldridge said, slipping the envelope into his pocket. She looked at Williamson for some kind of affirmation. The captain nodded slowly.

"All right. But I wouldn't get my hopes up."

"Hope is all I have, Captain. Don't take that away from me too."

Helen Van Geer left the room without saying another word and returned to her seat near her husband's casket. Baldridge and Williamson stood in silence for a few moments.

"He's guilty as hell, you know," Williamson said. "Probably just as worthless a son of a bitch as his father."

"Probably," Baldridge said with a nod.

"So why did you take the money?"

"We need the work."

"*You* need the work. I've got a packet line to run."

"Oh, so now you're no longer a partner?"

"I didn't say that. I just don't know what you expect to do for this woman."

"We'll ask a few questions. Talk to the son. Talk to the law. Hell, that will take two or three days," Baldridge said.

"And then what?"

"Then we'll politely tell Mrs. Van Geer that her son is guilty as sin, return maybe fifty dollars of her money for good faith, keep the rest, and go find a real case."

"I suppose it wouldn't hurt," Williamson said. "But we sail for New Orleans Tuesday night at five o'clock—"

"Sharp," Baldridge said simultaneously with Williamson.

"If you're going on the *Paragon* with me, you'd better have this wrapped up," Williamson said, opening the door to the chapel.

Inside, he took a seat for the service, but Baldridge begged off and went outside and walked to the rear of the chapel, where he retrieved his silver whiskey flask from his pocket. Baldridge hated funerals; the day he buried his wife, he had sworn that the next funeral he sat through would be his own.

In less than a half hour the back door of the chapel opened as the service concluded, and Baldridge watched the pallbearers convey Hudson Van Geer's casket out the door and into the hearse. He slipped his flask back into his pocket as Williamson found him, and they walked down Olive Street toward their horses. The two men were within a few feet of their mounts when the hearse, having moved almost fifty yards up the street, came to a sudden halt, causing the several carriages following to rein up suddenly. Baldridge, hearing a commotion, moved to the edge of the street, where he saw someone draw back the black curtain and leap from the rear of the hearse. While one of the undertaker's men held the horses in check, the other jumped down from the driver's seat and began pursuing a young boy headed directly for Baldridge. The man gave up his chase after only a few steps and returned to the hearse, cursing the boy, who had veered between two buildings. Climbing into the rear, he emerged a few moments later, jumped down to the dusty street, and walked back to the driver's seat. Before he mounted, he tossed something into the grass beside the road, then his partner whistled to the team and snapped the reins to start the hearse moving slowly forward again.

Baldridge thought it an odd series of events, and after he and Williamson had mounted and joined the funeral procession, he diverted Nashville Harry to the shoulder of the road and peered into the grass near where the undertaker had remounted the hearse.

"What are you looking for?" Williamson asked.

"I don't rightly know, but I saw that undertaker throw something away."

Leaning to the side in his saddle, Baldridge searched the ground.

"What is it?" Williamson asked, riding over beside him.

In a bare spot, amid a damp clump of dirt, was a light brown eggshell and smears of yolk splattered against the grass.

BENEATH THE WELCOME shade of a broad cedar tree near the center of St. Vincent Cemetery, a dozen white-uniformed crewmen from selected Van Geer packets stood shoulder to shoulder, their white-gloved hands folded before them, along one side of a freshly dug grave, singing in rich harmony. A Methodist minister spent less than a minute extolling the virtues of Hudson Van Geer and committing his body to the ground. The family each tossed a handful of dirt onto the casket as it lay in the grave, with Helen Van Geer, struggling through tears, tossing a second handful. Baldridge thought he heard her whisper, "for Stewart."

The service over, most of the family members and friends began making their way to their carriages, but several mourners remained at the cemetery, talking in groups of three or four. Several feet from Williamson, Baldridge stood observing the departing crowd and listened in on the conversation as Luke spoke with a couple of captains operating riverboats in two other shipping lines.

"I'm a little surprised to see you here, Luke," said Brent Pegram, captain of the *James Howard*, of the St. Louis–based Kountz Line.

"Just paying my respects," Williamson said.

"Weren't no secret how you felt about Hudson Van Geer."

"Then I guess I'm not paying top dollar, am I?"

"I keep wondering what will happen with Van Geer's line," said Captain Jude T. West of the *City of Quincy*, primary boat in the St. Louis and New Orleans Packet Company. "Who do you think's gonna run the show, Luke? Sure as hell won't be his son Stewart."

"Jude's right," Pegram said. "They'll hang him for sure."

"Won't be his son Robert either," West said.

"Why is that?" Williamson asked.

"I heard he's gone to work for some railroader," West said, lending a scandalous tone to the word.

"Railroad?" Williamson said.

"That's what I heard."

Williamson shook his head. "I don't know. But if it comes down to it, and they start selling off boats," he said, his eyes fixing first on Pegram, then on West, "you can tell Mr. Kountz, and you can tell your partners, that Luke Williamson will be in the bidding."

"Damn, Luke. Won't you let 'em bury the body before you start carving up the man's business?" Pegram said.

"Hudson Van Geer spent the last six years chopping on *my* business," Williamson said. "That son of a bitch can—"

"Luke," Pegram said, nudging Williamson on the shoulder, "hold it down." Williamson had not noticed Helen Van Geer, her daughter-in-law, and another woman passing nearby as they moved toward their carriage, but now he stood quietly as the group made their way past. Baldridge saw Helen Van Geer glance at Williamson, her eyes almost beseeching him, before continuing to the carriage. The men with Williamson were silent until she had made her way inside and the driver was underway.

Pegram revisited the conversation first. "Well, all this just means that we'll go after each other's business with one less player."

"That's the problem," Williamson said.

"How's that?" Pegram said.

"We're going after each other's business, all right. And I understand why. God knows, with this drought there's a limited amount of crops and goods to transport. But that's exactly what's wrong. We're going after each other, when the real enemy doesn't even operate on the river."

"You talking about the railroads?" West asked.

"Damn straight. Gentlemen, don't you see what's happening? We're hauling less freight than we did a year ago, not because one of us is undercutting the other but because the farmers and planters are starting to use the railroads more."

"Luke, the railroads ain't never gonna match a good steamboat for tonnage," Pegram said. "It'll never happen."

"It's already happening," Williamson countered. "And if we don't band together, set some rates, organize ourselves against the competition of the locomotive, we're going to find ourselves running weekday passenger excursions up and down the waterfront instead of hauling freight and passengers to New Orleans."

"There's not enough track, Luke," West observed. "Why, there's not even a rail line running to most parts of the country."

"But they're building more every day," Williamson said. "It's just a matter of time." He turned to Pegram. "Jude, you run the Ohio sometimes. What's the river distance from here to Cincinnati?"

"Oh, about seven hundred miles, depending upon the water stages and the cutoffs, and—"

"It's three hundred and forty miles by rail."

"How do you know that?" West asked.

"Because I've been checking. Now, if you're a farmer with perishable goods, are you going to ship those goods by boat, which takes a little under three days, or by railroad, which takes maybe thirty or forty hours?"

"But they can't match us in tonnage," Pegram said.

"Not yet. Not today," Williamson countered. "But what about five, ten years from now?"

"So, what are you saying we do about this?" West asked. "All go out and buy a railroad?"

"Well, for starters, we can stop tearing each other apart. We can quit undercutting each other's business. Quit trying to steal customers. Van Geer was the worst about doing that. You men know it as well as I do. You talk about me not liking Van Geer, I dare say not a one of you lost any sleep when you heard he was dead."

The cemetery had cleared, except for Williamson's group and one or two others. Baldridge noticed the two hearse drivers he had seen at the chapel, removing shovels from the hearse to complete the interment. He slipped quietly away from the group and walked to the graveside.

"Afternoon, sir," the shorter of the two men said as Baldridge approached.

"Afternoon." Baldridge watched quietly for a few moments as the two began shoveling dirt, the dry clods smothering the lid of the casket with a cold, abrupt thud, sending a cloud of dust slowly climbing from the grave. He lifted his flask from his pocket and took a swig, holding it out to the short man.

The man paused momentarily and looked both directions to see that most of the mourners had left. "Don't mind if I do have a little swallow," he said, taking the flask.

"You boys about scared the shit out of me," Baldridge said.

After one swig, the man handed the flask back to Baldridge and continued shoveling. "How's that?"

"I was following the hearse when you left the chapel back there, and I swear I thought ol' Hudson Van Geer had changed his mind and come back to life."

The other gravedigger looked at Baldridge. "What are you talking about?"

"When the curtain of that hearse all of a sudden parted and

somebody came jumping out. I'll tell you, even Harry, that's my ol' horse, just about spooked."

The small man looked at his coworker. "He's talking about that little pissant you caught messin' with the casket."

"Oh, him. I don't know when that little bastard crawled in there," the other gravedigger said. "Must have been when we came around the building."

"If you don't mind me askin'," Baldridge said, "what was he doing in the hearse?"

"Who knows?" the small man said, tossing another shovelful of dirt. "You see some strange things in this business. The boy probably never saw a dead body before. Hell, he couldn't have been over ten or twelve years old."

"He was trying to get the casket open, all right," the other man said. "I heard something in the back, so I figured the casket had shifted around. So I pulled the curtain back to check, and that's when I seen him." He tossed another shovelful of dirt, waving the rising dust away from his face. "That's when I seen him trying to put something on the body."

"What? Put what on the body?" Baldridge asked.

"Damnedest thing I ever saw. The boy was about to put an egg in that corpse's hand. I ran him out of the hearse, but I'll tell you one thing," the man said, sticking the point of the shovel in the loose dirt at his feet and leaning on the handle. "If I find out who he is, I'm gonna see to it his mamma and daddy blister his young ass real good."

The men returned to their work, and Baldridge watched them for perhaps another minute. He agreed with the gravediggers. The boy needed an ass-whipping.

3

SHORTLY BEFORE FIVE o'clock, Williamson and Baldridge entered the Washington Square jailhouse, a two-story brick building facing south on Clark Street. Baldridge had lost an argument with Williamson about stopping off for a quick drink before coming to the jail, leaving the ex-Confederate edgy and a bit short-tempered. After the two of them signed the visitors' log and Baldridge checked his revolver at the desk, they were introduced to Detective Horace Kenton, an eight-year veteran of the St. Louis Police, who had conducted the initial investigation of Hudson Van Geer's death. His version of events offered little more detail than the newspaper account; outside of Stewart Van Geer's own confession, Kenton admitted that the police had no other evidence. No witnesses to the shooting had been discovered, and no clear motive had yet been established; but with a confession in hand and no reason to pursue other suspects, Kenton seemed satisfied with the progress of the case. He seemed firmly convinced he had the murderer in custody, and Baldridge got the distinct impression that Kenton was not taking them seriously as investigators.

Since Kenton seemed certain of Stewart's guilt, Baldridge asked why Kenton had not tried to find out why Stewart Van Geer committed the crime.

"Ain't interested in why," Kenton told him. "Real detectives just want to know who and how. With three hundred and sixty-nine officers and eight detectives to keep the lid on a cityful of criminals, we have to spend our time where it can be best used. Chief McDonough's orders. I've got a confession. No need to look any further."

"Mrs. Helen Van Geer believes her son is innocent," Baldridge reminded him.

Kenton motioned toward the cell block. "I've got a building full of people whose mothers all think they're innocent."

Williamson asked that they be allowed to interview Stewart Van Geer, prompting a wry grin.

"Good luck," Kenton mumbled. " 'Cause since he walked in here and confessed to the killing, he's hardly said a word to anyone. He wouldn't hardly talk to his own mother when she came to see him. Won't even talk to his wife when she brings him supper. Just sits back there curled up in the corner."

Kenton instructed the jailer to lead the two men to a cell, the paint peeling on its walls, the afternoon sun slanting between the bars of a small, rectangular window perhaps ten feet from the floor.

"You've got visitors, Van Geer," the jailer said, but the man lying in a fetal position in the far corner of the cell did not acknowledge him. Instead he kept his face against the wall, one hand busily picking at the plaster as his body rocked slowly, almost imperceptibly, in place.

When the door was unlocked, Baldridge and Williamson stepped into the cell. "Van Geer! I said you've got visitors." The jailer shook his head and moved back outside, closing the cell door behind him. He stood watching Van Geer for several seconds, then said, "Crazy as a damn loon, if you ask me."

"Didn't ask you," Baldridge said flatly, locking on the jailer. He stared at him until the man got the hint and began walking down the hall.

"You know, you could have been a little nicer to the man that just locked us in here," Williamson observed.

"And you could have stopped off for a drink with me, too."

"It ain't like you haven't got any whiskey." Williamson tapped Baldridge's shirt pocket. "That flask of yours is seldom empty."

"That ain't the point."

"You're right," Williamson said, pointing at Van Geer. "He's the point."

Stewart Van Geer remained huddled in the corner. His trousers, though expensive and handsomely tailored, were torn at the knee, and what was once a clean, starched white shirt now showed the heavy wrinkles of at least three days' wear.

"Mr. Van Geer, my name is Captain Luke Williamson, and this is my associate, Mr. Baldridge." The man's eyes darted toward him momentarily, then returned to their close-up gaze at the wall. Williamson could see that his face was reddened and swollen. When he took a couple of steps toward him, Van Geer seized into an even tighter ball, his eyes widening in terror. Williamson halted. "We're here to talk to you about your father. We want you to tell us what happened."

With those words, the man began to sob softly, the rocking motion becoming faster. Both men watched him briefly before Baldridge reached into his pocket and produced his flask. But instead of taking a drink, he dropped awkwardly to one knee and leaned his face within inches of Van Geer. He spoke in a gentle voice.

"Stewart, how 'bout a little drink to calm your nerves?" He removed the top and waved the flask under Van Geer's nose. "It's good whiskey." Van Geer's head jerked back and he turned his face toward the wall. "All right," Baldridge said, replacing the top on his flask and slipping it back into his pocket. "If you don't want to have a drink with me, I can understand that. Hell, the captain here don't either." Instantly, his voice became harsh and threatening. "But you know, Stewart," he said, grabbing Van Geer's collar, "what I can't quite understand—" Baldridge got to his feet, pulling Van Geer out of the fetal position and onto shaky legs. "What I can't quite understand is why you don't grow a damn pair of balls and act like a man." He shoved him against the wall. "Instead of curling up in the corner and crying like a little boy." Baldridge backhanded him across the face.

"Baldridge!" Williamson shouted, moving to separate the two men.

"How 'bout it there, Stewart? Are you sure you don't want to talk to us?"

"Masey, let him go," Williamson said, pulling his hand from Van Geer's collar.

Baldridge grabbed the man's hair with his other hand and pushed his head against the wall before Williamson could stop him.

"Okay," Van Geer moaned as he tried to fight off Baldridge. "All right, I'll—I'll talk to you."

"What the hell's the matter with you?" Williamson asked Baldridge.

"He's talkin', ain't he?" Baldridge said, a satisfied smile on his face. "Just needed to get the boy's attention."

Stewart Van Geer anchored himself in the corner of the cell, his pale blue eyes alternating between Williamson and Baldridge as he spoke.

"What do you want from me?" The words were slow and effortful.

"The truth will do," Baldridge said.

"I, uh . . . already talked . . . to the police."

"Well, talk to *us* now," Baldridge said, but when he moved toward Van Geer, the man recoiled and hugged the wall even closer. "Hell, I ain't gonna hit you, unless you start that damn whining again."

Williamson noticed Stewart's slurred speech, like that of a man coming off a three-day drunk, yet the only smell of alcohol came from his partner. Stewart seemed to have trouble keeping his eyes focused, and his balance was unsteady. When his eyes grew heavy again, Baldridge moved in front of him.

"Are we boring you?" When Baldridge grabbed Van Geer again, Williamson started to intervene, but he realized that Stewart was at least responding to Baldridge. Lifting Stewart's chin, Baldridge snapped his fingers in front of his face. "Are we keeping you from your afternoon nap?"

"All right. I'm talking. I'm talking. What do you . . . what do you want to know?"

Baldridge seemed puzzled as he stepped back three or four feet, his hand on his chin, studying Van Geer.

"What is it?" Williamson asked.

Baldridge leaned closer to Williamson and whispered, "That son of a bitch is loaded."

"I'll agree that he acts like it, but I don't smell any liquor."

"Me neither, but believe me, Luke. I know a drunk when I see one."

"They don't allow liquor in jail. The man's been here three, maybe four days. There's no way he could be—"

"I can't tell you how he got that way, or what he's drinking, but I'm telling you this man is drunk."

For the next fifteen minutes Williamson and Baldridge tried to talk with Van Geer, who was never fully lucid. He seemed to remember nothing before coming into the Washington Square police station on Thursday afternoon. He recalled placing a pistol on the officer's desk and telling him he had killed his father. And though he never denied shooting Hudson Van Geer, he could offer no details of the crime. Baldridge was pressing him to describe what happened at the Van Geer home when someone opened the door into the cell hallway. Williamson leaned his head against the bars as a crude whistle from one of the other inmates echoed down the hallway.

"Shut your mouth," the jailer barked at a prisoner two cells down and across from Van Geer. "Act like you've never seen a lady before." Arriving at Van Geer's cell, the jailer inserted the key into the cell door and addressed Baldridge and Williamson. "I'll have to ask you men to leave now."

Williamson saw two women standing behind the jailer; the nearest, a brunette of medium build, carried a basket covered with a plaid cloth. The individual behind her, a younger, dark-haired woman, perhaps two inches shorter, held a pewter pitcher. Recognizing the first woman from the funeral, he was about to introduce himself when she preempted him.

"You're those men from Hudson's funeral, aren't you?"

He introduced himself and Baldridge as the jailer opened the cell door.

"What are you doing in there with my husband?"

"Our agency has been retained by Mrs. Helen Van Geer to look into the death of her husband."

"Mother Helen mentioned that she had hired a detective agency," the first woman said as she stepped into the crowded cell. Clutching the basket tightly with her left hand, she extended her right to Williamson. "I'm Claire. Stewart's wife." Stewart Van Geer began to sob when his wife spoke, and she stepped near to console him. "Now, now, Stewart. It's all right. See here? I've brought your supper." She indicated the woman standing in the doorway. "Marie has some cool lemonade for you, too."

The jailer interrupted. "Listen here, two of you are gonna have to leave. It's against jail policy to have that many people in a cell at one time." He muscled his way inside. "And let me check that basket again."

Claire Van Geer jerked it away. "You've already pawed

through it once. And don't think I didn't see you steal that chicken leg. You stuck your nasty nose practically inside the lemonade Marie brought. Would you care to swash your hand around in the pitcher? I assure you, officer, there's no gun hidden in the lemonade."

"Well, I guess it's all right," the jailer said. "But two of you still have to clear out of there."

Baldridge stepped into the hall first, followed by Williamson. Baldridge addressed the jailer as he locked the two women in the cell with Stewart Van Geer.

"Any policy that says we can't stand out here in the hall and talk?"

The jailer hooked the keys on his belt. "I suppose not. But you can't stand around long. It's thirty minutes to a visitor, and you two have already been here twenty. I'll be back for you in ten minutes." He called to the women as he walked down the hall. "And don't leave no mess in the cell."

Claire Van Geer placed a white linen napkin on the solid wood bunk chained against the far wall and set out Stewart Van Geer's dinner, complete with silverware and crystal goblet, as calmly as if the two were on a picnic along the river. The other woman poured a glass of lemonade and stepped a respectful distance away, still holding the pitcher.

"What has my husband told you, Captain Williamson?" Claire asked.

"Not very much. He doesn't seem to recall the shooting." Williamson watched as Claire fed each bite to her husband. "I don't understand, Mrs. Van Geer; your husband acts like . . . like—"

"Like he's drunk," Baldridge interrupted.

Claire Van Geer's eyes flashed at Baldridge.

"He's distraught, Mr. Baldridge. And given what he's been through, who wouldn't be? Look at him. He can barely eat. He doesn't sleep. Is it any wonder that—"

"How's he been getting whiskey?" Baldridge asked.

"Whiskey? I'm sure you know that the police don't allow spirits in the jail."

"Well, something's got him lit up."

"My husband has been charged with a terrible crime," Claire said, laying a chicken breast on the napkin and rising to her feet. "He's clearly upset. Is this how you detective people earn your money? I thought you were here to help free my husband. Instead you accuse him of being a drunk!"

Williamson tried to intervene. "Now, Mrs. Van Geer, Masey wasn't saying your husband—"

"He thinks my husband's been drinking, and I'll not have him insulted that way."

"Mrs. Van Geer—"

She spun around and picked up the basket, emptying its remaining contents, a piece of chess pie, onto the napkin. "Mr. Baldridge, do you see any whiskey in this basket?" She took the pitcher from the other woman. "Does this smell like alcohol to you? Unless, of course, you classify lemonade as hard liquor."

Baldridge leaned his face against the bars. Removing his handkerchief from his pocket, he wiped sweat beads from his forehead, eyeing the pitcher jealously. He reached his hand through the bars. "Ma'am, you don't suppose I could have a little sip of that—"

Claire Van Geer jerked the pitcher away, sloshing some of its contents on the cuff of her sleeve, then slapped his hand. "I should think not! Certainly not after the way you've talked about Stewart." She began rolling up her damp sleeve, revealing her smooth, pale skin. "Now look what you've done! You ought to be ashamed of yourself!"

Williamson pushed Baldridge aside. "Masey didn't mean to offend you, Mrs. Van Geer. We just need to know whatever you can tell us about Hudson Van Geer's death."

"Very little, Captain. Stewart and I have a modest home just down the street from his father. Marie and I"—she nodded at the woman in the corner of the cell—"Marie Trehan is my attendant—were at home when it happened. We only learned of the tragedy some two hours after it occurred. I was ill that day. As you can see, I'm carrying Stewart's child, and Mother Helen had come to stay with me. The first we knew of it was when a policeman arrived at our home. He indicated that Mr. Van Geer had been killed. Imagine my shock when he told me my husband was the murderer." She glanced back at Stewart Van Geer, who had not eaten a single bite since his wife walked away, but rather stared blankly at the wall. She addressed her companion before continuing to speak to Williamson. "Marie, would you feed him the rest of his dinner?

"Marie and I rushed to the Van Geer home to find Hudson dead in the foyer. There must have been a half-dozen policemen there already."

"Where was Stewart?"

"Apparently Stewart had already made his way here to the police station. He had already turned himself in by that time. He told them he killed his father. They locked him up immediately." Claire Van Geer began to sob. "It's all so tragic. So very, very tragic."

"Do you believe your husband is guilty, Mrs. Van Geer?"

She hesitated momentarily before answering. "I don't want to believe it. I don't want to ever believe that Stewart is capable of something like that. But look at him," she said in a near whisper. Marie Trehan was now feeding him. "He's been this way ever since the murder. It grieves me to say it, Captain, but Stewart behaves like a man who has committed a terrible act."

Baldridge moved nearer the cell. "He behaves like a man who's—"

"I'm well aware of your opinion, Mr. Baldridge, and I'll thank you to keep it to yourself." Claire addressed Williamson again. "Mother Helen hired you to prove her son's innocence. I suppose any mother would do the same. But unlike Helen Van

Geer, I am a realist, Captain Williamson. And with my husband having already confessed to murder, I should think you'd be lucky to keep him from hanging, much less set him free."

"But why? Why would your husband kill his father?"

"I don't know. As I told the police, Stewart and his father did not always get along, but I would never have dreamed it would come to this."

Williamson was about to ask another question when the jailer barged into the hall. "Time's up. You two have to leave now. Mrs. Van Geer, you can stay another fifteen minutes or so."

"Thank you, Officer." Claire Van Geer shook Williamson's hand through the bars, ignoring Baldridge. "My prayers are with you, Captain. Perhaps you and your associate can do something to . . . to keep my Stewart alive."

"We'll do our best," Williamson said. He realized he had left his hat in the cell, and when he peered through the bars, he noticed that Marie Trehan was holding it. Before he could ask her for it, she stepped toward him and wedged the hat through the bars, addressing him in a low, throaty voice, almost the tenor of a man's.

"Your hat, Captain."

Williamson accepted it, and he and Baldridge followed the jailer out the door into the front office, where Baldridge recovered his .45 Long Colt revolver and slipped it into the holster on his left hip, the butt of the weapon facing forward.

"Ain't nothin' like a woman that believes in her man," Baldridge observed as he placed a small leather strap over the hammer to hold his weapon in place. "Let's head back to the *Paragon*. Looking at all that food made me hungry."

WILLIAMSON PROBABLY SHOULDN'T have resented it. The man had a right to eat. And they were, after all, business partners. But watching the dining room steward place a second bowl of mashed potatoes in front of Baldridge annoyed the captain just the same. Sure, it was all part of the agreement. Passage for Baldridge and Salina Tyner was Williamson's contribution to Big River Detective Agency. Still, he kept wondering what Baldridge's contribution would be. For weeks now he'd had the run of the boat—playing cards most nights until well past midnight, sleeping the morning away, and running up a serious bar tab. Passage was one thing, but he wasn't about to keep Baldridge in liquor. That task alone could bankrupt him. Williamson figured one thing for certain: this case wasn't going to make any money past two or three days. At least Baldridge would be staying behind to wrap things up while Williamson took the *Paragon* to New Orleans. It would be up to him to hustle some business instead of living it up on the captain's boat.

"You need to find some new business while I'm away."

Baldridge took a sip from his wineglass, and Williamson noted that the bottle it came from was one of the rarest vintages on board. "Do you have to order the most expensive wine on my list?"

"Life's too short to drink bad wine," Baldridge said, cutting another slice of rare roast beef. "You be sure and tell Anabel how good this meat is." He held up the slice for Williamson to admire. "Look at that. Cooked just right. Still juicy and—"

"Business, Masey. I asked you about business. Did you hear me?"

"I heard you." He chewed the bite slowly and swallowed. "Just what exactly am I supposed to do? I mean, *after* I tell Helen Van Geer her son really is a murderer and her daughter-in-law's a bitch. Am I supposed to go door-to-door in St. Louis and ask folks if they could use a detective?"

"I don't know. That's what's bothering me about this whole thing. I know how to run a shipping business. You load the freight, take on the passengers, treat 'em like royalty, and if you're lucky, you make a profit. But I don't know anything about running a detective agency. I told you and Sally that when you came up with this notion."

"Having second thoughts, are you?"

Williamson looked at him several seconds and then stared out an open door to the starboard deck. "Maybe. Maybe not. I don't know—"

"Well, I'll tell you one thing," Baldridge said. "I figure a deal's a deal. We shook hands on this—me, you and Sally. But if you want out, you just say the word. 'Cause I'm getting tired of the bullshit."

"*You're* getting tired of it?"

"I've seen the way you look at me when I'm in this dining room."

"What's that supposed to mean?"

"It means this, Luke. If you want the Big River Detective Agency to stay in business, then stand by your word."

Williamson didn't like his tone. "You saying I don't keep my word?"

"You agreed to provide me passage on your boats. That's what you should do. And without the dirty looks every time I order a decent bottle of wine, or sit in on a card game. You ain't my daddy."

"I'm not trying to be your daddy. But passage means meals and a room," Williamson said, his frustration growing. "It doesn't mean a twenty-five-dollar bar tab, and it sure doesn't mean fleecing my passengers in some slick card game."

"Slick? You sayin' I cheat?"

"Hell, no, you don't cheat. You don't win often enough to be a card cheat. But the passengers don't know that. All I want you to do is carry your own weight around here and stop—"

Baldridge pointed his fork at Williamson. "I'll pay my own goddamned bar tab."

"When?"

"When I get good 'n' goddamned ready, that's when!"

"How about right now?"

"Now?"

"Yeah."

"Right now?" Baldridge tossed down his fork and stood up quickly, reaching into his vest pocket.

"Yeah, right now."

"I can't pay it right now," Baldridge said, abruptly lowering his voice and returning to his seat.

"Why not?"

" 'Cause I'm a little short."

"What happened to the horse-racing money?"

"I just couldn't get a decent poker hand last night. But I expect to rake the pot tonight if we can get up a good game, and I'll—"

"That's what I'm talking about, Masey."

Baldridge lifted the wine glass from the table and finished off the last sip. "You'll get your money." He took the bottle in his hand and stood up to leave, then reconsidered and returned the bottle to the table. "I won't be staying for dessert. The company has caused me to lose my appetite."

Storming out of the dining room, Baldridge disappeared down the starboard deck in the direction of the stern. Williamson arose to follow but decided it best to let him go. Everything he had said was the truth. He was right, and Baldridge needed to be told. He had nothing to be ashamed of. Yet still he felt bad about how he had said it.

THE NEXT MORNING Luke Williamson awoke early, as was his custom, grabbed some bacon between two pieces of toast in the ship's kitchen, and began his morning rounds—a daily ritual for the past eight years. Though he had slept well, the rest had not made him forget the way he had talked to Baldridge last night, and he determined to try and smooth things over later that morning. But given Baldridge's sleeping habits, it would likely be *much* later. Climbing to the crew level, he had just cleared the stairs when a young boy came dashing down the deck, ducked under his arm, and raced down the steps, nearly knocking him down. He was about to correct the young man when Jacob Lusk appeared out of one of the cabins, shouting as he ran.

"Boy, if I catch you, you gonna wish . . . McCauley, he's headin' down yo' way," Lusk shouted, slowing up as he met the captain.

"What's going on here?" Williamson asked. The boy cleared the bottom three steps with a leap and ran along the boiler deck.

Lusk was breathing hard. "I believe we got us a thief, Cap'n." He leaned over the rail. "There he goes! Down by the Virginia Room."

Williamson looked over the rail and saw a crewman closing in on the young man from the stern as Steward McCauley chased him. "I believe they gonna catch him, Cap'n," Lusk remarked. The boy, not more than twelve years old, struggled to gain entry to a locked stateroom as the two pursuers closed on him from opposite directions. The men were within arm's reach of the young culprit when he spun around, a look of terror upon his face, and leaped overboard. His small body plummeted twenty or more feet before splashing into the muddy water that separated the *Paragon* and the *Mollie Moore* by no more than six feet.

"Well, I'll be damned," Lusk said, removing his hat and slapping it on the rail.

The water churned for twenty to thirty seconds without any sign of the youngster.

"You want I should go in after him, Mr. Jacob?" the deckhand called up. Lusk offered no reply as he watched the water between the two steamboats. "Mr. Jacob?" the man repeated.

Suddenly, near the bow the water broke, and the boy emerged, sloshing his way along the muddy bottom calf-deep in a rush for the landing.

"I knew it," Lusk said. "The little scoundrel has done this before. I'd bet on it." He cupped his hand over his mouth. "Boy, don't you never come back on this boat, else I'll have the law put you *under* the jail." Once out of the water, the child disappeared between two wagons and melted into the crowd of rousters loading corn aboard the *Mollie Moore*.

"Where did you find him?" Williamson asked.

"You ain't gonna like the answer."

"What do you mean?"

Jacob Lusk replaced his cap. "Caught him around your cabin, Cap'n."

"My cabin?"

"Yes, sir. One of the chambermaids caught him coming out of your cabin when she went to bring you a fresh bowl of washing water. Ain't no tellin' how many cabins he was in. Good thing we're light on passengers right now."

"That's a *good* thing?"

"Well, you know what I mean, Cap'n. Less for the little trash to steal."

"Oh, it's all right if he made it to the captain's cabin. Just don't let the passengers be inconvenienced." Lusk appeared worried by Williamson's comment until a grin emerged on the captain's face.

"I doubt he had time to get anything, Cap'n. He wasn't carrying anything, or I would have seen it. Still, if I was you, I'd check around and make sure nothin's missing."

"I'll do that," Williamson replied.

4

Monday Morning, June 16

"OH, MR. KENNARD, you are just the kindest gentleman," Salina Tyner said, as the middle-aged businessman labored to carry her Saratoga trunk along the St. Louis landing. Sweat rolled down his cheeks and formed droplets on his chin as he hustled to follow the slender, dark-haired woman through the humid morning air.

"Anything for you, Miss Tyner," Kennard said, short of breath.

"Well, since you were determined to accompany me to the *Paragon*, you certainly could have hired a wagon, or one of these roustabouts to carry that trunk."

"No further than this?" Kennard said, still struggling with the balance of his load. "Wouldn't be a judicious use of funds."

A judicious use of funds. That was ol' Kennard's problem as far as Salina Tyner was concerned. He'd been a bit too judicious ever since they left Vicksburg on Friday. He had followed her around the *Mercury* all the first day of the trip, practically drooling at the mouth. Then when she did pay some attention to him, he turned out to be cheap. The only thing worse than an ugly middle-aged man looking for a poke was a stingy, ugly middle-aged man looking for a poke. Kennard wasn't about to get the poke, no matter what he did, but he didn't have to know that. At least not until they got to St. Louis. Tyner was out of that business. For good. The Big River Detective Agency was her chance, and though she had been unsuccessful in her search for business in Vicksburg, she wasn't about to give up. That didn't mean she couldn't enjoy the company of a determined suitor.

"What do you think, Miss Tyner," Kennard said as he struggled to keep up, "about the two, uh . . . the two of us maybe having dinner together this evening?"

Tyner did not look back but focused her attention along the row of steamboats, where she located the *Paragon* some fifty yards ahead.

"As delightful as that might be, Mr. Kennard, I'm afraid it's impossible for this evening."

"Well, then, how about—"

"Careful of that mooring rope, Mr. Kennard," Tyner warned, as she lifted her dress and stepped gracefully over the tightly stretched strand of four-inch, woven hemp.

Kennard got one foot over the rope, then almost dropped the trunk as he swung the other foot over. "Careful, Mr. Kennard. There are breakables in that trunk." *If that cheap bastard drops my trunk, he'll buy everything in it.*

Kennard collected himself, with a loud groan adjusted the trunk on his shoulder, and continued. "Then perhaps tomorrow?"

Tyner stopped and turned to face him. "Mr. Kennard," she said, offering a sugar-melting smile, "you're a businessman. And as I've told you, I'm in business myself. The detective business."

Kennard lowered the trunk to the ground as she spoke, took

a handkerchief from his pocket, removed his hat, and wiped his brow.

"Yes, ma'am. You're the only woman I've ever heard of being in the detective business."

"Well, be that as it may, surely you, as a businessman yourself, understand that there are times when one simply cannot break away."

"But Miss Tyner—"

"I do so appreciate you hauling my trunk all the way down here from the *Mercury*. God knows we wouldn't have wanted you to hire a wagon so we both could ride. But I'm afraid I simply won't have the time to join you for dinner."

From behind them and near the bow of the *Paragon*, clerk Steven Tibedeau approached. "Miss Tyner? Is that you?"

"Steven!" she said, whirling about, "how nice to see you again."

"I thought you were in Vicksburg."

"Well, I was. But Vicksburg and I didn't see eye to eye, so now I'm here." She noticed Tibedeau looking at the sweat-soaked gentleman. "Oh, Steven, this is Mr. Kennard. He owns a business here."

Kennard, still out of breath, extended a sweaty hand to Tibedeau. "J. P. Kennard," he said. "Kennard's Carpets and Curtains."

"Steven Tibedeau."

"J. P. was kind enough to walk with me all the way down the landing from the *Mercury* . . . *in this heat*," she added with a glare that Kennard could not see. "But he has to leave now," she said, winking at Tibedeau, who took the hint and called a rouster down from the *Paragon* to take Tyner's trunk aboard.

Tyner faced Kennard. "J. P.," she said, taking his hand. "What a pleasure meeting you. Now, you keep selling those carpets, you hear? And perhaps I'll run into you again on one of your future business trips."

Kennard removed his hat and attempted an awkward bow. "I'll check the landing regularly, Miss Tyner. I sure hope to see you again sometime," he called after her as she walked up the landing stage with Tibedeau.

"Not if I see you first," Tyner whispered.

Tibedeau laughed. "He didn't seem like such a bad guy."

"Cheap. Talked constantly about his carpets. I now know the difference between an oriental carpet from Burma and one from China."

"Captain Luke is going to be surprised to see you," Tibedeau said. "Maybe it'll get him in a better mood."

"What's the matter with Luke?"

"He's been on the warpath all morning. I think he and Mr. Baldridge had a big argument last night. At least, that's what Jacob told me at the crew's breakfast this morning."

"An argument? Those two? It's not possible," Tyner said with a smile.

"No, Miss Tyner, I think they're really mad at each other this time."

"About what?"

"It's got something to do with this detective business." The way Tibedeau said "detective," Tyner knew his opinion of their efforts had not changed. From the start, Tibedeau had been against his captain getting involved in such a scheme. And though he had never shared his view with Williamson, he had confessed his concerns to Tyner before her trip to Vicksburg.

"The captain's got enough to be worried about, trying to run the packet line," Tibedeau had told her. "He doesn't need a distraction like this."

But as Tibedeau knew from his years working as Williamson's clerk, and as Tyner had found out over the past year, Williamson was a man accustomed to doing what he wanted—a man unlikely to be pressured into anything.

"So, how do you know they're mad?"

"Because they aren't talking to each other," Tibedeau replied. "The two of them sat in the dining room ten feet away from each other this morning, and neither one said a word. That's not like those two. Maybe they argue, but at least they talk. Of course, I'm not sure Mr. Baldridge could've talked if he'd wanted to. He looked pretty hungover. I don't know what he was doing out of bed. One of the stewards told me he stayed up playing poker until after four this morning. Mr. Baldridge is seldom out of his cabin until noon. Jacob said he drug himself out of the sack this morning just to spite Captain Luke."

"What's this all about?" Tyner asked.

"Seems that the captain took a case, and—"

"A case?" Tyner's eyes lit up. "Luke got us a case?"

"As far as I know. It's got something to do with the murder of ol' Van Geer."

"Hudson Van Geer?"

"Yes, ma'am."

"I read something about that in the *Memphis Appeal.*"

"The captain got a letter from Van Geer's wife. He and Mr. Baldridge went to the funeral yesterday. I don't know for sure, but I think they're working on something to do with his death."

Tyner patted Tibedeau on the back. "You see? For someone who doesn't like the detective business, you've got a pretty good ear for what's going on."

Tibedeau smiled. "I don't miss too much that happens on this boat."

Thirty minutes later, Tyner located Luke Williamson in the engine room, where he and his chief engineer, Ham, were leaning over one of the cylinders and working on a broken steam pressure gauge. When a crewman started to speak to her, Tyner held one finger over her mouth to silence him and tiptoed unnoticed to within a couple of feet behind the two men. She cupped her hands around her mouth and uttered a loud *"Hisssssssss!"*

Both men jumped. "What the hell!" Ham shouted, as he and Williamson spun about to locate the source of the leak, causing Tyner to break out into boisterous laughter. Both men scowled at her, and for a fleeting moment she wondered if Ham planned to use that wrench that he stood slapping into his palm on her.

"What are you doing here?" Williamson demanded.

"That's not a very nice way to say hello, Luke."

"And scaring the shit out of somebody *is*?"

"Oh, relax. And you too, Ham." Though Williamson allowed himself a momentary smile, the chief engineer never quite found the humor in the situation. He turned back to the steam gauge, glancing over his shoulder once more just to make sure that Tyner was keeping her distance.

Tyner took Williamson by the arm. "Come up on deck and tell me about this case you've got."

After determining that Ham had the repair under control, Williamson followed Tyner up the narrow stairway to the main deck.

"Why aren't you in Vicksburg?" he asked as they emerged into the sunlight.

"There's no business there."

"No business? You said you knew people. You said you'd find some business in—"

"There's nothing to be found, Luke," Tyner said curtly.

Williamson folded his arms and leaned against the deckrail, his eyes studying hers. "Maybe you didn't stay long enough."

"I stayed plenty long."

"Did you talk to the wharfmaster like I suggested?"

"Yes, I talked to him, for all the good it did."

"How about some of the captains? Did you talk with any of them? Surely they—"

"I met with one or two."

"One or two? Sally, there must be—"

"That was enough."

Williamson wasn't buying it, and Tyner knew it. She wasn't surprised when the next question came.

"What's going on, Sally? Why did you come back so soon?"

Tyner stared at the steamboat docked adjacent to them. It wasn't like she hadn't tried. And there was no shortage of mischief going on around Vicksburg that somebody couldn't use their services. As she thought about her answer she felt a lump in her throat and fought back tears. She couldn't allow herself to cry. She wouldn't cry.

"They wouldn't listen, Luke."

"I thought you said you talked to them."

"I talked. I talked plenty. But nobody was listening."

"Did you tell them about what we've done? About you and Masey's work with the Pinkertons? About the situations you've handled?"

"I tried. I mean, I told them all that, Luke."

"Then why didn't—"

"Because . . . because when they look at me, they don't see a detective," Tyner said, her voice nearly breaking. Her gaze went down to the deck. "They see a woman." She laughed nervously. "No, I guess that's not really true either. Most of the captains know me from years past. Most of them don't even see a woman." Her eyes came up to meet Williamson's. "They just see a whore." A tear crept down her cheek, and she tried to wipe it away before Williamson saw it.

"I'm sorry, Sally."

"You're not half as sorry as I am," she said. Tyner stood silent for several moments before continuing. "You know, Luke, about five years ago I ran into this hellfire preacher on a boat to Cincinnati." Though her voice nearly broke, she laughed. "He said something to me at the time that I dismissed, but I guess he was right. He said, 'You can't outrun your past.' Do you think that's true, Luke?"

"Look, maybe that was just Vicksburg. Maybe a different town—"

"Do you really think someplace else will be different? People know me all up and down the river. The Ohio, too. Do you really believe they're going to give me a chance? They all respect you, Luke. But even using your name wasn't enough." No words passed between the two of them, as she stood listening to the distant thump of the deckhands hammering on the paddle wheel at the stern of the boat. Chambermaids' and crew members' footsteps sounded on the deck above. She wondered what Williamson was thinking. Was he sorry he'd agreed to this venture? Did he fear she would never pull her weight? Was he looking for a way out? Standing there crying about her fate would surely give him one, if that was what he sought, and since this was her only hope for a life that didn't include the bed of strangers, she determined not to make it so easy. She wiped her eyes and turned to face him. "Enough about me. Tell me what you and Masey have."

"Masey hasn't got anything except a hangover," Williamson said.

"What's going on between you two? Steven said you've been arguing. He also said you had a case."

"A case? Yeah, I guess you could call it that. At least for a few days, anyway. Baldridge is another matter. He needs to straighten up, Sally. He should be out talking to people about the case right now. But he's not. I suspect he's back in bed. The son of a bitch got up this morning and sat at breakfast just so I couldn't say he was loafing again. But I'll bet you a twenty-dollar gold piece he's back in bed."

"What about you? Why don't you work the case?"

"Look around you, Sally. I've got a few things to do here. Now, maybe I can break loose for a couple of hours this afternoon, but that's all the time I can give to it. We steam for New Orleans tomorrow evening at five o'clock, and there's still plenty to be done. When I agreed to this detective business back in Memphis, I told you two all along that I had to run my ships first. The river will always come first. Masey's got to get on the ball. Who's going to work this case when I'm gone tomorrow?"

"Masey and I will," Tyner said. "I'll straighten him out."

"Good luck."

Tyner pulled up a rocking chair for Williamson and another one for herself. "But first you've got to tell me about the case."

"Sally, I've a dozen different—"

"Luke, you're either in the business or you're not. If I can't convince people to hire us, I can sure as hell work the case. And I can light a fire under Masey, too. But I can't do either one if you don't tell me what you've got." Williamson took his pocket watch from his vest. "Put your watch away and talk to me," Tyner said, taking him by the sleeve and pulling him into the rocking chair. "And don't spare any details."

THE NEGRO CHAMBERMAID outside Masey Baldridge's stateroom was less than enthusiastic about using her passkey to open his door, even after Salina Tyner, whom she knew from several trips on the *Paragon*, told her the captain had given his blessing.

"Mr. Baldridge, he don't like to be disturbed 'fore noonday," the chambermaid said, producing her passkey from her apron. "I've seen him bless a cabin steward out for just knocking on the door, and I sure ain't in no mood for that." Her brow furrowed, she anxiously inserted the key in the door lock. "You be sure and tell Mr. Baldridge this was your idea, Miss Tyner."

"Thank you," Tyner said, pushing the door open once the chambermaid had retrieved her key. "I'll make sure he knows." The woman continued with her chores as Tyner swung the door open wide, the daylight fanning over Baldridge, who lay facedown across the bed, fully dressed less his boots, snoring loudly.

"Wake up!" Tyner shouted above the nasal gasps of Baldridge as he stirred on the bedspread. She replaced the top on a whiskey bottle minus some three-fourths of its contents, picked up a dirty shirt from the floor of his cabin, took a whiff of it, and held it at arm's length. "Masey, wake up!" She jostled his leg. When that brought forth only a low groan, Tyner moved to the washbowl on his bedside table, wet a washcloth, rolled it up, and slapped it against the back of Baldridge's neck just above his shirt collar.

"Uhmmmmm," he moaned, rolling over and grasping futilely at the back of his neck. "What's . . . what's going on . . ."

"It's time to get up, Masey. Come on, it's almost lunchtime."

"I ain't hungry," he groaned, feeling around until he located the wet washcloth, now lying next to him on the bedspread. He tossed it across the cabin, and it sailed out the open doorway and landed on the deck.

"Luke will make you buy that rag if you throw it overboard. And I wouldn't blame him one bit."

Masey sat up in the bed, squinted in the bright daylight, and said, "What are you doing here?"

"I'm here to work on the Van Geer case, that is, if I can ever get you out of bed."

"What about Vicksburg?" Baldridge asked, turning his face away from the light.

"Long story. I'll tell you on the way to see Helen Van Geer."

"Helen what?"

"Van Geer," she repeated, rescuing the washcloth from the deck. "Luke told me about it." She handed the washcloth to Baldridge. "Wash your face, comb your hair—"

"Climb that persimmon tree, eat your breakfast, and go to school, sir," Baldridge recited.

"What?"

"Oh, just something my daddy used to say to me." Baldridge wiped his face.

"What would he say about you sleeping all day?"

Baldridge pointed upstairs. "There's a fellow upstairs that thinks he's my daddy."

"What's going on with you two?" Tyner said. "I leave for a few days, and you're at each other's throats."

Swinging his feet over the edge of the bed, Baldridge cast about for his boots. Tyner handed them to him. "Everything's got to be done Luke's way."

"And what exactly is getting done? Looks to me like you've been in bed all morning," she remarked.

"I'll have you know I was present at the breakfast table," Baldridge declared as he slipped on his boots.

"Yeah. I heard about that. You nearly passed out in your scrambled eggs trying to impress Luke Williamson."

"Impress, hell! I was just showing him he was wrong."

"Wrong about what?"

"Wrong about me not pulling my weight."

"So you finished breakfast and came back to bed?" Tyner said. "Sounds like maybe he was right."

"Are you going to start on me, too?"

"Nope. But *we* are going to get something done." Tyner picked up the dirty shirt she had discovered earlier and an equally worn pair of pants and carried them out on deck. Attracting the attention of the chambermaid, she called to her, "Would you please have someone launder these, and charge it to Mr. Baldridge's bill?"

"Yes, ma'am," the chambermaid said. "Just leave them there by the door, and I'll see to them."

"What are you doing?" Baldridge asked.

"You can't be a businessman if you don't look like a businessman."

Baldridge stood up and buttoned his shirt. "What's this about Helen Van Geer?"

"We're going to talk with her. Luke said he would help later this afternoon. He says that—"

"Luke says," Baldridge echoed. "Luke ain't sayin' shit about who goes where and talks to whom. I'll have you know I was planning on going to see Helen Van Geer all along. I just hadn't gotten up yet, that's all."

Tyner walked over to Baldridge, gently placed her arms around his neck as if to kiss him, then abruptly delivered a light slap on his cheek. "Well, now you're up." She handed him his gun belt and hat. "Let's go."

THE BROAD, WHITE two-story home of the late Hudson Van Geer occupied a well-manicured tract of land facing south on Chestnut Street at the corner of Fourteenth. Baldridge and Tyner rode up the horseshoe-shaped drive toward a semicircular front porch, its roof supported by four massive, Grecian columns. On both sides of the front porch extended smaller covered porches, and on the extreme right an overhang wide enough for a wagon stood to protect arriving and departing guests from the weather. Tyner noticed that the massive structure was even deeper than it was broad, and she wondered how many rooms it contained. The home reminded her of a madam's house in Helena, Arkansas, where she had once spent a week recovering from the roughhousing of an abusive gentleman—a gentleman, she recalled with a smile, who now only saw out of one eye.

"What are you grinning about?" Baldridge asked her as they reined up before the towering white columns.

"Oh, nothing. Just admiring this home."

"It's something all right. More money than I'll ever see."

"Either of us," Tyner said, easing her mount alongside

Nashville Harry. "The river made Hudson Van Geer a wealthy man, Masey."

"Yeah. And look where it got him. The same place all of us are gonna end up."

A man dressed in a black dinner jacket, white shirt, and tie emerged from the huge double front door. Walking to the edge of the porch he spoke first to Tyner, then to Baldridge.

"Good afternoon, madam. Sir, may I be of service to you and the lady?"

"We're here to see Mrs. Helen Van Geer," Baldridge said.

"And whom may I say is calling?"

"Masey Baldridge."

"And Salina Tyner," Tyner added, tossing Baldridge a menacing stare. "We're with the Big River Detective Agency."

"Just a moment, please." The man reentered the house, and Baldridge swung his stiff left knee over the saddle and dismounted on the right between his horse and Tyner's. Dropping the reins at his side, he had limped two or three steps toward the porch when Tyner cleared her throat loudly. Baldridge looked back over his shoulder.

"What you waitin' on? Ain't you coming inside?"

Tyner remained seated sidesaddle on the small horse Baldridge had rented for her from a livery near the wharf, her hat canted slight to the left, her frustration growing.

"Masey!"

"What?"

"Aren't you going to help me down?"

"Hell, you don't need help off that little horse."

Tyner pushed off the saddle horn and dropped adroitly to the ground, gathering her skirt as she rushed up to Baldridge. "You just don't understand, do you?"

"Understand what?"

"It's not that I need help getting off the damned horse." She glanced over Baldridge's shoulder to make sure no one was listening, then lowered her voice. "We're supposed to be running a business here. You should help me down from my horse to show people you're a gentleman. To show them that we're running a classy business here."

Baldridge glanced around. "Nobody's watching, Sally."

"You don't know that for sure. You *never* know who's watching." Tyner sensed that she wasn't getting through to Baldridge. "Just try. Promise me you'll try to show a little class."

The heavy front doors opened wide and the man who had appeared earlier invited them in, promising to have the stable-boy see to their horses. Baldridge started forward, then stopped abruptly. Removing his hat, he surprised the doorman and Tyner with an exaggerated bow. "After you, Miss Tyner."

"Masey—"

"No, I insist," Baldridge said. Tyner forced a smile and started through the door. "Is that better?" he whispered as she passed.

"A little bit."

"Good," he said, surreptitiously slapping her on the ass with his hat as he followed her inside.

The doorman led them down the entry hall past an elegantly furnished sitting room, where Tyner had expected to see Mrs. Van Geer waiting for them. Instead, they continued down the hall and stopped before a second doorway.

"Mrs. Van Geer is in the billiards room," the attendant said, opening the door. "Madam Helen, I have Miss Tyner and Mr. Baldridge here."

Helen Van Geer, a small woman of little more than five feet in height, her black hair almost fully overcome by the encroaching gray, approached them from the far side of a black walnut billiard table.

"Did we interrupt your game, Mrs. Van Geer?" Baldridge asked, lifting a billiard ball from a corner pocket.

"Oh, no, Mr. Baldridge, I never play," she replied. "My

husband—that is, my late husband—played occasionally." She seemed slightly embarrassed. "I still can't get used to saying that."

Baldridge rolled the ball toward the opposite pocket, banking it narrowly off the rail so that it rolled back toward him. Tyner impatiently grabbed the ball before Baldridge could reach it and returned it to the pocket.

Baldridge met Mrs. Van Geer and shook her hand, introducing Tyner as his associate.

"Is Captain Williamson not with you?"

"No, I'm afraid he must attend to some matters on the *Paragon*," Tyner said. Sensing Mrs. Van Geer's disappointment, she quickly added, "But Masey and I keep Luke informed on everything we do. We all work together on cases." Tyner smiled broadly.

"Well, I suppose I understand about river matters, Miss Tyner," Van Geer said. "It seems that Hudson was forever distracted by some problem that only he could solve." Mrs. Van Geer smiled wistfully. "In our thirty-eight years of marriage, my husband only had one mistress."

Tyner was surprised by such a statement coming from a woman she had only just met. "Mrs. Van Geer—"

"But she was a jealous mistress, and one who wielded a spell over him that I could never break." Tyner's puzzlement must have been evident. "The river, Miss Tyner. The river was my husband's greatest love." Mrs. Van Geer seemed to delight in her little puzzle, one she had no doubt used before. "Can I offer either of you a drink?"

"Brandy," Baldridge said, Mrs. Van Geer's words scarcely out of her mouth.

"Nothing for me," Tyner said.

Mrs. Van Geer dispatched a maid to get Baldridge's drink. "Perhaps I should have received you in the sitting room, but I presumed you wished to speak of Hudson, and this room was a favorite of his."

The walls, which rose some twelve feet high, were paneled with cypress and oak, the lower third being cured, varnished cypress. The huge room held a faint aroma of lilac water, and several paintings of the steamboats plying the Mississippi decorated the walls. Along the wall opposite a case of billiard cues was a mahogany table that displayed detailed wooden replicas of the ships in the Van Geer Shipping Line. Above the table, deer antlers were mounted on a plaque that read "Hudson Van Geer — Captain on the Mississippi —1855."

Baldridge received his brandy from the attendant and took a sip, surveying the room full circle once again. "Mrs. Van Geer, what can you tell us about the night your husband died?"

For the next fifteen minutes, Helen Van Geer related the story of the night of June 12. About six o'clock, she had been called away from the house to see about Claire Van Geer, Stewart's wife, who had been having a difficult pregnancy. Hudson Van Geer was working in his study, she explained, producing a key from around her neck and showing Tyner and Baldridge through another door on the far side of the billiards room. Unlocking the door, she told them how, fearing that some of his important business papers might be disturbed, she had secured her husband's study immediately after the police left. No more than one-quarter the size of the billiards room, the study contained a low, wide desk, two wooden cabinets, and a chair positioned beside a wall-mounted oil lamp. Helen explained that when she returned to the house at approximately eight that evening, two of the household servants and three police officers were gathered on the front porch. When she climbed from her carriage, two of them met her and gave her the news that her husband was dead. When she came inside she found him lying on the floor, a blood-soaked sheet covering his body. She had an officer pull the sheet back and saw him lying in a pool of blood.

"I'll never forget that sight," Helen said. "It was so horrible." She swallowed and sought to maintain her composure. "But then things got worse."

She went on to explain that about thirty minutes later another policeman arrived to inform her that her son Stewart had appeared at the police station and confessed to the murder. Over the next couple of hours the police, led by Detective Horace Kenton, determined that Stewart Van Geer had entered the house at approximately six-thirty or seven that evening, quarreled with Hudson Van Geer, shot him four times, and fled the scene.

Baldridge finished off his brandy and called for another. "Mrs. Van Geer, you don't seem to have any shortage of help around here. What exactly did the help see that night? What did they tell the police?"

"Very little, actually, Mr. Baldridge. You see, Hudson always gave the help a night off. Once a week. Always on Thursday. He has been doing that for years. No servants were in the house that night, though several were in their quarters at the rear of the property."

"So no one actually saw Stewart Van Geer arrive?" Tyner asked.

"No."

"What about leaving? Did anyone hear the shots? See your son leave the house?"

"No, not to my knowledge. But that would not be unusual on a Thursday night, Miss Tyner. Detective Kenton talked to our household employees, and it's my understanding that no one saw or heard anything."

"Then who found your husband's body?" Baldridge asked.

"One of the maids came back into the house from her quarters shortly after seven o'clock to pick up some crochet thread she had left in the kitchen. She told the police that she wanted to check and see if Hudson needed anything. That's when she found him. She ran to get one of our other employees to go for a doctor, but it was too late. Hudson was already dead. The coroner who came with the police told me he thought my husband died quickly. At least that was merciful."

"I'll be real honest with you, Mrs. Van Geer," Baldridge said. "The confession that your son Stewart gave the police is going to be hard to handle. I mean, for a man to walk up to the police, hand them a gun, and say 'I did it' . . . it don't leave much room to wiggle."

"At least no one saw Stewart enter or leave the house that night," Tyner observed.

"Maybe not, Sally," Baldridge said, "but the man's own words—"

"There's something wrong with Stewart, Mr. Baldridge," Helen Van Geer declared. "He's not a well man."

"I could see that from talking to him in the jail," Baldridge said. "How much does he drink?"

"Stewart drinks occasionally, but never to excess."

"Any chance he got liquored up and lost control of himself that night?"

"I've never seen my son drunk a day in his life." Tears swelled in Mrs. Van Geer's eyes. "I don't understand why you're saying these things. I thought you were working to free my son, not build a case against him. Perhaps if Captain Williamson were here . . ."

Tyner could see that Helen Van Geer was becoming annoyed, yet she knew that Baldridge was trying to assess the case against her son. Baldridge must have sensed it too, for he stood up and, after winking at Tyner, asked permission to examine Hudson Van Geer's office more closely. With Helen Van Geer's leave, he returned to the study.

"Masey said Stewart looked bad when he saw him yesterday in jail. If he's not drinking, what do you think is wrong with him?" Tyner asked.

"I wish I knew," she said. "I pray to God to know. But

whatever it is, it is nothing that would make him harm his father."

"Then if not Stewart, who?" Tyner asked. Mrs. Van Geer swallowed hard and attempted to hold back tears as Tyner continued. "Luke—that is, Captain Williamson—said that a number of people may have held a grudge against your husband."

"A lot of people envied my husband, Miss Tyner. They wanted what he worked all his life to earn. They resented him because of his success, and some of them were jealous enough to do anything to take it away from him."

"Who? Who hated your husband that much?"

"Grant De Paul, for one. He couldn't compete with Van Geer Shipping. But instead of admitting it and staying with a short-run packet service, he kept challenging my husband on the St. Louis–to–Memphis run. But Hudson won," Mrs. Van Geer said, with a self-satisfied smile that made Tyner wonder if Helen Van Geer might not have enjoyed her husband's success almost as much he did.

"Are you saying Grant De Paul hated your husband enough to kill him?"

Mrs. Van Geer hesitated. "He certainly threatened him. Not more than three or four months ago, De Paul confronted Hudson at the company wharfboat down at the foot of Vine Street. Several people heard De Paul say he'd kill my husband if he lost his business. De Paul's last boat was repossessed by the Boatman's Savings Bank a little over a month ago. Hudson bought it at auction. It wasn't personal. It was just business to Hudson." Helen Van Geer walked over to the edge of the billiard table, where she stood running her hand across the felt. "I told the police all of this the day after my husband was killed, but I doubt they will even bother to talk to Grant De Paul." She looked at Tyner. "Why wouldn't they at least talk to him?"

"*We'll* talk to him, Mrs. Van Geer," Tyner replied, though she knew full well the answer to the woman's question, and she suspected that in her heart Helen Van Geer knew it too. With a confessed killer tucked safely away in the jail, the St. Louis police were not likely to spend countless hours trying to locate and question all the people that may have threatened Hudson Van Geer, even if they had had the manpower.

"Captain Williamson told me that Mr. Van Geer's business practices undercut a lot of boatmen, not only here in St. Louis but all up and down the river," Tyner said.

Helen Van Geer measured her words carefully. "Some have said that Hudson was ruthless. That he would do anything to further his shipping line. Perhaps he was, I suppose, somewhat cold. But Hudson was a businessman, Miss Tyner, first and foremost." Helen Van Geer gazed out the tall window on the far side of the room. "Hudson was a husband and father only as an afterthought. I guess that's what drove our other son, Robert, away."

"Did Robert not get along with his father?"

"Hardly. Since Robert was the oldest, Hudson expected him to eventually take over the shipping line. For years he groomed him for it, taking care to teach Robert the business. He was always taking him on trips, trying to give him increasingly more important positions within the company. But Robert just never seemed to want it. Stewart did, however. He couldn't wait to get involved in the business. Robert never loved the river like his father or his brother did, or at least if he did, he didn't show it. I think that bothered Hudson more than anything."

"Did they quarrel often?"

"Not until the very last."

"The last?"

"Until Robert left the company," Helen Van Geer said, picking lint from the corner of one of the billiard pockets. "When Hudson wouldn't agree to Robert's plan for expanding the company, Robert told him he wanted no part of his business."

"Exactly what did Robert want to do with the business?"

"The one thing his father would never agree to," Helen Van Geer explained. "He wanted to get into railroading. Claimed it was the future of the country. He actually told Hudson—*his own father*—a man who spent the last twenty-five years of his life building his shipping business—that he was doomed to failure."

"Is that when Robert left the company?"

"Yes. That was almost a year and a half ago. Then he broke his father's heart with the greatest insult of all," Van Geer said. "He went to work for Fieldhurst Freight—one of the biggest railroad outfits in St. Louis. He used the Van Geer name to help raise bond issues for several different railroads all up and down the river. Hudson was furious. But who could blame him?" Tears swelled again in Mrs. Van Geer's eyes, and Tyner quickly produced a handkerchief from the blue crocheted bag that hung from her waist. As she gave it to her, the woman continued. "Van Geer Shipping has no peer on the water, Miss Tyner. Except for Captain Williamson's packet line, and perhaps one or two others, my husband had no serious competition for freight and passengers on the river. But railroads are another matter. They're hurting everyone in the shipping business, including us. And when his own son set to working for his greatest competition, Hudson could never forgive him. He felt betrayed. He and Robert haven't spoken for almost a year now."

"What about Stewart? Did Mr. Van Geer get along with Stewart?"

"On most things, yes. Hudson had to count on Stewart more than ever before this past year after Robert left, and I think he was pleasantly surprised at how well the boy did. Oh, they disagreed from time to time on business matters, but generally speaking I'd have to say they got along . . . except over Claire."

"Stewart's wife?"

"Yes. Hudson never approved of Stewart's marriage to Claire. I was surprised the day he gave his consent."

"Why was he against the marriage?" Tyner asked.

"He just felt that Stewart rushed into things. He didn't think he knew enough about Claire."

"That Stewart knew enough?"

"Yes. But Hudson as well. Hudson was suspicious of everyone. He used to say that he didn't get where he got in the shipping business by trusting people. The whole courtship with Claire, and the marriage, it all came about so quickly. And all Stewart ever told him was that Claire was orphaned in her late teens, and that she came from well-to-do people in Louisiana. Robert introduced them, you know."

"Really?"

"Yes, Stewart and Robert were on the same boat going to New Orleans. Robert knew Claire previously in connection with some of his travels for the railroad. And truthfully, I think that was part of Hudson's suspicion. I'm not sure he ever really gave Claire a chance in our family. He just never seemed comfortable with her around."

"And you?"

"The girl seems all right to me," Van Geer said. "She's awfully quiet, but that's no crime. And if she makes Stewart happy, then—"

"Is he? Happy, that is?"

"Stewart adores Claire. He tries to meet her every need. Ever since they met on one of his business trips to New Orleans, he's been devoted to her. Whatever Claire wants, whatever she says, Stewart tries to do. And when they learned she was pregnant, Stewart was thrilled," Van Geer said, smiling proudly. "Almost six months along."

But her smile quickly faded. "That only makes this tragedy worse. And it's precisely why you've got to find a way to free Stewart. I simply won't allow my grandchild to grow up without a father."

Masey Baldridge emerged from Hudson Van Geer's study with yet another brandy in his hand. Tyner was beginning to think the glass was permanently attached.

"Find anything we can use?" Tyner asked.

Baldridge shook his head, gave Tyner a wink, polished off the remainder of the brandy, and spoke to Mrs. Van Geer. "You said your husband was working in his study alone the night he was killed."

"That's right."

"Tell me again why you weren't here."

"Masey—" Tyner was shocked at his implication.

Helen Van Geer lifted her hand as if to silence Tyner. "It's all right, Miss Tyner. I've hired you to do a job. At least you're asking questions. That's more than the police are doing. I'd been in town most of Thursday afternoon," she explained. "I had a luncheon with the Eastern Star ladies, then I went shopping for a while and finally arrived back home about five o'clock. I had planned to have Hudson return to town with me for dinner—the servants having the night off—but some time around six o'clock, Marie—that's my daughter-in-law's attendant—arrived and said Claire wasn't feeling well. She's been sick to her stomach with this pregnancy for the last few weeks, and she sent Marie to bring me to see after her."

"Why couldn't Marie see about her?" Baldridge asked.

"She could have, but Claire and I have gotten rather close since we learned she was pregnant, and she's just been more comfortable with me around. I guess since it's her first baby and all—"

"What was your husband doing when you left?" Baldridge asked.

"Working in his study. He seemed preoccupied and worried about something, but I supposed it to be the usual pressures of business. I asked him if he wanted me to get one of the servants to prepare him dinner while I was away with Claire, but he declined. He was not at all pleased that I was going to see Claire, but then he seldom ever was."

"And how long were you gone?"

"I guess, perhaps, an hour and a half. Maybe two."

"Can you show me exactly where they found Mr. Van Geer?"

Helen Van Geer walked over near the door through which they had entered the billiards room. "Right here," she indicated, beginning to sob softly. "When I returned home with Marie Trehan, the police had covered his body with a cloth. Some officer had wiped the blood from his face, or I couldn't have stood to look at him. Mercifully, they took him away rather quickly after that, but I cannot pass this spot in the house and not still see him lying there—such a powerful man so helpless . . . and for the first time that I can ever remember."

Helen Van Geer was growing more distraught by the moment, so Tyner recommended to Baldridge that they leave, insisting that they would return in a day or two and speak with her again. Tyner and Baldridge followed the doorman out to the front porch. A stableboy, partially hidden from view by Nashville Harry, stood between their two horses, holding a bridle in each hand. When Tyner reached her mount, the stableboy, his hat pulled low over his brow, handed her the bridle. When Baldridge came around Tyner's horse, the boy placed the bridle in his hand, quickly turned around, slipped between the two horses, and hurried off toward the stable. Tyner briefly hoped that Baldridge might do the gentlemanly thing and help her mount, but instead he stood staring at the stableboy as he crossed the front yard of the Van Geer estate.

"Masey?" Baldridge didn't answer, but kept watching the boy as he disappeared in the distance. "Masey?"

"What?" Baldridge said.

"Why are you staring a hole in that boy?"

"Is everything all right, sir?" the doorman asked, stepping forward to the edge of the porch.

Baldridge, still distracted, gathered his bridle in his hand and, because of his stiff leg, moved almost back-to-back with Tyner to mount from the right. She felt his ass bump against hers.

"Aren't you forgetting something?" she asked, hoping Baldridge might yet reveal some semblance of etiquette and assist her onto her mount.

"Oh, yeah." Baldridge dug into his pocket and pulled out a coin, then stepped into the stirrup with his right foot and swung his bad leg over the horse and into the saddle. "What's the stableboy's name?" he called to the doorman.

"We call him Tewley."

"Tewley," Baldridge repeated. "See to it that Tewley gets this," he said, tossing a coin to the doorman. Leading Nashville Harry to the left, he started off in a walk, glancing back over his shoulder at Tyner, who was still standing alongside her horse. "What are you waiting on?"

Tyner wanted to strangle him on the spot, but she flashed the doorman a plaster smile instead, quickly mounted sidesaddle, and followed.

5

MONDAY EVENING JUST before going down to dinner, Luke Williamson was seated in his cabin, finishing a letter of recommendation for a crewman who was leaving to take a job on a Missouri River packet. He said all the usual things, but he had found it hard to concentrate on writing with all the hammering going on next door. Having just that morning ordered the second mate to move to a larger cabin in the crew's quarters down the texas, he had instructed Manuel Ramirez, the ship's carpenter, to renovate the cabin next door and turn it into an office. He told himself he was doing it because *he* needed more room, what with managing two fully operational packets and the increased paperwork, though he had been handling the increased office work satisfactorily from the modest desk in his cabin. But when one or two of the crewmen, or Tyner, or Baldridge showed up in his room, Williamson felt too crowded and uncomfortable. He reasoned that he needed more space to properly sit down and discuss river business. He told himself the three-by-five-foot wall map of the Mississippi River—from Minnesota to Louisiana—he'd had mounted in the new room was needed for the business, though his packet line never operated above St. Louis. The high-backed chairs he had ordered from a furniture maker, to be picked up on his next stop at Cairo, Illinois, were to entertain important passengers, he told himself. And he had convinced himself that the locking file drawers Manuel had installed would hold any important shipping documents, even though Tibedeau filed all significant papers in the clerk's office. None of this was for the detective business, he assured himself, not even the hidden panel beside the wall map Manuel was building to store Williamson's Henry rifle and two or three handguns.

As he folded the letter of recommendation and placed it in an envelope on the edge of his desk, he scarcely heard the knock at his door above the construction work.

"Come in!" he shouted over the rhythmic grind of a saw. A piece of wood plinked onto the floor next door.

The door opened a few inches. "Luke? Are you in there?"

"Come in!" he said even louder.

Salina Tyner leaned in. "We saw your light on. Masey and I are back from talking with Helen Van Geer," she shouted.

Williamson invited them inside, then walked over to a blanket hanging in the spot where Manuel had cut a doorway into the wall between the captain's cabin and the new office. He pulled the blanket back from the unfinished entrance.

"Manuel." Neither the carpenter nor his assistant, who supported a board that Manuel was sawing, heard him, so he stepped through and called his name again.

"Si, Señor Captain?"

"Let's call it a night, Manuel."

The carpenter looked about him. "But Captain, I still have very much to do." He began pointing and explaining the tasks that remained. "And if you want me to finish by the time we leave tomorrow—"

"It'll be all right. You can't work much later tonight anyway without disturbing the passengers and crew. Start again first thing in the morning, and whatever you don't get done by the time we depart, you can finish en route."

"Si, Señor Captain." Manuel instructed his assistant to gather his tools.

"Just leave the lantern on," Williamson said. "I want to show the room to my friends."

Manuel beamed. "Si, si. I think they will like this room very much." With his helper close behind, the two of them left through the regular door to the deck.

Williamson peeled the blanket back from the doorway and invited Tyner and Baldridge inside the new room, which smelled of fresh-cut wood and varnish.

Baldridge surveyed the ongoing work. "What is all this?"

"I just needed more space. Figured it would make a good place to meet with people, you know, talk things over."

"You mean clients?" Tyner asked. "For our business?"

"For the *shipping* business," Williamson countered. "The jury's still out on the other, unless you found out something about Van Geer that we can use."

"Maybe," Baldridge said, moving to examine the captain's new wall map.

Williamson offered Tyner and Baldridge each a cane-bottomed chair borrowed from the sitting area on the deck below. "These will have to do for tonight. I've got some decent furniture on order."

Only Tyner and Williamson sat down, as Baldridge continued to study the map. Tyner related her interview with Helen Van Geer, Baldridge tossing in an occasional comment or clarification.

After listening intently for several minutes, Williamson spoke. "So no one saw Stewart Van Geer enter the house, and no one saw him leave?"

"That's right," Tyner said.

"And all the police have is Stewart's confession?"

"That's enough," Baldridge said.

"At least until we can find something or someone to prove it wasn't him," Tyner said.

"Or at least raise suspicion," Williamson said. "Create reasonable doubt. That's all we've got to show." Williamson looked at Tyner. "I assume he's got a good lawyer?"

"The best in St. Louis, according to Mrs. Van Geer."

"He'd better be," Baldridge added.

"You still think he did it, don't you?" Williamson said.

"Hell, yeah, I think he did it! What bothers me is *why* he did it."

Williamson nodded slowly. "If Hudson Van Geer dies, Stewart takes control of the business."

"Not if he's six feet under," Baldridge said. "And he will stretch hemp for sure. You wait and see."

Tyner agreed. "Masey's right, Luke. The murder of a man as powerful as Hudson Van Geer is bound to bring justice, and bring it swiftly. Even if his own son did kill him, this will go to trial and be decided fast. You can bet on it."

"It makes no sense that Stewart killed him for the business," Baldridge said.

"Then maybe he just got into an argument with his father. Maybe it got out of hand," Williamson offered. "Wouldn't be the first time something like that happened."

"I didn't get the impression from anything Helen Van Geer said that Stewart had those kind of disagreements with his father," Tyner concluded. "I'm sure they didn't see eye to eye on everything, but I got the feeling that Hudson Van Geer was pretty well pleased with Stewart, particularly since he stepped in when the other son, Robert, left."

"What about Robert?" Williamson asked. "Some of the rivermen at the funeral talked about him working for the railroad."

"Helen Van Geer said the two hadn't spoken in a year. Apparently Robert had no interest in his father's business. He wanted nothing to do with him."

"What about this Grant De Paul fellow?" Baldridge said. "Helen Van Geer said the man threatened her husband."

"I knew Grant De Paul when he was captain of his own boat," Williamson said. "He was a good man. When he lost his last boat, he took work as a pilot for some local carrier down around Vicksburg. As far as I know, he's still down there."

"But he lost his boat to Hudson Van Geer," Baldridge said. "That would make a man mighty angry. Angry enough to kill. Or have someone kill for him."

"I can't see Grant De Paul doing that," Williamson said, "but I guess it wouldn't hurt to talk to him. I'll look him up on the way down to New Orleans."

"We're going to need more than this," Tyner said. "There were plenty of people that disliked Hudson Van Geer, but right now I don't see how we can tie anyone other than Stewart Van Geer to his death."

"Maybe there is something," Baldridge said, turning again to look at the map.

"What are you studying on that map?" Tyner asked.

"Luke, where is St. Joseph, Louisiana?"

"It's about four hours south of Vicksburg, just below Grand Gulf. Why do you ask?"

"Something I found looking through Hudson Van Geer's papers," he said. Baldridge reached inside his jacket pocket and produced some folded pages.

"Masey!" Tyner said, almost rising from her chair. "Did you take those out of Van Geer's study?"

Baldridge nodded. "While you were talking to his wife, I looked through the papers Hudson Van Geer had been handling in the days just before the murder—you know, things still out on his desk. I thought maybe I could find something that would point to one of Van Geer's competitors."

"You found something? Something on De Paul?" Tyner asked.

"No, there was nothing there on De Paul."

"Then what?"

Baldridge unfolded a letter. "It appears that all may not have been happiness and sunlight between Hudson Van Geer and his son Stewart."

"What are you talking about?" Williamson said.

"I found this letter among Van Geer's papers. The letter is dated May 28. It's from someone named V. R. Sheldon in St. Joseph, Louisiana." Baldridge handed the letter to Williamson, and Tyner pulled her chair over to see the page.

St. Joseph, Louisiana
May 28, 1873

Dear Mr. Van Geer,

Your gracious offer of a 25% discount on shipping rates for my mercantile trade, in exchange for my habitual business with your packet service, finds me at a loss for words to express my appreciation. These troubling financial times give me cause to humbly accept your offer, and I look forward to a long and mutually prosperous affiliation with Van Geer Shipping Lines. As verification of our agreement, I shall show this letter to your clerk when the next of the Van Geer boats stops here.

Williamson waved the letter at Baldridge. "I don't get it. It's just Van Geer trying to undercut everyone else's business again. Same old shit. The man was always doing things like this."

"That's what I thought, too, until I read the rest of it."

Williamson's eyes returned to the page.

With reference to the favor you asked in your letter of the 25th ultimo, I have been able to determine the following. The family of Pierre Boulet lived near Lake Bruin in Tensas Parish, some six miles north of our fair town of St. Joseph. Having been acquainted with Pierre, and having occasionally done business with him over the past several years, I was quite saddened by the untimely death of he and his wife, Anna. In October of 1871, a fire at the Boulet home took the lives of both Pierre and Anna. Only their daughter, Claire, survived the tragedy. As to your question about Miss Claire Boulet's whereabouts, I cannot say with certainty. I have inquired of some friends who tell me that after she recovered from injuries in the fire, she left Tensas Parish in the company of two of the family's household servants. To my knowledge, she has not since returned.

I regret that I cannot offer you better information, but I extend to you every hope of success in locating Miss Boulet. Allow me to hasten to add one final note. While Miss Boulet did not return to Tensas Parish, the Boulet Plantation, that is, the four hundred acres and outbuildings less the mansion, which was a total loss from the fire, has since been sold. I am told by the clerk in the parish land office that Miss Boulet did not return to Tensas Parish to conduct the transaction, but that the entire matter was executed through attorneys and handled by mail.

Per your request, I shall hold your inquiry in confidence until you arrive. I again wish you every success for the future, and shall be delighted to treat you to dinner upon the occasion of your visit. In the meantime, do not hesitate to call upon me should I be of any additional service.
Respectfully,
V. R. Sheldon

Williamson looked up at Baldridge. "Why would Hudson Van Geer send a letter to Louisiana supposedly looking for his own daughter-in-law, who was right here in St. Louis?"

"I was kind of wonderin' that myself," Baldridge said.

Tyner stood up and walked over to the door, peering through the unfinished window frame at the lights of an adjacent steamboat. "Helen Van Geer told me that her husband never liked the fact that Stewart married Claire." She glanced over at Baldridge. "Right before you came back into the room at Van Geer's place, Mrs. Van Geer said her husband thought Stewart rushed into the marriage. He said it was the one major disagreement between the two of them."

"So, his father is checking up on his new wife," Baldridge observed, "and maybe Stewart found out about it. Maybe he argued with his father and ended up shooting him. It still points to Stewart Van Geer."

"Or maybe Stewart didn't know anything about it," Williamson said, as he carefully reread the letter. "Hudson Van Geer may have been a son of a bitch, but he was a *thorough* son of a bitch. When it came to business, I never knew him to miss a detail. If he was checking up on Claire Boulet, you can damned well bet he had a good reason. And the Hudson Van Geer I knew wouldn't have told a soul until he had everything in order."

"Sounds like you halfway admire this Van Geer," Baldridge said.

"Admire him? No. But I've butted heads with him enough over the past five or six years to get a feel for how he operates," Williamson said. He tapped the page with his finger. "It sure sounds to me like he was planning to go to Louisiana to follow up on this."

Baldridge spoke to Tyner. "Do you think Helen Van Geer knows anything about this?"

"I doubt it. She had nothing harsh to say about Claire. She even said she had gotten closer to her daughter-in-law since

Claire became pregnant. She said Hudson didn't care for Claire, but I feel sure she would have mentioned it if she had known about the letter."

"Not necessarily," Williamson said, rising from his chair. He stepped beneath the blanket in the new doorway and disappeared into his cabin, speaking loudly enough for them to hear him. "Van Geer was known to be as tight-lipped as they come." He returned momentarily from his cabin with a pen and paper in hand, then began copying information from the letter.

"What's that for?" Baldridge asked.

"I'm going to check this out," Williamson said without looking up.

"You're going to St. Joseph?" Tyner asked.

Williamson shook his head. "Nope. Hardscrabble Landing. It's about eight miles north of St. Joseph."

"Why stop there?" Tyner asked.

Memories of a face from his past produced a slight smile, but he kept the sweeter details to himself. "I was there with Commander Ellet for a week during the war. We made our headquarters on Hardscrabble Plantation at the home of the owner, Monroe Routh. As I recall, the Rouths know most everybody in those parts."

Baldridge grunted. "Oh, I'll bet they'll be glad to see you. I got a firsthand look at what was left of a few houses you Yankee officers turned into 'headquarters,' and they weren't fit for a pack of Gypsies."

"It wasn't like that," Williamson countered. "We didn't—"

"So they were Union people? Is that why you didn't destroy the place?"

Williamson stopped writing. He thought about not answering. To say more would only provoke Baldridge, but he wasn't about to sit there and let this Southerner lump him in with every unscrupulous Federal soldier or sailor he had ever seen. "No. The Rouths weren't for the Union. But my men carried themselves with dignity—"

"While they carried off the silver, the furniture, the music—"

"Damn it, Baldridge," Williamson said, rising to his feet. "Do you have any idea how sick and tired I am of hearing you talk like the Rebels had a monopoly on decent behavior? I've seen Southern partisans like you steal the horses and mules from their own people and leave a family with forty acres of crops and no mule to plow them."

Baldridge moved toward him, with Williamson meeting him, the two men standing nose to nose. "Who you callin' a partisan thief? I was in the Seventh Tennessee Cavalry, and we never—"

"Stop it!" Tyner shouted, stepping between them and pushing them apart. "Both of you just stop it!" Baldridge and Williamson glared defiantly at one another. "I'm not about to watch the war fought out again tonight in this room. We've got plenty to do without this." She looked at Baldridge. "Masey, I think it's a good idea for Luke to see what he can find out about this. Maybe it'll help. Maybe it won't. But he's going south with the *Paragon* anyway, so he might as well check into it."

"Well, I wouldn't want to put him to any trouble," Baldridge said. "He is a busy captain and all . . ."

"I said I'd do it, didn't I?" Williamson was still glaring at Baldridge. "I mean, I have got a shipping business to run, but I said I'd do it. It's not like I sit around all day with nothing to do, like some people."

"You talking about me?" Baldridge replied.

As Baldridge closed toward Williamson, Tyner pushed them apart again, turning to Williamson. "Masey and I will see what else we can turn over around here. We've still got to talk with Robert Van Geer, and Claire, and—"

"Don't worry yourself, there, Captain," Baldridge said. "We'll wrap this thing up for you while you're gone."

Williamson shoved the letter back at Baldridge, who took it from him. "I'll wire you if I find out anything." He made an excuse about having to begin his late rounds; he'd had enough of Baldridge for the night. Before departing, Baldridge brought up the matter of his and Tyner's "business expenses" while the *Paragon* and the *Edward Smythe* were both away from St. Louis. Williamson took twenty dollars of the advance money Helen Van Geer paid him and bypassed Baldridge's outstretched hand to give it to Tyner. Had Baldridge gotten hold of it, Williamson had visions of the advance turning into a stake in another all-night poker game. And although he promised to meet both of them for breakfast in the morning, he figured Tyner would be the only one likely to make it, with or without stake money. Closing his cabin door behind them, Williamson leaned against it and picked up his pipe, tobacco pouch, and a friction lighter from a table beside the door. Pressing in some fresh leaf, he lit the pipe and puffed until a robust smoke swirled about his head. He took a long draw, leaned his head back against the door, and blew the smoke toward the lantern. The light flickered and made the shadows dance about the walls of his cabin.

Detective business. What in the hell am I doing?

6

Tuesday, June 17

THE TEMPERATURE WAS well over ninety degrees, with a near-smothering humidity in the air that cast a haze about the boxcars as Baldridge walked Nashville Harry up to a horse trough at the southeastern end of the St. Louis rail yard. As the animal drank, Baldridge surveyed the tracks in search of the office for Fieldhurst Freight, where he expected to find Robert Van Geer. The smell of burning coal permeated the air, as a short blast from a locomotive whistle alerted working freight handlers that a line of cars would be moving several feet down the track. Baldridge watched the workers quickly grab a drink of water from a nearby barrel as the next two empty boxcars eased up and halted beside a loading dock. The men resumed rolling barrels aboard the car, much as he'd seen the crewmen on the *Paragon* do hundreds of times. Still, there was a difference—a difference Baldridge wasn't sure he would have paid much attention to before he met Luke Williamson. He had been riding trains all his life, and even helped to capture a few back during the war. Though trains had been important to local travel and business in the forties and fifties, anyone wanting custom accommodations and trying to move large amounts of freight during those days would almost certainly use the river. But the war had changed all that, showing just how far and how fast troops and equipment could travel over a decent rail system. Railroad agents were everywhere now, many of them former Union and Confederate officers using their popularity and influence to raise bond issues to build new railroads in every direction. Like an adolescent youth, the railroad flexed its muscles and tested its strength as it reached into new towns and villages all over the country. And Baldridge would probably have thought of it all as progress, as everyone else seemed to, if he hadn't come to know Luke Williamson. Spending time on the packets and living in the elegance of the riverboats made him share some of Williamson's dislike for the railroads' iron monstrosities. His gaze fell upon the locomotive at the head of the dozen cars the freight handlers were loading. It sat on the track, occasionally snorting steam from beneath its wheels like an unruly bull, hungry to leave its pen and charge up the distant track. Black smoke rose from its smokestack, lingering momentarily until what little wind there was wafted its cloud past the depot and over Baldridge, leaving a sooty film that he could feel on his hands and face. He had been there less than fifteen minutes, and he already felt dirty.

When the line of railcars moved again, Baldridge caught a glimpse of a sign beyond the tracks for Fieldhurst Freight, so he coaxed Nashville Harry from the water trough and walked him slowly across the track, cutting a wide swath behind the caboose of the train he had been watching. As he approached a small wooden building, he recognized Robert Van Geer from the funeral. His blond hair was neatly combed, and both sleeves of his white shirt were rolled up to precisely the same level just above both elbows. He pointed to some papers in his left hand as he spoke to a half-dozen men standing with their backs to Baldridge. Masey halted his mount some twenty feet away, as an animated Van Geer waved the papers vigorously and gestured in the direction of the train Baldridge had seen being loaded, his men nodding in agreement. The way Van Geer's bright blue eyes flashed when he spoke, he reminded Baldridge of a preacher. If he knew Baldridge was there, he gave no indication, consumed as he was in his rhetoric, so Baldridge waited until Van Geer had finished his remarks and the men had hustled away. Van Geer started down the four steps leading from the building.

"Mr. Van Geer!"

"Yes?" Van Geer halted.

"I'm Masey Baldridge. I was wondering if—"

"From my father's funeral."

"Yes, that's right."

Van Geer folded his arms. "What can I do for you?"

"I've come to talk to you about Stewart."

"My mother sent you, didn't she?" He glanced impatiently at the men who had just departed, then back at Baldridge.

"No, I wouldn't say she *sent* me."

"You're some kind of detective, aren't you?"

"I'm with Big River Detective Agency," Baldridge said, noting a sense of pride at having actually said it to someone for the first time.

"Well, she told me she was hiring you—you and that Captain Williamson," Robert said. "Against my advice, I might add."

"Mr. Van Geer, we're just trying to find out what happened to your father."

"I know what happened to my father, Mr. Baldridge. My father was murdered. He was gunned down by my own brother. Now if that's not bad enough, if that's not embarrassment aplenty, my mother has to drag the whole thing out by hiring

some detectives to run around asking questions and kee[everything squarely in the public eye."

Baldridge eased Nashville Harry closer to the steps wl Van Geer stood. "Your brother is going on trial for murder morrow."

"As well he should." Robert started down the steps. "I got to see about some new boxcars, Mr. Baldridge. I really do have the time or the desire to talk to you about the evil ı brother has done."

"But what if he's innocent?"

Van Geer halted beside Baldridge's horse. "Innocent? M Baldridge, Stewart confessed to the police! Now, I don't kno why he did it, so there is nothing I can tell you that will help And as far as I'm concerned, my mother's hiring you was a wast of time and money, because there's nothing you can find out thal will change the facts."

"Maybe not," Baldridge said. "But there are some things that don't add up about this whole affair, and I was hoping you could help me clear them up."

"I'm a busy man. I've got to see about these boxcars—"

"You wouldn't mind if I came along, would you? I'd just like to ask you some questions."

"It won't do any good. It's a waste of time."

"You're a businessman, Mr. Van Geer. Don't you believe in getting what you pay for?"

"Of course I do."

"Well, your mother's paying me, whether you like it or not. So do you have any objections to her getting her money's worth?"

"Very well, then," Van Geer said, strolling off toward the loading dock. "But you'll have to talk while I'm working. And don't get in the way."

Baldridge tied up Nashville Harry and fell in behind Van Geer, his limp drawing Van Geer's attention, though he made no mention of it. They arrived at a length of track where a brake-

man stood atop a stationary boxcar as a locomotive slowly backed another car toward it for coupling. Baldridge grew anxious as a second brakeman stepped beside the coupler and positioned himself between the two boxcars. Even with the buffers on both cars, there was precious little clearance for a man to stand. He watched the brakeman's hands moving quickly around the link-and-pin coupler as the two cars closed, the loud, metallic clank signifying a successful join, followed by the brakeman adroitly sliding the pin into place.

"Make the brake connection," Van Geer ordered the men, and the brakeman on top of the boxcar signaled toward the locomotive as the other brakeman connected a hose between the two cars. The sound of rushing air startled Baldridge, and he stepped quickly backward, though the crewmen seemed quite pleased and Van Geer broke into a broad smile.

"What the hell's that?" Baldridge asked, pointing to the hose.

"The newest thing," Van Geer said. "Air brakes. A man named Westinghouse invented it. It'll stop a train in one-third the distance it takes these brakemen to manually turn the brake wheels." Van Geer smiled proudly. "And we've got the first air brakes in St. Louis. I convinced Mr. Fieldhurst to buy them." Van Geer began walking along the train toward the locomotive, and Baldridge followed.

"About your father—"

"My father," Van Geer repeated reflectively. "What do you want to know about my father?"

"Do you have any idea why someone would want to kill him?"

"Surely you're joking, Mr. Baldridge. By now you must know that a lot of people hated my father."

"Enough to kill him?"

"My brother did."

"How about you?"

Van Geer stopped. "I beg your pardon?"

"I said, what about you?"

"Don't think for one minute that I don't know what you're up to, Baldridge. You're looking for someone, anyone other than Stewart, to blame for Father's death. That's how you detectives make your money, isn't it? You run around stirring up trouble, making accusations—"

Baldridge ignored the diatribe. "Your mother said you and your father didn't get along. She said you haven't spoken in almost a year."

Van Geer revealed a modest smile and shook his head. "Dear Mother. She has such a knack for understatement."

"How's that?"

"She said we didn't get along." Van Geer looked Baldridge squarely in the face. "I hated the son of a bitch."

"Is that why you left the steamboat business?"

"I guess you could say that." Van Geer leaned up against the ladder attached to the rear of a boxcar. "My father was a difficult man, Baldridge. He was a cold man. I've seen him fire crewmen and throw their families out on the street with nothing but the clothes on their back. And I can think of any number of people who wanted to see him dead, including me on occasion. But I discovered the best way to deal with my father was not to deal with him at all, so I went my own way."

"Into railroading."

"That's right."

"But why leave shipping altogether?"

"Because I can see where this country's going, Baldridge, that's why. People hated my father because he was a good businessman. I hated him because he wasn't good enough."

"I don't understand," Baldridge said.

Van Geer signaled to the brakemen that he would rejoin them in a moment, then turned to Baldridge. "Hudson Van Geer was blinded by the river. It's all he knew and all he wanted to know. Look around you—" Van Geer gestured over the railyard. "Anyone with any sense at all can see where the future of the passenger and freight business lies—the railroad."

"Your father wasn't interested in the railroad?"

"Never. Despite my best efforts to convince him. Hudson Van Geer was a wealthy man, but he could have been enormously wealthy if he had only diversified his business. He could have purchased a controlling interest in any of two dozen railroads being built across the Southeast. I tried to tell him, but he wouldn't listen."

"So you left the company."

"He gave me no choice. I refuse to be a part of the past, Baldridge. My father was the past. I am the future. I, along with the railroad."

"But now you work for someone else. You're no longer—"

"Temporarily. I supervise the purchase of new equipment, evaluate investment opportunities in other railroads, and help Mr. Fieldhurst raise bond money to expand his railroad. Mr. Fieldhurst understands the value of a man of my talent and vision."

"Or the influence of your father's name."

"So? There's no crime in that."

"Apparently Hudson Van Geer thought so."

"My crime in my father's mind was not being obsessed with the river the way he was. Frankly, I think he was jealous," Van Geer said, "and maybe a little bit nervous. Freight shipments in the steamboat industry are down almost fifteen percent this year. And do you know where it's all going? The railroad. Baldridge, do you realize that this country will probably lay three thousand miles of new track in the next year? Why, it takes half the time to go from here to Cincinnati by train that it takes by river. I think my father was starting to feel the pressure of all that. Had he lived, he would have had to admit I was right, though I doubt he would ever have done so."

"You don't seem too bothered by his death."

"What do what want from me, Baldridge? If you're looking for the grieving son, you're looking in the wrong place. Go talk to Stewart. He practically celebrated, the day I left the company. Stewart couldn't wait to get his hands on the daily affairs of Van Geer Shipping. Daddy's little boy come to save the day. I'm sure he'll grieve enough for the both of us, particularly when he thinks about what he's done. Between him and that Tewley, I'm sure they'll cry us a river."

"Tewley? That's the stableboy, right?"

"Yeah. The boy's father worked on Van Geer ships for almost fifteen years. My father took the boy in when his father died in an accident on one of the boats. I guess the old stone-hearted Hudson Van Geer got to feeling guilty, though I'd never seen it in him before. The boy's mother was gone. The kid had no one. Beats anything I ever saw the way he made over that kid. He sure as hell paid more attention to that boy than he ever did to either Stewart or me. Hell, my father was scarcely home when I was growing up. And when I was old enough to help him run the shipping business, he chose to pay no attention to my advice. When I tried to start my own life, he responded by shunning me like a leper. What am I supposed to feel? Tell me, Mr. Baldridge. What exactly am I supposed to feel?"

"What about Van Geer Shipping? If Stewart hangs, who will run the company?"

"That's not my problem. My father made it quite clear that it wouldn't be me. When I told him I was going into the railroad, he went out of his way to put it into writing that Stewart would succeed him as head of the company." Van Geer smiled momentarily, picking some rust off the handrail of the boxcar. "If Stewart hangs, I guess that makes my dear mother the owner and president of Van Geer Shipping Lines. That ought to be fun to watch." Van Geer glanced toward the locomotive. "I've got work to do, Baldridge. If you'll excuse me—"

"There is one other thing I need to ask you about."

"Make it short, Baldridge."

"How well do you know Stewart's wife, Claire?"

"I think highly of Claire. Mother probably told you that I introduced her to Stewart."

"She mentioned something about that."

"It's probably the only thing my brother will ever thank me for."

"How did you know Claire?"

"I met her returning from Natchez well over a year ago. I was evaluating a railroad project for Mr. Fieldhurst."

"You still travel on your father's boats?"

"I'm a businessman, Mr. Baldridge. Perhaps it is one thing I got from my father—I never let emotion get in the way of business. Stewart came on board at Helena. I introduced him to Claire, and well, you know the rest."

"So you do get along with Stewart?"

"Obviously, Baldridge. It's my father that I chose not to deal with. I still communicate as needed with my brother and my mother. Why are you asking me about Claire?"

"Were you aware that your father had some concerns about Claire Boulet?"

"Concerns? What kind of concerns?"

"I'm not sure. But I think your father had some questions about her."

"You're making no sense. What kind of questions?"

"It's probably nothing, but I found a letter your father wrote to a man in Louisiana. He seemed to have been asking questions about Claire's parents."

"I was under the impression that Claire's parents are dead."

"Yes, I know that."

"Why would my father ask such a thing?"

"I don't know, Mr. Van Geer. I thought you might be able to tell me."

Van Geer seemed annoyed. "How should I know? I've already told you that I haven't talked to my father in nearly a year. Hudson Van Geer didn't like a lot of people. He probably resented the fact that I introduced the two of them. But I fail to see what Claire's parents have to do with my father's death."

"Maybe nothing."

"Then why are you wasting my time? And my mother's money? I'm going back to work now, Baldridge. I'm sure you can find your own way out of the rail yard."

7

Wednesday, June 18

SALINA TYNER HAD just about had enough. She tapped her fingers impatiently on the window of the carriage as she waited for the sudden thunderstorm to pass. The carriage sat beneath a spreading oak tree, the driver huddled under an oil-cloth and trying to calm his nervous animal. Rain slapped against the roof as Tyner peered through the window at the home of Stewart Van Geer, one block away. This was her third trip, and she had yet to speak with Claire Van Geer. Once yesterday morning, and again yesterday afternoon she had been turned away by an odd-looking woman calling herself Marie Trehan. Tyner remembered the name from talking with Helen Van Geer and from Luke's description of his visit with Stewart in jail. Helen Van Geer had called her Claire's attendant. Guard would have been a more accurate term, as far as Tyner was concerned. Trehan, a woman with the dark skin of a Creole, had informed Tyner on both visits with a hint of a French accent that "Madam is ill." Of course she was ill, Tyner figured. Her husband was to be tried tomorrow for murder, and the chances were pretty good that he would hang. But for her to be too ill to talk to someone trying to help Stewart seemed unusual to Tyner.

Baldridge had returned that afternoon to the Washington Square jail in another attempt to get some sense out of Stewart. Last night at the Dearborn Hotel—Tyner and Baldridge's home upon the *Paragon*'s departure—a frustrated Baldridge had revealed that nothing from his conversation with Robert Van Geer would shed light on the elder Van Geer's curious letter about Claire. So with the trial beginning on Thursday, everything pointing to Stewart as the killer, and no other leads to track down, Tyner was determined to see what she could find out— if she ever got inside the house! It would be at least two days before Luke Williamson reached Louisiana, and there was no guarantee he would turn up anything even then. She and Baldridge were fast running out of time. As the rain slackened, she hatched a plan.

As the driver eased up to the front of Stewart Van Geer's home, Tyner dropped the curtains over the windows of the carriage. The rain having stopped, the driver shed his oilcloth and dismounted, walking slowly toward the dozen or so steps that led to the front door. The home had two stories, with a porch running across the front and down the left side. Modest when compared to Hudson Van Geer's, it was still more house than most people would ever afford, the grass well kept and flowers adorning boxes mounted along the porch railing. Tyner watched as the driver stopped at the bottom of the steps, removing his hat just as the door opened. Marie Trehan, wearing a deep maroon dress and a black, Spanish-looking lace hat, came outside.

"What is your business?" she demanded in a low monotone.

"Uh, ma'am," the driver said, "there's someone here to see you." He pointed toward the carriage with his hat.

"You were here yesterday. Tell the lady that Madam remains ill."

"The lady says she wants to see Mrs. Van Geer real bad," the driver said. "She says she won't take no for an answer."

Trehan placed her hands on her hips, glaring at the carriage. "Then I shall tell her myself," she said, pushing past the driver. Rushing around her, he grabbed the door just ahead of Trehan. He swung it open to reveal an empty carriage.

"What are you doing?" Trehan demanded. "What is this all about?"

The driver, perhaps more surprised than Trehan, pulled the curtains back as if they might yet conceal Tyner.

He struggled for words. "Ma'am, I don't know. The lady was ... she was ..."

"Leave here now. I have no more time for your jokes. And if you return, I shall get the police."

Taking advantage of Trehan's distraction, Tyner emerged from her hiding place alongside the house and slipped up the side steps, tiptoeing around the porch and slipping in the front door, which she quietly locked behind her. She pulled back the drapery and stifled a laugh as the driver walked circles around his carriage in search of his vanished fare, while Trehan chastised him in a hodgepodge of English and French.

Tyner crept down the hall and peered into the parlor, but found no one. Hearing a sound up the stairs, she moved quickly to the second floor. In the first bedroom on her right she saw a woman, down on one knee, adjusting the foot pedal on one of those new-model home sewing machines. She thought it an odd position for someone so gravely ill.

"My, my," Tyner said, "you've made a miraculous recovery." She closed the bedroom door behind her.

A startled Claire Van Geer spun about, her hand moving to her mouth to stifle a scream that never came.

"Who are you!" she said. "Marie! Marie!" she shouted.

Tyner could now hear Trehan pulling at the front door.

"Claire!" Trehan shouted from downstairs.

"Marie!" Claire responded, backing away from Tyner.

"Oh, relax," Tyner said, moving confidently into the room. "I never thought you were as sick as that ugly woman claimed you were."

"I demand to know who you are and what you're doing in my home," Claire said, having retreated to the window as far from Tyner as she could get.

"I'm sorry I had to come in this way," Tyner said, the front door downstairs still rattling as Trehan struggled to open it. Then the noise was gone.

"You're that woman. That woman who Marie said came by to see me."

"That would be me," Tyner said matter-of-factly. "Twice, in fact."

"Tyner," Claire said. "You work with the detectives my mother-in-law hired."

"Right again," Tyner said, moving over and taking a seat on the corner of the high four-poster bed. She peeled back the mosquito net and ran her hand over the satin sheets. "Nice bed." Another time, another place, it would have been a good spot to work.

"Are you in the habit of breaking into people's homes?"

Tyner could hear Marie Trehan, having made her way in the back door, bounding up the steps. "I didn't break in your house," Tyner said. "I walked right in the front door."

"Claire!" Trehan burst into the room.

"Now *that* woman," Tyner said, pointing, "I believe *she* broke in."

"I don't find any of this the least bit humorous," Claire said.

"Who is she?" Trehan demanded. Tyner thought her tone rather presumptuous for a household attendant.

"She's with the detectives Helen hired."

"Honey, I'm not *with* the detectives, I *am* a detective."

"You must leave now," Trehan said. Tyner noticed a look in her eyes unlike any she had ever seen. She was angry, for certain, but something about the way the woman stared at her made Tyner shiver. For a brief moment she thought Trehan would come after her. "Madam is ill," she again declared.

"Yeah, that's what you kept telling me. Imagine my surprise when I found her practically standing on her head under that sewing machine. And her pregnant, too."

"It's all right, Marie. I'll speak with her," Claire said.

"But Ma—Madam—"

Claire raised her hand. "Really. It's all right." She looked at Tyner. "I'm afraid you've caught me in a bit of a lie." She moved over to Tyner. "With all that's happened to Stewart and to my dear father-in-law, I just felt it would be better to remain in seclusion." She forced a smile. "I really haven't felt very well. It's been a difficult pregnancy, you know. I offer you my apologies. I should have taken the time to speak with you yesterday."

"Considering that we're running out of time, I'd say you're right."

Marie Trehan, never ceasing her evil glare, left the room.

"How is Stewart?" Claire asked. "I was unable to visit with him last night. Marie took his supper, and she said he was still feeling poorly."

"I haven't seen your husband. But Masey Baldridge, my associate, is probably at the jail right now."

"That Baldridge seems like a nasty man."

"Masey does good work."

"Well, I do hope Stewart's doing some better. He just hasn't been himself since . . . since this awful tragedy."

From the moment she entered the bedroom, Tyner had noticed an odd smell, almost like someone cooking with vinegar. She now figured she had spotted the source of the odor. Despite the afternoon light coming through the partially raised window, Tyner noticed three short, thick lavender candles burning on the dresser. They sat atop a coconut, which in turn rested on a piece of paper.

"Are those scented candles?" Tyner said, walking toward the dresser.

"Leave that alone," Claire blurted, moving between Tyner and the dresser, her motion creating a draft that caused the candle flames to flicker. Claire placed her hands around the flames until they recovered and turned to face Tyner.

"What is that?" Tyner asked.

"Each of us grieves in our own way, Miss Tyner. If you must know, this is for the soul of Hudson Van Geer."

"From what I've heard about him, you need a couple more coconuts."

"Hudson Van Geer deserves to be remembered, Miss Tyner, despite what others may say about him. Stewart cared for his father, and his father for him."

"And you?"

"Me?"

"Did Hudson Van Geer care for you?"

"I was his daughter-in-law." She placed her hand over her stomach. "Soon to be the mother of his grandchild. Of course he cared about me."

"I understand he wasn't exactly thrilled about you marrying Stewart," Tyner said.

"Hudson Van Geer was a very strong-willed man, Miss Tyner. The only problem I ever had with Mr. Van Geer was over the way he dominated Stewart. He had already succeeded in running off one son, and he scarcely gave a listen to anything Stewart had to say."

"That must have made Stewart mad."

"Sometimes."

"Mad enough to kill his own father?"

Claire hesitated. "It would appear so, wouldn't it, Miss Tyner?"

"Helen Van Geer doesn't think so."

Claire forced a smile. "Poor Mother Helen. She wants so hard to believe in Stewart."

"And his own wife doesn't?"

"I resent your tone, Miss Tyner." Claire's voice softened. "A wife knows." She folded her hands and rested them on her protruding abdomen. "I've seen the pressure building in Stewart for weeks now. His father was just asking too much of him. He's not Robert, you know. He didn't ask for all the responsibility of the business."

"You know Robert well, do you?"

"No. No, not really. Just from the times I've seen him with Stewart. Although I did meet Robert first, as you probably know."

"Yes. On one of Van Geer's boats."

"That's right. He introduced me to Stewart and . . . well, you know how love is."

"Not lately," Tyner muttered.

"I told the police all this. I told them about all the pressure Stewart was under." She glanced out the window. "I felt bad about telling them, but . . . they just kept asking me why. 'Why would he do it?'" Tyner noticed that Claire appeared suddenly to be in tears. "Excuse me, Miss Tyner. It's just that . . . with the baby coming and everything, I simply don't know what I'll do without Stewart."

"They haven't hung him yet. Even if they find him guilty—and they probably will—Masey and I still have some time to see what we can find out."

"But what is there to find out?" Claire asked, wiping the tears from her eyes. "Do you honestly believe you'll be able to keep Stewart from hanging?"

"Well, for one thing, Masey and I want to know why Hudson Van Geer was asking questions about you."

"Me?" Claire's tears ended as abruptly as they began. "What are you talking about?"

"Apparently Hudson Van Geer wrote a letter to Louisiana a few days before his death. To a man named Sheldon, clerk of

Tensas Parish. He was asking about the Boulet Plantation. About you."

Claire's face, tear-streaked only moments before, now grew fierce.

"How could he do such a thing! How could he insult his own son like that?"

"Why would he be asking about you?"

"How should I know?" Claire nearly ran into the sewing machine as she stormed across the room. She pointed at Tyner. "He couldn't stand to see Stewart happy. That's what it was, you know. From the day he was told we were to be married, Hudson Van Geer was against it. We hadn't know each other long enough, according to him. I told Stewart all about my life, and I told his father too. My parents died in a fire. I barely escaped, myself. I came from a decent home and decent parents. Hudson Van Geer knew all he needed to know."

"Then why would he keep asking?"

"Who knows? Suspicious old fool."

"Do you think Stewart might have found out about his father checking up on you? Could they have quarreled about it?"

"I don't know. Perhaps. You'd have to ask Stewart."

"Well, we'd like to, but your husband hasn't said a sensible thing since the murder."

"Well, then, Miss Tyner, I really don't have any idea." Claire leaned against the sewing machine. "I'm sure Stewart is quite distraught."

"He's more than distraught. He's downright—"

"Look, I'm starting to feel rather nauseous. I need to lie down. I'm afraid I don't feel up to any more questions right now. You'll have to leave, Miss Tyner. Marie will show you out." Claire sat on the edge of the bed. "Marie!"

Within three seconds the door opened and Marie Trehan stepped into the room. Tyner suspected she had been outside listening the entire time.

"Madam?"

"Please show Miss Tyner out."

"That won't be necessary," Tyner said, winking at Trehan. "I got in without her help. I can find my way out."

Marie Trehan followed Tyner closely down the stairs. Stepping out on the front porch, Tyner realized that her carriage had long since departed, the driver no doubt angry despite the two dollars she had advanced him. The humidity seemed to have worsened after the earlier rain and Tyner did not relish walking the half mile back to the hotel. She spun around and addressed Trehan with the best fake smile she could muster.

"I don't suppose you'd have a driver who could—"

Trehan slammed the door in her face and stood glaring at her through the long, narrow window beside the door.

"I guess not."

Lifting her skirt enough to clear her ankles, Tyner moved down the steps and started walking toward the hotel. What possessed her to look back at the Van Geer house she wasn't sure, but what she saw puzzled her. She was perhaps half the distance to the spot where the carriage had waited out the rain earlier when she turned to see Marie Trehan emerge from the house and walk into the grass where she had crossed the lawn to reach the street, then pick up what appeared to be dirt and place it in a white cloth. Just as quickly as she appeared, Trehan returned into the house. Tyner had a momentary chill—a strange sensation, she thought, for such a hot day.

8

Thursday, June 19

WITH HIS CABIN door opened out onto the deck, Luke Williamson could hear Manuel Ramirez chastising his assistant in rapid-fire Spanish. Although his command of the language was minimal, Williamson could tell that Ramirez was disappointed with the work the man had done on the outside of the door that led into the newly built, adjoining office. For three days now Ramirez had been "finishing up," and Williamson knew that unless he directed him to some other task, he'd be refining his work for another week. All the sawing and hammering had begun to take its toll on Williamson's patience, and even though Ramirez had installed a door to replace the blanket hung between the cabin and the office, the noise next door still distracted him.

Over the sound of Ramirez's voice Williamson heard rousters singing as they jogged along the wharf to load a farmer's early crop of beans aboard the *Paragon*. He knew from the lyrics that First Mate Jacob Lusk's voice would soon follow.

> Mamma, Mamma, look at Sam
> Eating up the meat, 'n' soppin' the pan.
> Oh, Mamma went to beatin' and a-bangin' on Sam,
> He kep' on eatin' like he didn't give a damn.

Not five seconds passed before Lusk shouted at the rousters from the lower deck.

"Here, you men! Mind what you're singing!"

Williamson smiled. Lusk always tried to prevent the more ripened lyrics of the rouster work songs from offending what he called the "sensible ears of the passengers." Though Williamson had heard far harsher words sung by rousters, he was glad Lusk was paying attention. But then, Jacob Lusk was always watching and listening to the deckhands, and he made sure they knew it. The only negro first mate on the river, Lusk had been with Williamson for more than seven years, and he was Williamson's most trusted officer. Next to himself, no one knew the river better, and no one worked harder to make the *Paragon* the premier packet on the water.

The rousters had changed their tune, and Ramirez had calmed down somewhat, when Williamson heard a knock at his door: a chambermaid, requesting permission to clean the captain's cabin and change his bedsheets. Williamson, convinced it was impossible to get any work done at the moment, bid her come inside. Pouring himself a drink of water from a pitcher beside his bed, he stepped outside into the late afternoon sun. The tiny landing at Victoria, Mississippi, had only a deteriorating pier to which the *Paragon* nudged up its landing stage. The rousters had to navigate the decrepit pier to reach the bank, secure the cargo, then cross back over the pier to the landing stage and onto the boat. The water was too shallow most times of the year to nose up to the bank, and three months ago Williamson had threatened to cancel the stop unless the land owners that used it fixed the pier; but he knew they depended upon him to get their crops to market, and feed their kids, and plant for the next season, so he kept making stops, promising himself each time that on the next trip he would bypass. The rousters he had been listening to earlier paused momentarily to get a drink from a barrel, sent out, no doubt, by Lusk. In heat like this, a man could pass out after no more than two or three loads.

Williamson kept staring at that ragged pier, getting angrier by the moment. It was only a matter of time before a rouster fell through those rotten boards. He would be damned if he'd lose a man over this cargo stop.

"Ramirez!"

The carpenter appeared beside him from the new office. "Si, Señor Captain!"

Williamson pointed toward the shore. "You see that pier down there?"

"Si."

"Don't you have some extra lumber you haven't used on my office?"

"Si, Señor Captain. *Un poco.*"

"I want you to take your assistant here, and get two good deckhands from Jacob, and shore it up."

"The pier?"

"Yes."

The carpenter looked at his assistant and back at Williamson. "Right now?"

"That's right."

"But Señor Captain, there is still work to do on your office."

"No. You're finished with the office."

"But the moulding, the trim—"

"It'll wait. I want that pier fixed before I lose a deckhand on it." Williamson checked his watch. "I can give you half an hour, but not a minute more."

"Half an hour?"

"That's what I said. Can you do it in half an hour?"

Ramirez studied the pier momentarily, and Williamson suspected he enjoyed the challenge. The carpenter began nodding his head slowly. "Si, Señor Captain. Manuel can fix it."

"Good. Then get to it." He showed him his watch. "The clock's ticking."

Ramirez grabbed his tools from the office and trotted down the deck, rattling off instructions in Spanish to his assistant. In less than five minutes Jacob Lusk had emerged from the stairway and was calling to Williamson as he walked toward him.

"Cap'n! Ramirez just told me to give him two men. He said he was gonna fix that pier. Has he done lost his mind? We ain't got the time to be sittin' 'round here while he—"

"We will make up the time," Williamson said.

"Beg your pardon, Cap'n?"

"Jacob, how long do you think it'll be before one of your hands drops right through that pier?"

Lusk gazed at the rousters bringing aboard the last load of the cargo from shore. "Well, Cap'n, it probably won't be long. But I thought you said we wasn't stopping here no more." Lusk removed his hat and wiped the sweat from his forehead. "How come *we* fixin' that pier? How come the men what owns it don't fix it?"

"I figure they would if they could, Jacob. They've got their hands full just getting the crops in."

"If we let their beans sit there on the next pass, I bet they'll fix that pier."

"We need their business, Jacob. If we don't stop, somebody else will, and we'll likely lose them for good."

"I suppose you're right, Cap'n."

"I'm gambling they'll remember who fixed their pier when one of our competitors tries to win their business."

"Yes, sir. If you reckon that gamble's worth a few minutes of Ramirez's time—"

"It's worth it to me just to get Ramirez working on something else for a while."

Lusk laughed. "All that noise gettin' to you, is it?" Williamson nodded. "That man don't ever seem to get finished with no carpenter project, does he?"

"He's a perfectionist, Jacob." Williamson pointed at the pier. "But he's only got twenty minutes left to—"

Williamson's words were interrupted by a scream from his cabin. Both men turned to see the chambermaid stumbling out the open door.

"What's the matter with you, woman?" Lusk said.

She pointed inside. "The cap'n got a . . . he got a—"

Lusk held the woman by her shoulders. "A what? What, Betty?"

The frightened woman struggled for words. "He got a . . . a mojo under his bed."

"Are you sure?"

"I done seen it myself, Mr. Jacob," the chambermaid replied, her voice trembling. Lusk released her and stepped inside the cabin, Williamson right behind him.

"What in the world's got her spooked like that?" Williamson asked as Lusk dropped to one knee and lifted the bedsheet.

"Uhmmm, uhmmm," Lusk groaned as he stared under the bed.

The captain knelt beside him in the narrow cabin. Pressed up between the springs, not more than a few inches from the head of the bed, Williamson saw a cloth bag some four or five inches long, and less than half that in width. The bag appeared to be made of red flannel. "What's that?"

"Betty, go bring Anabel here," Lusk said. When she did not immediately respond, his voice grew harsher. "Straighten up there, woman, and go on and get Anabel like I told you."

"Why are you sending for Anabel?" Williamson asked.

Lusk sat back on his rear and crossed his legs as if he planned to remain on the floor for a while. " 'Cause Anabel knows about them things, Cap'n."

"Knows about what?" Williamson reached under the bed to retrieve the bag. "Hell, Jacob, it's just a piece of cloth."

"Don't touch that, Cap'n!" Lusk said, grabbing Williamson's arm with a force and urgency he had never seen his first mate display. "I believe Betty's right. I believe that's a mojo."

"Mojo? Do you mean like a curse or something?"

"Could be, Cap'n."

"Come on, Jacob," Williamson said with a chuckle. "You must have told me a dozen times before that you don't believe in those swamp curses and spells."

Lusk was still gripping Williamson's arm, and though he released the pressure somewhat, he did not let go. "I ain't sayin' I do, and I ain't sayin' I don't. But I want Anabel to see this before we move it."

Within minutes, chief cook Anabel McBree arrived with Betty and two other deckhands who had caught wind of the incident. Lusk remained on the floor, watching the bag as if he thought it might disappear, while Williamson stood up and made room for Anabel. The others waited outside, trying to steal a glance through the doorway.

Williamson noted that Anabel did not offer her usual cheery greeting; instead, she knelt quickly on the floor beside Jacob.

"Is that what Betty thinks it is?" Lusk asked her.

Anabel nodded, slowly looking up to meet Williamson's eyes. "Somebody done throwed at you, Cap'n. And they throwed at you hard."

"Threw what? A bag?"

"A mojo, Cap'n. That's the work of a hoodooer. Now, I don't know until I look in it, but right off I'd say somebody is out to bring you harm."

"That's crazy. I don't believe in voodoo," Williamson said. He didn't say it, but he figured only coloreds believed in conjurers and curses, the exception being Jacob Lusk.

"The Cap'n is right. Ain't no such thing as hoodoo," Lusk added.

"Well, *somebody* believes it, Cap'n," Anabel replied. "And whether you believe in it or not, I think we'd best get this out of your cabin."

"Do you want me to reach under there and get it?" Lusk said. There was something in his voice that made Williamson believe he was hoping Anabel would say no.

"You want to fetch it out of there?" Anabel said, the first hint of a smile emerging on her face.

"If . . . if you want me to."

"Lordy, Lordy, man, you wouldn't admit you was scared for nothin', would you?" Anabel said.

"I *ain't* scared," Lusk said. "I just, uh . . ."

"I'll get it myself."

As they looked on, Anabel took a clean, white cloth from Betty's linen stack outside the cabin and carefully reached under the bed. Wrapping the cloth around the bag, she pulled it from the springs and carried it outside with the delicacy usually reserved for handling gunpowder. The crew members gathered outside stepped a respectful distance away as Anabel laid the cloth on the deck. Slowly and deliberately she opened the pouch and emptied its contents onto the white cloth. A shiny button matching the ones on Williamson's uniform came out first, followed closely by a dried lizard head, penetrated on all sides by pins. A murmur passed among those watching, but Williamson was growing impatient.

"What's all this supposed to mean, Anabel?"

Anabel explained that, based upon the contents of the pouch, someone had set out to harm and possibly even kill him. While not a "hoodooer" herself, as Anabel described one, she had grown up in a part of the country where the power of certain individuals to put a curse on others was highly respected. She told how a hoodoo doctor was marked from birth, being a child born with a veil or perhaps the seventh son of a seventh son. Learning their craft from others, their teachings were passed down orally, with no one daring to write what Anabel called the "recipes" for various curses.

"There's seven pins in this lizard's head," Anabel told Williamson. "That means someone is out to see you dead, Cap'n, and they want it mighty bad."

"But I don't believe in that stuff."

"It don't matter, Cap'n. A mojo can hurt you whether you believe in it or not. And if you thinking it's just colored folks that hoodoos, you're wrong. The strongest hoodoo doctor I ever heard about was a white man. Lived way back up in the hills. Now, all hoodooers ain't bad, and all mojos ain't bad. They can curse or they can heal, depending upon what the one that made it intends. But I'd have to say this was made to curse."

"So am I supposed to drop dead or something?"

"It don't usually happen that way."

"Good," Williamson said with a laugh.

"Most folk get drinelin' sick. They get all stooped over, slow moving, and weak in the bones. They just drinel away to nothin'."

"Well, I'm feeling just fine. So why don't we clear everybody out and get this thing out of here. Throw it overboard or something, and let's go on about our business."

"That would be the thing to do all right, Cap'n," Anabel said. "We'll drop it in the running water and never look back. That's a good way to get rid of a mojo."

Williamson reached down toward the cloth. "Fine. But I want my button back."

"Cap'n," Anabel said, putting her hand between Williamson's and the button. "If it's all the same to you, I'd feel a whole lot better if you let me toss it *all* in the river."

"Seems like a lot of trouble," Williamson said, "not to mention wasting a perfectly good button. But I'm not going to argue with you about it. Do what you please."

"Thank you, Cap'n. And I'll have Betty boil those sheets of yours in some red pepper and salt to ward off—"

"That won't be necessary," Williamson said.

"We got to change them anyway."

"Fine. Change the sheets."

Reluctantly, Betty reentered the captain's cabin and removed his sheets, then rushed down to the lower deck to follow Anabel's instructions. Anabel prepared to leave with the red flannel bag and its contents but stopped and turned to Lusk.

"You don't believe in mojos—ain't that what you told me one time, Jacob?"

Lusk looked rather sheepish. "I believe I might have said that one time."

Anabel shook her head. "But you sho' didn't waste no time callin' me up here when you saw one, now did you?" She didn't wait for his answer before disappearing down the deck.

Williamson stared at the springs on his bed. "All that commotion, and I still don't have clean sheets."

"I'll have them brought up here for you real soon, Cap'n," Lusk said, his face still a portrait of concern as he surveyed the captain's bed.

"You still spooked by that so-called mojo?"

"It ain't so much the conjuring business that bothers me, Cap'n."

"Then what's wrong?"

"I want to know who put that in your bed and how they got in here to do it."

The simplicity of Lusk's concern caught Williamson off guard. All the talk about conjurers and "hoodoo" had caused him to overlook that very point. Believe or don't believe— but who could have had it in for him enough to go to all that trouble?

Williamson quickly checked the buttons on his uniform and, finding that he was missing none, stepped over to the shallow closet on the far side of his cabin. Opening the door, he immediately discovered a button missing from the left sleeve of a clean uniform. Someone had been in his cabin unobserved long enough to plant that ridiculous bag and even trim a button from his clothes to place inside it. He showed the sleeve to Lusk, and the two of them began to consider who could have had access to the captain's quarters since the uniform had been washed. Washday for the crew's clothing was always Saturday, and with clear weather for drying, uniforms were usually returned on Sunday morning. He and Lusk concluded that whoever planted the mojo had to have been in his cabin sometime after noon on Sunday. Williamson knew that the chambermaids were careful to lock his quarters after coming and going, and though he recalled them refilling his water pitcher or attending to other minor matters on a daily basis, he could think of no one else with access to his cabin. The only exception was the carpenter before he installed the door to the adjoining office, but neither he nor Jacob Lusk could imagine Manuel Ramirez having anything to do with voodoo, and they doubted that his assistant was ever out of Ramirez's sight long enough to make such an entry.

For ten minutes they discussed who might have been inclined to such an act, and they had been able to come up no one, until Jacob Lusk snapped his fingers.

"That boy," Lusk said, his eyes sparkling at the realization. "The one we chased off the ship."

"That was early Monday morning, wasn't it?"

"It sho' was, Cap'n. He was in your room. I'm almost sure of it. I don't know how long he was here, but you told me that afternoon that you weren't missing anything."

"No, I made a quick check of my area. Nothing seemed to be missing."

Lusk grinned. "That's 'cause he wasn't takin' nothing. He was leavin' it behind."

"But why? And who was he?"

"Lots of children run up and down that wharf at St. Louis. Some of 'em ain't got a home."

"You figure he was one of them?"

"Could've been. Those boys live off of odd jobs and what they can steal from the boats. I know quite a few of them boys by sight. I've even let them do some cleanup work from time to time, keepin' a real close eye on them, mind you."

"And did you recognize him?"

Lusk shook his head. "I didn't get a real close look, but right now I'd have to say I've never seen that boy around the landing before."

"But except for perhaps a half-dozen people in the dining room, the passengers had cleared the boat by that time of day."

"I know what I saw, Cap'n. And from the way that boy cut and run, he was up to no good. He'd be a good bet to have stuck that mojo in your cabin."

"Since when do children work voodoo curses?"

"They don't," Anabel McBree commented from just outside the cabin. She had returned to inform the captain that she had disposed of the mojo, and she had been standing there long enough to hear part of their conversation. "Every hoodooer I ever heard about was an adult," Anabel said. "But sometimes they use children to throw down a mojo. Often times a child can get into places an adult can't."

Anabel's comment reminded Williamson of Sunday afternoon at the funeral for Hudson Van Geer. He told her and Jacob about the child who jumped from the hearse just as the funeral procession was leaving the chapel.

"Do you think it could be the same boy?" Lusk asked.

"I guess it's possible. But what's the connection?"

"What was that boy doing in Mr. Van Geer's hearse?" Anabel asked.

"Masey told me the strangest thing after the funeral," Williamson explained. "He got to talking to the gravediggers as people were leaving the cemetery. Apparently, the boy we saw climbing out of Van Geer's hearse had tried to get inside the casket to the body."

"Why? Why was he messin' around with the body?" Anabel asked, her attention growing in intensity.

"Masey said the gravediggers told him they caught him with an egg in his hand. A egg, of all things!"

"This ain't good, Cap'n."

"How's that?

"The ol' time hoodooers say that if somebody dies by murder, and you put an egg in the hand of the person who died, the murderer can't get away. They say he'll wander all about the scene of his killing."

All this talk about voodoo was beginning to make Williamson jumpy, despite his disbelief. Yet he had to admit that it all seemed to be tied to Van Geer's death, and that fact alone made it worth pursuing. Still, it made no sense that someone would attempt to curse a murderer so that he would be found, then turn around and curse the man hired to find him.

He made that point to Anabel, adding, "The police have had Stewart Van Geer in jail since the day Hudson Van Geer died. He's even confessed to the crime. And even though the dead man's wife hired us to investigate, right now we have no evidence that Stewart wasn't the killer."

"Well, somebody sho' don't think so," Anabel said. "Wouldn't be no reason to thrown down that egg conjure unless somebody figured the real killer was still on the loose."

"Sounds like maybe somebody knows something they ain't telling," Lusk added.

After a few more minutes Jacob and Anabel excused themselves to attend to their duties, leaving Williamson alone to ponder what young boy might have a connection to the case. The only person he could come up with was the stableboy that Tyner had mentioned living on the Van Geer property. He considered, upon his return to St. Louis, getting Tyner or Baldridge to talk with the boy; but the more he thought about that lizard head with the seven pins jammed into it, the more the situation bothered him. He didn't believe in swamp curses and mojos, he told himself. That was not the question. But the fact that somebody was trying to interfere with the investigation was important enough that Baldridge and Tyner know about it. That they might think him foolish was a strong possibility, but he decided to telegraph them with the new information and let them think he had lost his mind if they pleased. After all, nobody had put a lizard head in *their* beds.

9

Thursday, June 19
St. Louis Municipal Courthouse

"ALL RISE," THE bailiff said, and the occupants of the crowded courtroom scrambled to their feet. Sitting on the next to last row, along the center aisle, Salina Tyner watched as Stewart Van Geer was helped onto shaky legs by his defense attorney.

"Oyez, oyez, oyez," the bailiff continued, "this court for the City of St. Louis, County of St. Louis, State of Missouri, is now in session, the Honorable Winslow Grove presiding."

The judge took a seat, and the crowd followed suit. He rapped his gavel. "This hearing in the case of *The People versus Stewart Van Geer* is now in session."

Tyner surveyed the courtroom, noting what a well-dressed crowd had gathered. Most of them, she suspected, were friends of the Van Geer family, or perhaps business associates. She recognized no more than a half-dozen faces out of the more than fifty people present. Helen Van Geer, dressed in an expensive-looking dark blue dress, sat in the row immediately behind her son, separated from him by a low railing. To her right was Claire Van Geer and immediately behind Claire was Marie Trehan, her wide, feathered hat nearly blocking Tyner's view. No one was present who matched Masey's description of Robert Van Geer, but Baldridge should have been here by now to see that for himself, she thought as she glanced at the door in the back of the courtroom. He knew the trial was today. She had made a point of telling him. Surely he hadn't started drinking and forgotten.

Judge Grove addressed Van Geer's lawyer. "Counsel, at our preliminary hearing Mr. Stewart Van Geer indicated that he wished to plead guilty to the murder of Hudson Van Geer. Is that still the case?"

Van Geer's lawyer, a portly, bearded gentleman, rose to his feet. "Your Honor, Mr. Van Geer still wishes to plead guilty to the charge."

A murmur spread through the crowd, and Tyner could see Helen Van Geer attempting to say something to her son. Judge Grove again rapped his gavel. "I'll have quiet, ladies and gentlemen." But as the noise from the crowd died down, Helen Van Geer's voice could be heard beseeching her son to alter his plea.

"Please, son. I'm begging you to at least—"

"Mrs. Van Geer," Judge Grove said, "you must sit back and remain quiet."

"But, Judge, Stewart is not well. Anyone can see that. Just look at him. He's—he's not thinking straight. He simply—"

"Depressed, Mrs. Van Geer. Your son is depressed." The judge thumbed through some papers. "And, according to the doctor's examination made upon his attorney's request two days ago, your son suffers from a 'general malaise.' Not at all surprising, considering the crime to which he is pleading guilty."

"But, Judge—"

"Please attempt to control yourself, Mrs. Van Geer. I realize this must be a terrible time for you, given the nature of the crime, but I must ask you not to interfere in the conduct of this trial."

Even at the distance she sat from the defense table, Tyner could see why Helen Van Geer was concerned. While Stewart's behavior was not as severe as what Masey and Luke had described during their visit at the jail, she could plainly see that something was wrong. He sat next to his lawyer, leaning forward on his elbows, staring straight ahead—not at any particular person or thing, simply gazing into the air. Not once since entering the courtroom had she seen him turn and speak to either his mother or his wife. He communicated only with his lawyer, and that consisted of a slow, deliberate nod of his head. Perhaps the doctor was right. Maybe he was depressed. Killing one's father would certainly give a person grounds to be depressed; yet somehow Tyner wondered why, even in the anger and sadness of such an act, a person's instinct for survival—the mere desire not to hang—wouldn't take over. And if he *did* kill his father, would he not want his mother's forgiveness? That he would be confused and frightened in the days immediately after the killing was understandable, but surely he knew by now what was going on around him. Part of Tyner's concern was out of frustration more than any particular sympathy for Van Geer. How dare he plead guilty with his mother hiring Big River to investigate the crime? It was a waste of everyone's time. She again looked toward the rear door.

Where was Baldridge?

Judge Grove turned his attention to Stewart Van Geer, who, upon hearing his name called, stood up only with his attorney's assistance. "For the record, then, Mr. Van Geer, how do you plead to the charge that you murdered Mr. Hudson Van Geer at his residence on St. Charles Street, Ward Six, in the City of St. Louis, on the evening of June 12, 1873?"

Van Geer's response was barely audible, but Tyner could tell from Helen Van Geer's reaction that he had responded

"Guilty." Claire, with her arm around Helen, attempted to console her as she began to cry.

Judge Grove looked at the prosecuting attorney. "You have heard Mr. Van Geer's plea of guilty to the charge of murder. Does the state have any additional evidence to enter?"

The prosecutor arose, glanced at Stewart Van Geer with utter contempt, then slowly strolled to the center of the courtroom and addressed the judge.

"Your Honor, in the interest of justice, and to underscore the true fierceness of this horrible crime, the people of the State of Missouri would ask to hear, in the defendant's own words, his account of his deed. We have provided to the court the confession that Stewart Van Geer offered to our officers at the Washington Square police station on the evening of the crime. If it please the court, I would ask that the clerk read the defendant's account for the public record."

Judge Grove acknowledged the prosecutor's request and turned to Van Geer. "So granted. And I shall ask you, Mr. Van Geer, upon the conclusion of the reading of your statement, to affirm or deny the truth of that statement in light of your guilty plea."

Tyner listened as the court clerk read the statement, wishing that Baldridge were there to hear it as well. She was getting angrier by the moment at his absence, as she envisioned him limping across some saloon to buy yet another bottle, completely oblivious of where he was supposed to be and what he was supposed to be doing.

Stewart Van Geer's statement to the police was rambling and awkward, with only a bare mention of entering his father's home on St. Charles Street and walking toward the study. His father, according to Van Geer, must have heard him coming through the billiards room, for he emerged from his office to meet Stewart, saying something that Stewart could not recall. Tyner noted that the statement made no mention of an argument or even any harsh words. In fact, Stewart made no indication that he even spoke to his father that day. He told the police that he "must have fired two, three shots" in rapid succession into his father's chest. As the clerk read the words, a murmur drifted through the courtroom, and he paused until silence had returned. The confession further stated that Stewart remembered nothing until he entered the police station. Short and to the point, the statement was, and at no time did anything the clerk read offer insight as to motive. Tyner again wished Baldridge had heard the statement, for it made no sense to her that a man would walk up and kill his father without ever saying a word. If he had been angry enough to kill him, how could he have resisted telling him why? She noted a degree of frustration in the judge's voice, too, as he addressed Stewart Van Geer, and she sensed that he was equally at a loss for why the man would commit such a crime.

"Mr. Stewart Van Geer," Judge Grove began, "you have heard the reading of your confession regarding the murder of your father, Mr. Hudson Van Geer. Have you anything to add or to change about your account?" He paused to allow the man to offer some explanation of his act, and Tyner sensed that the judge would have welcomed some new revelation, or at the very least some suggestion of remorse. But Stewart Van Geer simply leaned against the table on shaky legs and said nothing. "Very well. Do you then attest to the truth of the statement as read?"

Van Geer's lawyer whispered something into his ear, and Stewart Van Geer mumbled, "Yes."

Judge Grove shook his head in bewilderment as the prosecutor arose again. "Your Honor, let the record reflect that officers at the Washington Square police station took from the hand of Mr. Stewart Van Geer that night a forty-five-caliber revolver that had recently been fired. Four expended cartridges remained in the cylinder. The coroner determined from an examination of Hudson Van Geer's body, both at the scene of the crime and later in his office, that the victim's death resulted from four gunshot wounds, delivered at close range, from a forty-five-caliber weapon. Mr. Hudson Van Geer received two wounds to the chest, one wound that broke his right arm, and a fourth wound to the head. And, Your Honor, in the coroner's opinion, let the State declare that while the body wounds were exacting, the coroner indicates that the wound to Mr. Van Geer's head was the fatal shot. It is also important to understand, Your Honor, that this last shot was delivered in cold blood to the back of Mr. Van Geer's head as he lay on the floor, desperately gasping for breath and struggling to hold on to any glimmer of life."

"Very well," Judge Grove said, turning to the defendant. "I will take the matter of sentencing under advisement until Saturday, at which time I will render a sentence based upon Mr. Van Geer's confession of guilt and the state's presentation of the circumstances surrounding the crime. Mr. Van Geer, is there *anything* you would wish to add to the State of Missouri's account of the crime before I consider your sentence?"

While Stewart said nothing, his lawyer, standing, did respond. "Your Honor, Mr. Stewart Van Geer's mother would like to address the court on behalf of her son."

The judge nodded and motioned Helen Van Geer forward. Assisted by Claire, Helen made her way from the first row of seating, and as she passed Stewart, she stopped and put her arms around him, hugging him, sobbing, and saying something to him that Tyner could not hear. Judge Grove allowed her several seconds with her son before he urged the bailiff to separate the two and have her step forward toward the bench. Tyner felt terribly sorry for this petite woman, dwarfed by the immense courtroom and the black-robed judge sitting on a raised platform before her. Her hands trembled as she spoke in broken sentences, torn by her grief and fear for her son's life.

Masey should be here, Tyner thought. He should see this.

"Judge, I believe," she said, struggling to hold back her

tears, "and I shall always believe, until the day I die, that my son Stewart did not kill his father. Stewart loved his father, and Hudson . . . Hudson took care of his family."

"All the more reason to view this as a particularly heinous crime, Mrs. Van Geer," Judge Grove responded.

"Something is terribly wrong here, Judge," Helen said, raising her arm and pointing her finger at Stewart, who sat beside his attorney, his chin against his chest, staring blankly at the table in front of him. "Look at him! Look at my son, Judge. He doesn't even act like my son. He's sick, Judge. Anyone that knows him can tell you he's sick. Ask them. Ask anyone."

Judge Grove said, "A doctor has examined your son, Mrs. Van Geer, and—"

"I heard all that. But it doesn't matter. Don't you see? Stewart could not have committed this crime!"

"Mrs. Van Geer—"

Helen Van Geer lifted her hands and clasped them together as if in prayer as she stepped nearer to the judge. "I know . . . that . . . you have decided he's guilty. I know that." She looked at Stewart desperately, then back at the judge. "I can't change that. But please, Judge, please, I beg you not to take his life. I've already lost my husband. That should be grief enough for anyone. Please don't take my son away from me too. Please, Judge, spare his life. That would give me a chance to find out who really killed Hudson. I've hired my own detectives to work on finding out what really happened. I might have enough time to make things right. Please, Judge, I beg you. In the name of everything that is decent and fair. Please." She remained before him a few moments, staring up in silence, then turning around, with a lingering glance at Stewart, she returned to her seat.

A rumble passed through the audience. Judge Grove lifted his gavel and declared, "This court stands in recess until ten o'clock Saturday, at which time we shall reconvene for sentencing." With a rap of his gavel, Judge Grove disappeared through a rear door almost before the onlookers could rise to their feet.

Tyner looked once more at the crowd exiting the building, halfway expecting Baldridge to come pushing his way into the building, like a salmon swimming upstream, stumbling into the courtroom. Still he didn't appear, so Tyner worked her way through the crowd toward Helen Van Geer. She waited for almost five minutes as friends and supporters spoke to the despondent woman, attempting to console her. Tyner's eyes met Claire's while she waited, and she sensed immediately that her presence wasn't welcome. Marie Trehan flashed her usual angry stare. But when Helen Van Geer eventually saw her, the woman's face seemed to lighten somewhat—more in hope, Tyner figured, than in any joy at seeing her.

Helen moved to the end of the aisle and took Tyner's hand.

"Miss Tyner, have you found out anything? *Anything* at all?"

Tyner ignored the stone faces of the two women standing behind Helen. "We're working on it, Mrs. Van Geer."

Helen quickly searched the dwindling crowd. "Where's Captain Williamson?"

"He had to go to New Orleans with the *Paragon*." Sensing her disappointment, Tyner quickly noted, "But he's working on a lead down there."

"In New Orleans?" Helen asked.

"Yes, ma'am."

"And that other man? The one that's always so frumpish?"

"Masey?" Tyner forced a smile to hold back her anger. "Well, I don't know exactly where he is at the moment," she said, adding quickly, "but I'm sure he's busy working on the case."

"Why did Captain Williamson go to New Orleans?" Helen asked.

Tyner eyed Claire and Marie, choosing her words carefully. "He didn't exactly go all the way to New Orleans. He went down to north Louisiana."

"But what's in Louisiana that has anything to do with Hudson's death?" Helen asked.

Helen's comment convinced Tyner that the woman knew nothing about her late husband's questions regarding Claire Boulet. "I was hoping I might talk to you about—"

"Nothing, I'm quite sure," Claire said, her eyes darting to Tyner. "Because nothing is exactly what these people have done since you hired them. I don't understand why you're wasting your time and money, Mother Helen. They can't be serious about helping Stewart, or they would have a *real* detective here instead of this annoying woman."

"Now, you listen to me," Tyner said, approaching Claire, prompting Marie Trehan to step between them. Trehan grasped Tyner's wrist, and instantaneously Tyner delivered a backhand across Trehan's face, staggering her.

"Oh my heavens!" Helen shouted. Several of the visitors who had not yet filed out of the courtroom stopped and stared. Recovering from the blow, Trehan lifted her hand as if to strike Tyner, but she stopped abruptly when Helen cried out, "Please! Please!" Tears were welling in her eyes. "I don't think I can stand any more of this." She noted the people watching them. "Haven't we had enough embarrassment without you ladies quarreling in public?" She spoke first to Claire and Marie. "Stewart's life is hanging by a thread, and you two are acting like schoolgirls." She turned to Tyner. "And you, Miss Tyner. This is hardly the behavior I would expect from a professional."

"I really need to ask you some questions," Tyner began, but Helen was clearly not in the mood to respond.

"Not now, Miss Tyner. Not now. This has all been too much for me," she said. "Claire, will you take me home?"

"Yes, Mother Helen. Right away."

Helen started away, holding the arm of Marie Trehan, but called back to Tyner. "Perhaps I can speak with you later, after I've had a chance to lie down."

"That will be fine, Mrs. Van Geer."

Claire hung back as Marie walked Helen toward the door. "May I speak with you a moment . . . in private?" Claire said.

Tyner surveyed the room. "Looks like it's getting private in here pretty quickly."

"I think it's despicable that you would take advantage of my mother-in-law at a time like this. I'm not really sure what you're up to, unless you're just trying to take her money."

"And you? What about you, Claire? What exactly are *you* up to?"

"If you're referring to that ridiculous business about Hudson Van Geer checking up on me, you can forget it. I'll not have you upsetting my mother-in-law with such things. Perhaps he was checking on me. It would be just like him. But I assure you, he would have found nothing but the truth, and I had already told him that. If he chose not to believe it, that is not my problem."

"Maybe. Maybe not."

"I don't think my mother-in-law can stand any more bad news right now, and she certainly doesn't need to hear wild accusations that her husband distrusted her own daughter-in-law." Claire ran her hand over her stomach and smiled wryly. "Besides, she's got a grandchild on the way. She's not apt to listen to any of your foolishness."

"We'll see about that."

The smile disappeared from Claire's face. "I want you to stay away from Helen. You're not helping Stewart anyway. He's already been found guilty, and there's nothing more you can do."

"You seem to be all torn up about that."

"I only pray that he doesn't hang."

"Lighting up a few more candles, are you?"

"Miss Tyner, your work, if you ever did any, is over."

"Helen Van Geer will decide when this case is over."

"Well, I have a feeling that won't be very long in coming.

And now if you'll excuse me, I have no more time for idle chit-chat. I have to see to my mother-in-law and send Marie to take Stewart his meal. It's the one thing the poor man has to look forward to."

Claire left the courtroom, and Tyner stood by for another twenty minutes, hoping that Baldridge might yet show up, but when only she and a cleaning man remained, she determined it was hopeless and set out to find him.

10

Friday morning, June 20

MASEY BALDRIDGE LAY in the alley beside the Boatmen's Savings Bank on Fifth Street, choking on his own spit between snores. The resulting coughing fit jolted him to consciousness, and he bumped his head on the brick wall he had been sleeping against most of the night. Shielding his eyes from the morning sun, he tried to estimate the time. It was most likely midmorning, for an unsympathetic sun was already rising over the buildings at the end of the alley, and threatening any moment to mercilessly bathe him in direct light. His head pounded, and his skin felt warm as he struggled to his feet, still trying to clear his throat of the lingering spittle. At his feet he saw his companion from the night before, an empty whiskey bottle from a saloon—no, several saloons—along Carondelet Street. He hadn't planned on drinking so long, but then, he never did plan on it. His knee had been bothering him more than usual, and the first few drinks had dulled the pain so well he figured a few more would make it disappear altogether. Limping along toward the street, he realized that for the first time in months he did not notice the pain in his leg. Perhaps it was the dull ache throughout his body that kept him distracted; he was feeling far worse than after any other all-night drunk he could remember.

Emerging from the alley on Fifth Street, he almost ran into a woman leading her child along the wooden sidewalk. His sudden appearance startled her, and she grasped the child's hand tightly and sped along, glancing back disapprovingly at Baldridge before entering the bank. Removing his hat, he brushed his brown hair back in a futile effort to make it lie down, then he, too, stepped inside the door of the Boatman's Savings Bank. Several customers were standing in line at the three teller windows along the far wall. He noticed that the woman he had nearly collided with moments before was talking with the bank guard and pointing in his direction. Within moments, the guard, a pistol conspicuously strapped onto his hip, confronted Baldridge.

"May I help you?"

"Yes, you can," Baldridge replied. When the guard took a step back and frowned, Baldridge realized that the thick film on his tongue must be giving him bad breath. He turned his head slightly as he spoke. "The time, sir. I was just wondering what time it is."

"Do you have bank business?"

"No, sir."

"Then it's time for you to leave," he said, taking hold of Baldridge's arm.

Baldridge jerked away. "Don't be grabbing ahold of me—"

"I want you out of here," the guard demanded, reaching again to usher him out.

"I just want to know the time."

"Then buy a damn watch." The guard had grabbed him again. "Now, move along."

Baldridge struggled free. "Not until you tell me what time it is."

For a tense moment, Baldridge thought the guard might reach for his gun, and he wondered how he would respond. The man had no call to treat him like that, but Baldridge knew equally well that having the whole thing end up in the two of them drawing guns in a crowded bank was ridiculous. All he wanted was the time. This was a fight he didn't need. So Baldridge slowly lifted his hands and backed toward the door.

"All right. I'm going," he said, reaching for the door. Baldridge wasn't sure why—perhaps he was satisfied to have prevailed—but the guard held the door open for him. "Let me show you out," he said, then, pointing to a large wall clock on the far side of the room, added, "Ten-thirty." Baldridge offered no reply but continued down the street toward the hotel.

People seemed to always treat Baldridge this way when he had been drinking, and lately he'd been treated badly often. He had taken a Federal minié ball in his left knee three days before his unit, the Seventh Tennessee Cavalry, surrendered in May 1865. He had tried to return to his occupation as a farrier and blacksmith, but he discovered that he couldn't stand for long periods of time without pain. So for the first three or four years after the war he had drifted from odd job to odd job, hoping and praying the leg would get better, and only occasionally drinking when the pain became too much. When the doctors eventually told him there was nothing they could do, Baldridge lost hope of ever walking straight again. And as they had predicted, the ache in his leg, once occasional, became a near-constant companion, and his friendship with the bottle grew proportionately. As Baldridge clumped down the wooden sidewalk in the direction of his hotel, he recalled the doctors' offer to give him laudanum. But he had refused it, having seen too many men become slaves to that drug after the war—men with wounds far worse than his. At least with liquor *he* was in control—or so he thought. Mornings like this made him wonder.

About three blocks from the Dearborn Hotel, Baldridge

stopped and leaned against the wall of a dentist's office. He felt as if he had been kicked by a mule, every muscle in his body aching, and as he paused to gather his strength, the realization of what he had missed hit him.

Van Geer's trial. He was supposed to be at the courthouse yesterday to meet Sally. Lowering his chin to his chest, he stared down at his dusty boots, swallowing hard. How could he have forgotten that? He wasn't thinking straight. He hadn't been thinking or feeling right for two days now. But missing the trial? What would Sally say? What would Luke Williamson think? He ran over the events of the past two days in his mind. It was Friday. Williamson was gone with the *Paragon*. At least he wouldn't have to face him for a few days. But Sally. *Oh, God, Sally's going to be madder than a scorned bride.* Catching himself glancing up and down the street to see if she was coming, he felt like a child. She had most likely been looking for him all night. Sally Tyner was the last person he wanted to face this morning, particularly given the way he looked and smelled. Baldridge determined to make it back to the hotel, clean himself up, put on some fresh clothes, and wait for her at his room. That would give him time to think up an excuse for where he had been. He couldn't say he had been talking to the Van Geers; they would all have been at the trial. Maybe he could say he went to see the police. All night? No. As he moved up to the front door of the hotel, he surmised that he could tell her some fellows jumped him and took his money. She might believe that. He certainly looked and felt like he'd been beaten. No. Sally Tyner wouldn't be taken in by that tale. Peeking inside the lobby of the hotel, he did not see Tyner, so he walked quickly toward the stairs.

"Mr. Baldridge!" the desk clerk called from across the room. Baldridge pulled his hat down over his face and kept moving. The clerk rushed over and intercepted him after he had cleared only three steps. "Mr. Baldridge, is that you?"

Baldridge stopped and turned around. "What do you want?"

"Sir, your friend Miss Tyner's been looking everywhere for you."

"Is she here?" Baldridge asked reluctantly.

"No, sir." Baldridge was relieved. "She went out a little over an hour ago. She said if you came in to just wait here for her."

"Oh, she did?"

"Yes, sir. She was real worried about you last night, sir."

"Last night?"

"Yes, sir. She said you was supposed to meet her yesterday. She seemed quite upset until I checked the stable and found your horse was still quartered."

"Is Harry all right?" Baldridge asked.

"Your horse, sir? Oh, yes, sir. He's just fine."

"And Miss Tyner? What kind of humor was she in this morning?"

"Oh, she's not worried about you any more."

"She's not?" Baldridge said, somewhat disappointed.

"No, sir. She's downright *mad* today," the clerk said. "Madder than I've seen a woman in a long time."

Great. That was just what Baldridge wanted to hear. All the more reason to get upstairs and get cleaned up before she returned. He produced a half-dollar from his pocket.

"How about having somebody draw me a bath.? And make it fast." He tossed the money to the clerk.

"Yes, sir. I'll see to it right away."

"Thanks." His joints felt stiff as he turned to continue up the stairs, but the clerk followed after him.

"Mr. Baldridge, there's one more thing."

"What?"

"This telegram arrived for you and Miss Tyner a few minutes after she left this morning."

Baldridge took an envelope from the clerk and continued up the stairs, opening it as he went. Once inside his room, he located a freshly washed shirt and pair of pants the hotel maid had returned and hung in his closet and, taking a seat on the edge of the bed, laid the clothes next to him. Slipping his suspenders down, he removed his shirt, which by now even smelled bad to him. After removing his boots, he wiped the dust off both of them with the dirty shirt, then wadded it into a ball and tossed it into the corner.

While he waited for his bath to be drawn, Baldridge opened the telegram and read it.

JUNE 20, 1873
9:00 A.M.
VICKSBURG, MISSISSIPPI

BIG RIVER DETECTIVE AGENCY
C/O DEARBORN HOTEL
MR. MASEY BALDRIDGE
MISS SALINA TYNER

GRANT DE PAUL NOT INVOLVED STOP   FOUND
EVIDENCE THAT SOMEONE SEEKS TO STALL
INVESTIGATION STOP   YOU AND SALLY COULD
BE IN DANGER STOP   MASEY, VAN GEER
STABLEBOY MAY HAVE BEEN IN THE HEARSE
STOP   ASK HIM ABOUT PUTTING MOJO IN MY
CABIN STOP   FIND OUT WHAT HE KNOWS STOP
WILL WIRE AGAIN FROM ST. JOSEPH STOP

LUKE WILLIAMSON

Mojo? In his cabin? What the hell was he talking about? Since when had Luke Williamson become a believer in curses and signs? It was bad enough that the lead on Grant De Paul amounted to nothing, but this business about mojos had

Baldridge scratching his head. Who wants to stall the investigation? And what does that stableboy have to do with any of this? Tewley. That's what the attendant at the Van Geer mansion called the boy.

After a knock upon his door, a gentleman announced that his bath was ready, so Baldridge folded the telegram and slipped it into the pocket of his clean shirt. He picked up the fresh clothes and followed the attendant to the bathroom, where the humidity of the morning mixed with the steam around his bathtub, nearly taking his breath away. Recalling an ugly incident in Natchez last year, he ordered the attendant to open a window and clear the air. Pushing a chair beside the bathtub, he laid his revolver on its seat and climbed into the narrow metal tub. With the temperature on its way into the nineties today, he thought it odd that the warm water would give him a chill as he immersed himself, but he hoped the bath would chase his headache away.

In his room a half hour later, Baldridge's head still pounded as he dressed and took a seat by the window overlooking the street in front of the hotel. As he watched for Tyner, he tried to polish his story, but nothing sounded good enough to tell her. There was always the truth, but he wasn't sure it was worth the pain. He had no excuse. Sure he felt bad, and the hot bath had done little to assuage his aching body, but ultimately it was his own fault. He shouldn't have gotten drunk. He should have been at that courtroom. From his jacket pocket he produced five dollars of Helen Van Geer's advance money and fiddled with it in his hands. He began hatching a plan to keep watch until he saw Tyner coming, then hurry downstairs and meet her at the front door of the hotel. He would catch her off guard. He would apologize and immediately buy her lunch. He would just tell her the truth and that would be that. So he got drunk. So he passed out. So he felt like shit. She would understand. Besides, he couldn't have missed that much. Nothing important ever happens on the first day of a trial anyway, Baldridge reasoned. Satisfied with his solution, he propped his feet on the window sill and monitored the traffic on the street below.

About five minutes passed before he saw her coming west along the street toward the hotel. She moved with a sense of urgency in her steps, glancing ahead toward the hotel. He leaned back from the window when he thought she was looking up to their floor. Baldridge stood up, tucked his shirt into his pants, and put on his hat, watching her approach all the while. This was it. He would rush downstairs and meet her. He would apologize. She would accept. He picked up a half-empty silver whiskey flask from the chest of drawers beside his bed and tucked it into his pocket—a little something for later. He knew he could not afford whiskey on his breath now. Glancing out the window again, he noticed that she was within thirty yards of the front door, her dark green dress swaying with her determined step. But as he watched, he realized he was wrong. She wasn't determined. She was mad.

Baldridge walked reluctantly to the door and opened it, fully intending to hurry downstairs and meet her. But just as suddenly as he had resolved to confront Tyner and tell her the truth, Baldridge had a change of heart. He removed Williamson's telegram from his pocket, placed it in the middle of the bed where she would be sure to find it, and hurried out of the room, leaving the door open. Instead of walking down the hall to the stairs leading to the lobby, Baldridge rushed in the opposite direction, descended the back stairs, and limped out to the stable. Pressing the attendant to quickly saddle Nashville Harry for him, he eventually took over the job when the man moved too slowly, keeping watch for Tyner all the while. Once the horse was ready, Baldridge rode away from the rear of the hotel and headed for the late Hudson Van Geer's home. She would read the telegram and know he was hard at work on the case. She couldn't be mad at him about that. After all, he would be back by suppertime. There would be plenty of time for the truth and its consequences. Besides, Baldridge reasoned, he might find something out that would help Stewart Van Geer. He convinced himself he was doing the right thing and pressed his knees together, urging Nashville Harry along.

THE DOORMAN AT the Hudson Van Geer home told Baldridge that Mrs. Van Geer was lying down. He said she had been recovering from the difficult day at the courthouse yesterday. Not wanting to appear foolish, Baldridge tried to get the attendant to say what had happened at the trial, but the man offered him no specifics. Still, Baldridge could tell from his tone and demeanor that things had not gone well. When he asked to see Tewley, the stableboy, the attendant indicated that he thought he was in his room above the stable, so Baldridge rode slowly around the side of the Van Geer home along a well-worn path that led some hundred yards away from St. Charles Street and well behind the main house. On his left he passed four small frame buildings that he suspected housed the staff, and he caught the sweet fragrance of the violet and yellow summer flowers blooming around the front door of the building nearest the path. Observing no one in or around the servant quarters, he rode on toward the stable—a low, wide building painted a deep red and framed on both sides by large beech trees—that occupied the extreme edge of the Van Geer property. Baldridge figured the small window above the broad double doors marked the stableboy's room, and he kept an eye on it as he approached. As he dismounted, he felt slightly dizzy, yet he regained his balance, opened the gate, and led Nashville Harry inside the rail fence that surrounded the stable building. Although his knee wasn't hurting, every other muscle ached as he walked beneath the archway and into the stable. A bay in the stall to his right took note of his presence, leaned down to snap up some hay in two quick bites, and munched on it as he watched Bald-ridge tie Nashville Harry to a support post. Baldridge heard someone descending a narrow stairwell that led to the room he had noted above the entrance. Soon after, the stableboy emerged.

"Tewley?"

"What—what are you doing here?" Startled, the young boy stepped back into the shadows of the stairwell as if it would protect him.

"Aren't you Tewley? Don't you keep this stable?"

"Yes."

Baldridge sensed fear in his voice.

"My name is Masey Baldridge. I'm—"

"I know who you are," Tewley said. His comment seemed to Baldridge more an accusation than a declaration, and he moved toward the boy.

"You do, huh?"

Tewley took two steps backward up the stairs. "Yes."

Baldridge stopped. "Where you going, son?"

"I'm not supposed to talk to you."

"What?" Although the light was poor in the stairwell, Baldridge could tell that the boy was frightened. He moved slowly toward him, leaning over slightly to get a better look into the stairwell. "Son, I just want to ask you some questions. How about stepping out here in the light so I can see you?" When Tewley made no move, Baldridge took two or three steps back-ward. "Look, son. I don't know what you're scared of, but—"

"I ain't scared," Tewley whispered back.

"Then show me. Come on out here and let me talk to you."

Slowly, the boy moved down the last three steps and emerged into the daylight of the stable archway. He was a small, lean youngster, with sandy hair and bright blue-green eyes that seemed to shine from his dark-complexioned face—the prod-uct, no doubt, of hours of work in the sun. He looked away from Baldridge and down at the ground.

"You said you know who I am," Baldridge began. Tewley nodded but still did not look him in the eye. "And who do you think I am?"

"You're here about Mr. Hudson," he said, almost inaudibly.

"That's right. How old are you, son?"

"Twelve."

Baldridge thought him rather small and frail for twelve, but he knew from what Robert Van Geer had told him that the boy's life had been hard. "I understand Mr. Van Geer took you in here when your father died." Tewley nodded. "How long ago was that?"

"Almost two years," he said.

"Your father worked for Mr. Van Geer?"

"He worked on the *Silver City*. He was an engine man."

"You mean an engineer?" Tewley nodded, still refusing to look directly at Baldridge. "And your mother?"

"She's *been* dead. Don't hardly even remember her," Tewley said. "Why you askin' me all this? I got chores to do."

Baldridge pondered Williamson's telegram, wondering what possible connection Luke thought this boy could have to the investigation. Even though he had finally gotten a good look at him, he still couldn't be sure that Tewley was the boy he had seen jumping from Hudson Van Geer's hearse. Even if he was, what difference did it make? His head was still pounding, but he tried to concentrate on his questions.

"You thought a lot of Mr. Van Geer, didn't you?"

"He took care of me," Tewley replied. "He give me this place to live."

"Why do you think he did that?"

"I don't know. I guess 'cause he figured nobody else would."

"I understand that Mr. Hudson Van Geer thought the world of you, Tewley." Baldridge let his words sink in, noting that the boy turned his face farther away, attempting to hold back tears. "He treated you almost like one of the family, didn't he?"

"I guess so."

Baldridge saw the boy's lip quiver. "So, I guess when you heard he was killed, you were pretty upset."

"Mr. Hudson was good to me," Tewley said. "He shouldn't have been shot like that."

"Well, I agree with you, Tewley. That's what I'm doing here. I trying to find out who killed him."

"No, you're not," the boy said, now fighting back tears. "I *know* why you're here."

"Oh, you do? And why is that?"

"You're here to say bad things about Mr. Hudson," he said angrily. "You and that boat captain—you're gonna fix it so that Mr. Stewart don't hang for what he done." Tewley started to walk past Baldridge, who grabbed the boy by the sleeve.

"Whoa there, son. Hold on."

"Let go of me," Tewley said, trying to pull free.

"Who told you something like that?"

"It don't matter who told me," Tewley said, still wrestling to free himself. "And I ain't sayin' nothin' else to you. I ain't even supposed to be talking to you. You're . . . you're evil. You just want to hurt Mr. Hudson's good name. You just want Mr. Stewart to—"

His body aching, Baldridge grew tired of wrestling the boy and pushed him firmly to the ground. He awkwardly knelt in front of him on his good knee and forced the boy to look him in the eye.

"Now listen to me, Tewley. I don't know where you got this notion about Captain Williamson and me, but it ain't true." Tewley tried to look away, but Baldridge held his chin firmly forward. "I was hired by Helen Van Geer to find out the truth about what happened to her husband."

"I don't believe you," Tewley said.

"Who's been telling you these things? Who told you not to talk to me?"

"Miss Claire," the boy whispered.

"Claire Van Geer?" When Tewley attempted to nod, Baldridge realized how tightly he had been holding the boy's chin. He released him. "Stewart Van Geer's wife told you not to talk to me?"

Again Tewley nodded. "Can I go now?" Tewley said tearfully.

"If you answer one more question. What were you doing in Hudson Van Geer's hearse on the morning of the funeral?" Tewley looked shocked. "It *was* you, wasn't it?"

At first Baldridge thought he would bolt and run, but eventually he spoke.

"I wasn't doing nothin' wrong," he whispered.

"Then what *were* you doing?"

"I was seein' after Mr. Hudson."

"Seein' after him? What does that mean?"

"Nothin' you'd understand."

"Oh, I might—that is, if you'd tell me," Baldridge said softly, then added, "What's it got to do with an egg?" Fear showed in Tewley's blue eyes, and Baldridge knew he was getting somewhere, so he pressed him. "What do you know about mojos?"

At those words, Tewley struggled to his feet and darted past Baldridge toward the archway. Baldridge grabbed at his trouser leg but missed, managing only to tumble forward into the dirt. Kicking up dust as he ran, Tewley cleared the door and emerged into the sunlight. He halted momentarily and picked up a handful of dirt, then continued running toward the woods that bordered the Van Geer property. Baldridge got to his feet and walked outside, watching Tewley disappear into the trees. For a moment he considered mounting Nashville Harry and going after him, but he barely had the strength to get into the saddle, much less pursue him. And he figured the boy could lose him easily in the woods or among the distant houses. Baldridge felt as if his head was burning up, yet he shivered as he dusted himself off and tried to locate the spot where Tewley had paused momentarily during his escape. The handful of dirt he had seen the boy grab came from one of Baldridge's footprints. "That's one scared young'un," Baldridge said aloud. That he knew more than he was telling, Baldridge was sure; what he didn't understand was why Claire Van Geer would have so soured the young man against him and Williamson. He resolved to talk with Claire, just as soon as he rested a while back at the hotel. Sally Tyner or no Sally Tyner, he had to get off his feet before he passed out.

11

Friday, June 20

DURING THE YEARS since the war he had thought of her from time to time, particularly on those late afternoons when the dying sun lays an orange blanket over the rippling river. Hundreds of trips down the Mississippi to New Orleans had brought him past Hardscrabble Landing, and never once had he passed that he didn't catch himself scanning the distant bank, searching from the edge of the willows to the top of the landing levee, wondering if by chance she might be there. For almost two years after the war Hardscrabble had been a regular freight stop, but not once during that time had she ever come down to the water. Eventually, when the freight dried up, he stopped landing at Hardscrabble, but he never ceased looking for her as he traveled past. Once, perhaps a year ago, he even considered stopping. He thought he might make his way up to the house and see how she was getting along; but the way he had left things made the return all the more difficult, and with the schedule tight, he ordered his pilot to hold steady to the channel on their return north. Days would pass, and she would never come to mind, at least until his next trip south, and then as his ship cruised past Hardscrabble Landing the thoughts would return, and the image of her face would rise like a mist over the water on a cool morning. Yet mists burn away with the heat of the day, and life goes on; and so did Luke Williamson, every time he passed Hardscrabble Landing. Every time but this time. Today he would land, and he couldn't help but wonder what he would find.

Luke Williamson ran the final cloth patch through his Henry rifle and checked that it came out clean, then wiped down the barrel with a rag. Whenever he went ashore in swamp country, he was never sure what manner of varmints he might encounter, and having his Henry along gave him peace of mind.

"We're almost there, Cap'n," Jacob Lusk said, knocking outside the open cabin door.

Holding the rifle in his right hand along his side, and a saddlebag in his left, he stepped out on deck.

"Lord a'mighty, Cap'n," Lusk said, "you're looking sharp." Lusk referred to the freshly washed and pressed dress uniform. "They're gonna sho' be impressed with you."

"We'll see," Williamson replied as he walked to the stairs. Lusk followed along. Though the first mate knew Williamson had spent some time at Hardscrabble Plantation during the war, the captain had never spoken in detail of his time there, only mentioning the Routh family in passing.

"You're riding on down to St. Joseph after you visit with the Rouths, right?" Lusk asked, continuing before Williamson could answer. "And you'll be back here at the landing to meet the *Edward Smythe* on Sunday about noon?"

"Noon, on Sunday. That's right."

The two men descended the stairs. "Now, Cap'n, I can put you ashore at St. Joseph if you want. It would save you a ride back here."

"That's not necessary, Jacob."

"I don't understand why you're so all-fired determined to stop at Hardscrabble. You said yourself that the man you want to see is in St. Joseph."

"I've got my reasons," Williamson said. He had told his first mate about Hudson Van Geer's letter, and he had confessed to having no idea where his inquiry might lead. But he knew Jacob was worried. Lusk watched out for the captain, and since Williamson's association with Masey Baldridge and Salina Tyner, Lusk had been kept busier than usual. Apparently Lusk was thinking the same thing.

"Are you sure you don't want me or some of the men to go with you?"

"All I'm going to do is visit with the Rouths and ask some questions in St. Joseph," Williamson assured him as they emerged onto the lower deck.

"Every time you get to doing this investigation business something seems to happen," Lusk declared in an unusually accusatory tone. "If you ask me, all this—"

"Didn't ask you, Jacob," Williamson said, as a deckhand led a saddled horse up to the landing stage.

Williamson slipped his Henry into a rifle sling and latched it on the horse along with the saddlebag. Their long years on the river told both men the exact moment when the *Paragon* would reach the bank, and they shifted their weight in anticipation of the slight bump against the hull.

"Well, you're the cap'n. But leavin' this boat and ridin' off on some wild goose chase don't hardly seem the thing to do."

As two deckhands positioned and secured the landing stage, Williamson noted how the silt and sand bank of Hardscrabble Landing had been slowly and steadily caving into the river. The pier they had serviced during the war was now missing, with only the support poles sticking up some two or three feet from the water. It was as though the eroded bank had slipped away in the night.

"If it's a wild goose chase, why do you think you should go along?" Williamson asked, as he led the horse across the landing stage and onto the sandy shore with Lusk right behind him.

Lusk held the horse as the captain mounted. " 'Cause you got a way finding trouble, Cap'n."

"No trouble this time, Jacob."

Lusk grinned. "Well, seein' as how that Mr. Baldridge ain't around, you're probably right."

Williamson laughed. "I'm sure Masey will manage to find plenty of his own back in St. Louis." He took the reins in his left hand. "But I'll be fine, Jacob." Williamson followed an overgrown trail that snaked up the side of a forty-foot levee. He reined up atop the levee and watched as the *Paragon*'s huge paddle wheel chopped the water and backed her away from the shore. Momentarily her unique five-tone whistle sounded across the water as she steamed south. The captain sat watching her for almost ten minutes, until she disappeared beyond a sandbar overgrown with willows and made her way toward Boundurant Landing, St. Joseph, and on to New Orleans. Moments like this made him wonder if Jacob Lusk was right. Maybe he was in the wrong place doing the wrong thing. Maybe he should've stayed on the boat and forgotten about Van Geer's letter. Perhaps he should have let Baldridge and Tyner handle the investigation. But Helen Van Geer had come to him. She had trusted him because of who he was, and to have refused her—to do less than his best to help her—would violate the unwritten code among rivermen. You never left another riverman in trouble. Whether a boat ran aground, or caught fire, or just needed a tow, you always tried to help. And Hudson Van Geer, for all his faults, was a riverman. He didn't deserve to be gunned down in cold blood, and if his son did it, he should hang. But if he didn't—if Van Geer was on to something in his letter—Williamson had to find out. He owed that much to another man who had muddy water in his veins.

A brief stop in Vicksburg had determined that Grant De Paul could not have been involved in Hudson Van Geer's death. Not that De Paul wouldn't have liked to kill Van Geer, but the man had spent the past month in an insane asylum near Grand Gulf. One of the rivermen Williamson had talked to in Vicksburg had visited De Paul within the last few weeks. He indicated that losing his business had cost De Paul his mind as well, and that instead of chewing out rousters and deckhands on his packet line, he now spent his days chewing paint he managed to chip off the walls of the asylum. Another victim of Hudson Van Geer, some might say. Still, the man's story in no way lessened Williamson's desire to follow up on Van Geer's letter. Besides, that mojo left under his bed meant that somebody wanted him off the investigation, and that alone was enough to make him continue. He only hoped his telegram to Baldridge and Tyner would result in them finding something out.

The trail led down the levee, and as Baldridge followed it toward Hardscrabble Plantation, he recalled passing over the same ground during the war. This landing had been the center of operations for Ellet's Marine Brigade during the two weeks they patrolled the area for bushwhackers and guerrillas. By January and February of 1865, the Confederacy had lost control of the river down to New Orleans, and with no organized force to oppose Union shipping and troop movements, isolated bands of Confederate soldiers, many renegades and deserters from other units, would snipe at the troop transports or ambush unescorted ships as they plied the river between New Orleans and Vicksburg. Admiral Ellet had established his headquarters in the home of Mr. Monroe S. Routh, owner of Hardscrabble Plantation and Hardscrabble Landing. When not on duty as a pilot for one of Ellet's gunboats, Williamson had passed the hours at Hardscrabble, and he had come to know the Routh family— some of them better than others.

The road led down the west side of the levee, and Williamson ducked beneath tree limbs that had grown over the trail as he reached the flat land. Some three hundred yards away, at the end of a tree-lined road, surrounded on both sides by abandoned fields, sat Hardscrabble, the two-story home of the Routh family. The house sat upon stone pillars some seven feet high, allowing the Mississippi to overtake the levee during high water, which it frequently did, and run under the house without damage. But the fields on both sides of the road suffered from anything but too much water. Everywhere was dryness, and Williamson could tell the fields had not been planted this season, perhaps even in the last two years. At first he thought it was just the distance— that he wasn't seeing Hardscrabble clearly through the summer haze—but as he neared the home he began to sense the change.

The four towering white columns now seemed gray, and somehow smaller than he remembered, and the balcony above the entrance listed slightly to the right, with several of the vertical posts missing from the railing. The dark green shutters beside the two front windows were badly worn, and one was missing altogether. Momentarily Williamson wondered if he might have taken the wrong trail and come upon a different plantation. Nearing the house, he noticed the familiar walkway, lined on both sides with rocks, but where once a smooth brick path had led up to the front porch, spots of grass now protruded in several places where bricks were missing. There was not a sign of life as he scanned the surrounding grounds, so he halted his horse at the edge of the walk and dismounted. Tying the animal to a low-hanging oak limb, he moved up the brick path, calling out as he went.

"Anybody home? Mrs. Routh? Abby?" He hadn't spoken her name in over eight years, yet as he said it, he felt as though he'd gone back in time. Unspoken all these years, it had yet remained somehow familiar. "Abby!" he called again, almost as much to hear it as to get a response. When no one answered, he

continued up the steps and onto the front porch. He knocked on
the door, its dark green paint chipped away and severely weath-
ered in several places, and waited a full minute before knocking
a second time. Still no one answered, and he surveyed the land
in front of the house. He could almost see the rows of Sibley
tents spread over the grounds and the soldiers going about their
daily business as they had in 1865, when his unit occupied the
plantation. Walking toward the right front edge of the porch, he
recalled the exact spot where his crew was quartered and even
recognized a stump where he had played poker and seven-up
with the men. As a pilot, he frequented the Routh home where
Admiral Ellet and his staff were quartered, and he remembered
the first time he saw Abigail Routh. Indignant at the Federals
taking over their home, she refused to speak to him for three
days, and then only to suggest in something less than ladylike
terms that he step out of her way. He had liked her fiery tem-
perament, but as the days passed, he gradually discovered that
this bright, confident young woman had a softer side.

Williamson heard something around the side of the house.
He was moving closer to the edge of the porch when a rider
suddenly came galloping around the corner. Upon seeing him,
the startled rider pulled up sharply, and Williamson caught only
a glimpse of the revolver being drawn and cocked. Instinctively
he dove off the edge of the porch a split second before the
weapon discharged, burying a bullet in the huge column just
behind where he had been standing. The shrubbery broke his
fall, the twigs scratching his neck and chin, as he crawled to his
feet. He saw the head of the horse emerge around the porch as
the shooter urged the animal forward to get a better shot. Williamson could see his horse, frightened by the gunfire, struggling to free itself from the oak limb where he was tied, and he
realized he had to get to his rifle before the animal broke and
ran. Knowing it would be only seconds before his assailant got
off another shot, Williamson rushed for his horse, running in a

low crouch, as a second shot struck near his feet and ricocheted off the brick walkway. When he reached the animal, he struggled to hold it steady as he retrieved his rifle from the sling, all the while hearing the rider galloping toward him. Taking the Henry in both hands, he worked the lever to chamber a round and dropped to one knee beside his horse. Shouldering the weapon, he scanned to fix on the approaching target and would have fired immediately had not the rider veered off to the other side of the oak tree. As Williamson moved around behind his horse to the opposite side of the tree, he heard a voice that instantly halted him.

"You better come out from behind that tree where I can see you," a woman demanded, "else I'll blow your head off!"

Eight years may have passed, but he would have known her voice anywhere.

"Abby! Hold your fire. Abby!"

Several seconds of silence passed before he saw her walking her mount slowly into view as she approached cautiously around the tree, weapon extended, pointed toward him. He could not have recognized her from a distance, hat pulled low over her brow, string cinched tightly under her chin. But as she neared, her face betrayed her, despite the men's pants and checkered shirt she wore.

"Luke? Luke Williamson?"

"Don't shoot, Abby," he said, holding his rifle high in one hand.

She rocked in the saddle as her horse slowly approached.

"My God, Luke, I could've killed you," she said.

"You just about did," Williamson said, examining the tear in his dress uniform sleeve and wiping the trickle of blood from the scratches on his neck.

She dismounted, holding the smoking pistol at her side as she approached him. "I'm sorry. I thought you were—"

"It's all right," Williamson said, walking toward her. He

started to raise his arms instinctively to embrace her, but she stopped abruptly, and her apologetic tone suddenly disappeared.

"What are you doing sneaking around here, anyway?" Abby demanded. "How was I to know that was you? You could have been anybody. It's a thousand wonders I didn't kill you."

Williamson smiled. "Your aim is going to have to improve."

"There's nothing wrong with my aim, I'll have you know. You just spooked me, that's all. You shouldn't have spooked me like that."

"Do you shoot at all your visitors?" Williamson said.

"We don't have visitors anymore," Abby declared. "We just have trespassers."

The voice was as he remembered, as were the fiery eyes and the lovely face, but there was an anger—almost a fear in her voice that he did not recall. Having seen the condition of the house and grounds, he was tempted to ask what had happened.

"It's been a long time," he said.

"I thought you'd be back, you know," she said. "At least for the first six months."

"Abby, I—"

"And when the war ended, even Mother thought you'd be back. She liked you. Still does. Can you believe that?"

"How *is* your mother?"

"She's sick. Between the arthritis and her heart, I doubt she'll make it through the year. But what difference does that make to you?"

"Abigail?" a frail voice called from the front porch. "I heard the shooting, and . . . Abigail, is that . . . is that Captain Williamson?"

Abby shook her head. "There's nothing wrong with her eyesight." She called toward the house. "Yes, Mother. It's Captain Williamson."

Mrs. M. S. Routh, leaning on a walking cane at the top of the steps, called to her. "Well, bring him to the house, child."

Williamson could tell that Abby was less than thrilled by her mother's invitation, but she tied her horse next to the captain's and escorted him to Mrs. Routh.

"My, my, Captain, you look wonderful," Mrs. Routh said, managing an awkward embrace in spite of her shaky balance.

"It's good to see you, Mrs. Routh."

"All dressed up in your uniform. You're not still in the navy, are you?"

"No, ma'am. I run a steamboat line."

"Oh, that's right. I believe Abby said something about that." Mrs. Routh examined the sleeve of his dress jacket. "Why, you've torn your jacket, Luke."

"I ran into a little trouble," he replied, eyeing Abby.

"Well, please come into the house and visit a while. Abby will mend your sleeve for you."

"Mother, I don't think—"

"I'd do it myself, but these hands don't work the way they used to," she added, urging the captain inside. "Have you had lunch, Luke?"

"Yes, ma'am."

"Very well, then. You must come and tell me how you've been. I want to hear all about your exploits."

For the next half hour Mrs. Routh talked with Williamson while Abby sat tight-lipped, mending his sleeve. The years after the war had been difficult, and Mrs. Routh apologized for the run-down look of the place. With her husband killed in the war, only she, Abby, and two of the former slaves remained; the rest of the hired help was released a year ago. They had been unable to put in a crop last year, and high water had ruined most of the cotton and corn the year before. Still, despite her litany of woe Mrs. Routh sat as erect and proudly as her arthritis would allow, and Williamson detected occasional flashes of her wartime courage. But life was different now, as were Mrs. Routh and Abby. He remembered the mother as a constant optimist, even during the Federal occupation of her home and grounds. She had accepted her fate during the conflict with grace and dignity, maintaining all along that a reversal in the Federal fortunes of war was only a matter of time and patience. Perhaps it was her illness that had so dulled her, but Williamson never once heard Mrs. Routh mention the future or suggest how they might emerge from these hard times. And Abby—a woman who had never hesitated to confront either him or his fellow sailors during the occupation—seemed subdued. Not only had she little or nothing to say to him, she seemed genuinely frightened. After all, she had taken a shot at him for the crime of standing on her front porch, and that behavior, perhaps more than anything, seemed out of character for the Rouths.

Williamson eventually got around to his primary purpose—asking about the Boulet family—and just as he had suspected, Mrs. Routh knew all about them. She confirmed that the Boulet home had burned almost two years earlier, and that both Pierre Boulet and his wife were killed in the fire. Their only daughter, Claire, though injured, had survived the fire, only to leave Louisiana three months after the tragedy.

"That young Claire was a sweet girl," Mrs. Routh said. "Abby and her would sometimes spend time together at social events and church picnics back during the war. We saw her on occasion after the war ended—that is, until . . . until she stopped attending services. I guess Abby knew her about as well as anyone. Wouldn't you say so, Abby?"

"I suppose." Abby placed her needle and thread in her sewing kit, tucked the kit under her arm, stood up, and walked over to Williamson. She handed him his uniform jacket without speaking to him, picked up her revolver from an end table, and started out the front door.

"Abby, dear, where are you going?" her mother asked.

"To see to the horses," she replied, "and keep watch on the road."

Mrs. Routh looked away with an embarrassed smile. "Captain, I don't think Abby means to be ill toward you," she began, "but . . . but frankly, she's a bit disappointed in you."

Williamson knew what she meant. In the days he had been stationed at Hardscrabble during 1865, there had grown a respect between them that led to friendship, and a friendship that led to attraction, and attraction that led one night to even more. The last three days he was there, Williamson spent all his available free time with Abby. They laughed and talked and shared their dreams. But as suddenly as he had entered her life, Ellet's Marine Brigade received orders to leave, and he was sure Abby had not forgiven him that. Over and over in his mind he had reviewed his words to her, and he was sure he had never promised her anything, particularly that he would return. But spoken promises are often only the shadow of the unspoken, and he knew from her behavior that she was hurting, despite her facade of indifference.

"Why did Abby say she would be watching the road? Watching for what?"

"We've had some trouble, Captain."

"Horse thieves?"

"Hardly, Captain. We have no stock left, except for Abby's horse, one other, and one mule."

"What kind of trouble?"

"Land troubles. And I'm not talking about getting the crops in or taking care of the place. A lot of it goes back to the situation with the Boulets."

Mrs. Routh explained how, after Claire Boulet left Tensas Parish, word came that she was selling Boulet Plantation to a Northern businessman. Soon after, a man named Tallis came to supervise the place.

"It was all supposed to be done on the hush, but folks found out about it."

Williamson recalled Van Geer's letter. "You mean like V. R. Sheldon?"

"Do you know Vincent?"

"I came across the name."

"Vincent Sheldon runs the mercantile in St. Joseph. He knows just about everybody—at least, anybody who needs supplies."

"So he would know about the land sale?"

"I suppose so. But word has pretty much gotten around how it was handled. A couple of months after Claire left the parish, the magistrate in St. Joseph was contacted on the sale of the land by this Tallis fellow. Then the whole thing was done through the mail. Claire never returned, and the next thing you know this Tallis is running Boulet Plantation."

"So Tallis doesn't own the land?"

"No. I'm sure he's just managing it for someone else."

"How does that affect you?"

"Because he's not satisfied with just Boulet Plantation, Captain. This carpetbagger, or whoever he works for, wants our land, too. And everybody else's he can get his hands on. And he's already bought up most all the property around us." Mrs. Routh pointed a gnarled finger. "On all sides of us Tallis supervises the land now. It's all been bought up. Abby heard in St. Joseph that somebody is planning to build a railroad. But because of the way the swamp runs, they can't do it without Hardscrabble." She looked at Williamson, that wartime grit again displayed in her eyes. "We don't want to sell our land, Captain. It's been in the family for nearly a hundred years."

"I can understand that."

"And we've told him so, but he won't listen." Mrs. Routh looked away, struggling for composure. "And then there's his threats—"

"What kind of threats?"

"Tallis rode over here with a half-dozen men about a week

ago. We refused to sell again—this made the fifth or sixth time—so Tallis said he'd give us a week to reconsider. If we didn't, Hardscrabble would be knee-deep in ashes." She looked him squarely in the eye. "That's what he said, all right. 'Knee-deep in ashes.' He threatened to burn us out, and I reckon he means it."

"That explains why Abby was so jumpy when she saw me on your porch today," Williamson said. "Have you contacted the law?"

"The law's not much use this far out in the swamps, Captain. There's not much the two deputies in St. Joseph could do, anyway. They can't very well live out here with us, now can they? You know, Captain, this whole thing with selling Boulet Plantation is so unlike Claire. She was a decent girl. I guess the fire changed her. It would probably change anyone, especially with the injuries she received."

"Injuries? What kind of injuries?"

"Fire's a terrible thing, Captain. But being in the steamboat business, I suspect you know that. Claire was burned pretty seriously on her arms. They say she was trying to pull her parents out of the blaze. I suspect she'll carry those scars the rest of her life."

"You've seen the scars?"

"Oh, yes. About four or five weeks after the fire, I visited her with some of the women from the church—back when I could get around better." She pointed to her wrist. "She was burned from here all the way up to the elbow, on both arms."

Williamson leaned forward on the edge of his high-backed chair, his mind returning to the day he had talked with Claire in the jail in St. Louis. When Baldridge asked for lemonade that day, she had jerked it away so quickly it spilled on her sleeve. He remembered watching her roll up her wet sleeve almost to the elbow.

No scars.

"Mrs. Routh, are you *sure* about Claire Van Geer's injuries? I mean, you know for a fact that she has burn scars on both arms?"

"I told you, Captain. I've seen them myself."

Hudson Van Geer was on to something. Williamson would have given most anything for a photograph of Claire Van Geer, or Boulet, or whoever she was, to show to Mrs. Routh. But if the woman in St. Louis wasn't Claire, then who was she? And where was the real Claire Van Geer? Williamson realized there wouldn't be time enough before the *Edward Smythe* arrived to get to both St. Joseph and the Boulet Plantation, and he figured there was little the Sheldon man would add to what Mrs. Routh had told him anyway. Mrs. Routh's story about the rapid departure of Claire from Tensas Parish, together with the sudden sale of Boulet Plantation, made it seem to Williamson that Tallis was the one person most likely to give him answers about Claire Van Geer. So when Abby returned to the house, Williamson related his suspicion about Claire Van Geer and his desire to travel to Boulet Plantation. Abby surprised him by immediately offering to take him there.

"Boulet Plantation is surrounded on three sides by Lake Bruin, a horseshoe lake that used to be the old riverbed," Abby explained. "The trip by horseback takes about three times as long because you've got to pass what used to be the Boundurant place. Except that Tallis runs it now. We can go by jonboat, using Catfish Bayou. That is, if you're up to working the oars."

"When do we leave?" Williamson said, answering her challenge.

"Daylight," Abby replied. "It'll be dark in less than an hour, and I'm not about to run Catfish Bayou at night."

"Suits me," Williamson said, noting that Abby seemed to relish the idea of getting face-to-face with Tallis.

"What about your mother?"

"We should make it back by midafternoon. Demetrius will watch out for her until then. Is that all right with you, Mother?"

"I'll be fine, dear. Demetrius will take good care of me." She turned to Williamson. "Do you remember Demetrius? He was one of our slaves when you Yankee boys came."

"I remember him."

"He and Jewell, that's his wife, stayed with us after the war. I scarcely can conceive what we would have done without them." She glanced up at her daughter, who stood almost a foot taller than her and only slightly shorter than Williamson. "But I think we should feed the captain some supper now. You two will want to get to bed early if you're leaving at daylight." Abby nodded, as her mother added, "My Abby's become quite the cook, Captain. Jewell has taught her all manner of things."

"I don't recall you cooking at all back during the war," Williamson said.

Abby looked at Williamson sternly. "I do a lot of things now that I didn't used to do. I guess we should thank the Yankees for all our newfound skills, but somehow I just can't bring myself to do it." She walked into the hallway and headed for the kitchen.

The meal that night was modest—cornbread, fried pork, new potatoes, and butter beans—but even so, Williamson suspected it was heartier fare than usual. He spent most of the meal talking with Mrs. Routh, though he kept trying to draw Abby into the conversation. When she did speak, her comments were short and direct, and rarely did she initiate an exchange. Williamson kept stealing glances at her, recalling the woman he had known so briefly during the war and thinking how she had changed. Reconstruction had clearly hardened her, and he suspected that inside she was struggling to retain her pride amid the demise of Hardscrabble. He wanted to help her, but he wasn't sure how. Maybe if he confronted this Tallis fellow it might help. Maybe not. But the worst thing he could do, he figured, was lead her to believe he would help her and then disappear on Sunday aboard the *Edward Smythe*. And Williamson knew himself well enough to know that was precisely what he would do. Why give the woman false hope, only to dash it? Once or twice during the meal, however, his eyes met hers, and though she wouldn't hold the glance, he thought he saw something in those blue eyes that made it seem as if the eight years had never passed.

After the meal Abby gathered some fresh bed covers under one arm, took a lamp in the other hand, and showed Williamson to the upstairs guest room.

"Mother would've brought you up herself," Abby said, "but the stairs give her trouble."

"I understand," Williamson said. "It's good to see you again, Abby."

She folded the lightweight quilt at the end of the bed. "I doubt you'll need this, as hot as it's been." She walked over to lift a window, but it was stuck.

"Let me help you."

"That's all right, I've got it," she curtly replied, still struggling to break the seal.

Williamson tapped the base of the window on both sides, and in doing so brushed her hand. She lingered in contact with him momentarily, then pulled away. When they tried the window again, it rose two or three inches, kicking up dust on the sill.

"I'm sorry about this dust," she said. "We weren't exactly expecting company. And I'm afraid we've sent you to bed without a very good supper—"

Williamson took her by the hand and pulled her to face him. "Abby, I don't care about the dust. And the supper was just fine."

"I really need to go now," she said, turning away, but Williamson turned her back to face him.

"I just wanted to tell you that I *have* thought about you over the years." He could see tears forming in her eyes.

"That's real nice, Luke," she said, pulling her hand free from his grip. "I thought about you, too—for the first six months. Maybe a year."

"I've been real busy trying to build my shipping business—"

"Well, I've been rather busy myself," she said, fighting back tears.

"I never pass Hardscrabble that I don't think about you. I wonder how you're doing. I wonder—"

"Well, now you know," she said, half laughing and half crying. She walked across the room and picked up one of the lamps. "I've got to see to Mother now. I'll wake you about four-thirty."

"I'll be up," Williamson said. As Abby nodded and started out the door, he added, "You don't believe me, do you?"

She paused in the doorway, the light from the lantern playing off her face. "Believe what, Luke?"

"That I think about you when I pass the landing."

She nodded slowly. "Oh, I believe you. But that's the problem, Luke. You *pass*. All these years you've *passed*. And that tells me all I need to know." And she walked out of the room.

"Good night, Abby," he called, but she did not reply.

12

Saturday morning, June 21

EITHER THIS WAS the worst hangover she had ever seen, or something was wrong with Masey Baldridge. He was as pale as a sheet as he sat next to her in the St. Louis Municipal Courthouse, his eyes sunk in their sockets, his breathing heavy, barely able to stay awake as they waited for the judge to enter the courtroom. He'd really done it this time. A man could only drink so much whiskey until he paid the consequences, and if the blank stare on Baldridge's face was any indication, it was costing him a fortune. Thinking back on last night, perhaps she had been too hard on him, but she was mad, and she figured she had every right to be. It was bad enough that he had missed the hearing on Thursday, forcing her to lie to Helen Van Geer about him working on the case. She only hoped word didn't get back to the woman that Baldridge had gotten drunk and passed out— at least that's what he told her he had done during his more lucid moments Friday night. How was she to know that was the truth? Still, it was exactly the kind of thing Baldridge was wont to do.

He'd also babbled on about visiting the stableboy at the Van Geer home—something about the Tewley boy and Claire Van Geer. She had read Williamson's telegram, but not much of Baldridge's rambling made sense. So she had resigned herself to let him sleep it off, hoping to get more information from him Saturday morning; but it had taken all her effort just to get him up and dressed for Stewart Van Geer's sentencing hearing. Given his general listlessness, she considered just leaving him at the hotel, thinking he might embarrass her further. But she was not about to let him out of her sight again so he could go off and get drunk. Despite his condition, he would eventually pull out of it, she reasoned, and when he did she would need him on the case.

"Masey's not feeling well today," she told a nervous and frightened Helen Van Geer before they took their seats in the courtroom that morning. Baldridge managed a weak handshake and said nothing to Helen, and he would have lost his balance completely and perhaps tumbled into the aisle had not Tyner supported him.

The courtroom was filling up as she surveyed the room: Claire Van Geer and Marie Trehan were sitting just behind Helen Van Geer, but there was no sign of Robert.

"They're bringing him in," Tyner said, nudging Baldridge as the jailer escorted Stewart Van Geer to a chair beside his lawyer. Noting how the dazed look on his face resembled her partner's, she leaned over to Baldridge, whose breathing was labored, his eyes half open.

"Would you please wake up and pay attention?" she whispered, pushing her knuckle into his side. He moved slightly, but he didn't jump as he should have.

In a moment Judge Grove entered the courtroom. Reading from a prepared statement, Grove again detailed the crime, mostly in Stewart Van Geer's own words. When he had finished, he asked the prosecutor if he had anything he would like to add.

The prosecutor indicated that he did not, so he turned to the defendant. Stewart Van Geer's lawyer rose, helping Stewart to his feet beside him.

"Your Honor," the lawyer began, "my client deeply regrets his crime and the sorrow it has caused his family and the St. Louis community. Mr. Stewart Van Geer throws himself on the mercy of this court to spare his life, not only for himself but for his family, which has already suffered so much, and so that he might live to see his unborn child."

When the lawyer paused, Judge Grove prompted him.

"Anything else?"

"No, Your Honor."

"Very well, then. Mr. Stewart Van Geer, this court has found you guilty, by your own admission, of the brutal murder of your father, Hudson Van Geer. Because of the heinous nature of the crime—the deliberate manner in which you fired not one, but four shots into your own father—you showed no concern for human life. I, therefore, representing the people of the State of Missouri and the City of St. Louis, shall show equal concern for your life. Mr. Stewart Van Geer, for the crime of murder, on Saturday next, the 28th of June, 1873, at 3:00 P.M., you shall be hanged by the neck until dead." A low rumble swept through the crowded courthouse. Judge Grove stood up behind the bench. "And may God have mercy on your soul. This court is adjourned. Bailiff, return the prisoner to custody."

Just that quickly, it was over. That Stewart might hang—that he likely would hang—had always been a possibility; yet, despite his confession to the police and the evidence against him, Tyner felt as if she had failed, as though the Big River Detective Agency could at least have done something to change the sentence.

As the bailiff led Stewart Van Geer from the courtroom, his mother pushed open the gate in the railing and rushed to him. The officers of the court initially started to separate them but hesitated as the grieving mother embraced her son. Stewart wept openly as he hugged his mother, but Claire did not approach him. Rather, she stood beside Marie Trehan, her stony face never giving way to a tear. When the bailiff eventually separated Helen from her son, Claire finally stepped forward, and though Stewart beseeched her with his eyes and even called her name, she scarcely acknowledged him. Instead she took the distraught Helen Van Geer by the arm and began leading her down the center aisle toward the back door of the courtroom. As they approached, Tyner stepped to the edge of the aisle.

"I'm sorry, Mrs. Van Geer," Tyner offered. Baldridge stood behind her, steadying himself on the back of a bench seat. Helen Van Geer paused and looked at Tyner.

"Why couldn't you help? Why didn't you—"

"Mrs. Van Geer, we're still working. Masey and I are—"

"Mother Helen, I told you it was a waste of time and money hiring these people," Claire interrupted, urging her mother-in-law to continue toward the door. Marie Trehan followed Claire and eyed Tyner suspiciously. "She's insulted me, she's insulted Marie, and she and that whiskey-breathed friend of hers have done nothing but bring shame on the Van Geer name."

Tyner tried to speak over Claire. "This isn't over yet," she called to her. "Luke Williamson is working right now to—"

"Oh, I'd say it's pretty well over," Claire shot back. "My baby's father has been sentenced to hang in a week. I doubt there's anything you can to do stop that."

"Don't count on it," Tyner called to Claire. "Masey and I will—"

Suddenly Tyner felt Baldridge's full weight against her shoulder, and before she could turn to support him, he had slumped against the bench and tumbled to the floor between the rows.

"Masey!" Tyner knelt over him and shook him. "Masey, for God's sake get up." But his skin was cold and clammy; he was unconscious, and Tyner knew something was terribly wrong. She had seen plenty of drunks in her life, and spent more time than she cared to remember with men who passed out right in front of her. But this was different. This was trouble. "Would somebody help me? Somebody?"

Two men who had been observing the hearing, along with one of the court officers, rushed over to her.

"What's the matter with him, ma'am?" the officer asked.

"He's sick. He needs a doctor," Tyner said.

"Who is he?"

"His name is Masey Baldridge. He's with me. Can you find a doctor and have him meet me at the Dearborn Hotel?"

"Yes, ma'am," the officer said.

Several other people gathered near Baldridge, so close in fact, that Tyner had to ask them to step back so he could get some air. One of the onlookers offered the use of his carriage to take Tyner and Baldridge back to the hotel, and Tyner quickly accepted. Two men lifted Baldridge out to the carriage and slipped him inside, Tyner hurrying inside right after him. She laid his head in her lap as the owner of the carriage climbed into the driver's seat and snapped the reins. As they rounded the corner, Tyner saw Marie Trehan standing beneath the street sign watching them, a satisfied smile on her face.

ABOUT TWELVE-THIRTY Tyner was standing at the end of the hallway, staring out the second-floor window of the Dearborn Hotel, the building now busy with businesspeople dropping in to eat lunch in the dining room. A doctor named Hollister emerged from Baldridge's room and called to her.

Baldridge's shirt lay open, unbuttoned to his navel, tiny droplets of sweat clinging to the hair on his chest. He remained unconscious, his skin pallid.

"What is it, Doctor?" Tyner asked.

The doctor wiped his hand on a washcloth and returned some instruments to his bag.

"I'm not exactly sure, Miss Tyner. It could be alcohol poisoning, and from what you've told me about Mr. Baldridge's drinking habits, that would be my best guess right now."

"You say it *could be*?" The concern on the doctor's face worried her.

"It's certainly not a classic case of alcohol poisoning," Hollister admitted. "Didn't you tell me that he's been suffering from a general malaise for the last couple of days?"

"That's what he told me. Masey didn't say much last night, but he did mention feeling weak for the past few days. In fact, he could barely get out of bed this morning."

"And are you sure he didn't drink any more on Friday?"

"Well, no, I'm *not* sure. I mean, he may have at some time on Friday. But he didn't drink anything after I found him Friday night. I know. I was here."

"If Mr. Baldridge went on a binge on Thursday, most of the alcohol should be out of his system by now. Oh, he'd be uncomfortable all right. You know, nauseous, that kind of thing. If he'd had too much to drink, I can't see how he could have gotten out of bed, gotten dressed, and made it to the courthouse with you."

"You don't know Masey Baldridge."

"Maybe not. But the weakness he complained of bothers me. And this sweating, it's not usually associated with too much whiskey."

"Do you think he's caught some kind of fever?"

"That's what's got me puzzled," the doctor replied. "The best I can tell, his temperature is normal. In fact, if anything, he's cool to the touch."

"So, what are you saying?"

He closed his bag. "I'm saying I don't know. I don't know exactly what's wrong with your friend."

"But you're a doctor. You're supposed to know."

"I'm leaving you these tablets, Miss Tyner," the doctor said, taking a bottle from the dresser. "Chances are, he'll sleep it off. Give one of these to Mr. Baldridge when he comes to."

"What if he doesn't come to?"

"I'm afraid I'm going to have to give him nikethamide. But I'd rather have him come out of it on his own. If it's alcohol poisoning, he should eventually come around."

"And if it's not?"

"I'll check back on him tonight about eight. Just keep an eye on him in case he wakes up. Wouldn't want him to start vomiting and get choked. Turn him over onto his side if he does. Right now, it's best just to let him rest. Let him sleep it off."

Tyner thanked the doctor and showed him to the door. She returned to Baldridge's bedside, pulled up a chair, and took a seat next to him.

"Now what I am supposed to do?" she asked aloud. "How am I supposed to work on this case and keep an eye on you at the same time?" She sat in silence for several moments watching his labored breathing, his eyelids occasionally quivering from what she guessed was a delirious dream.

"What are you dreaming, you silly man?" She took his hand and squeezed it. "And what in the world have you done to yourself?"

13

LUKE WILLIAMSON'S DREAM was so vivid, he actually got out of bed and looked out the window to be sure his wartime unit wasn't camped on the lawn of Hardscrabble Plantation. But as he gazed out the window, the yard was still and silent, only the light of a half-moon bathing the willow tree as it slowly rocked beneath a gentle early morning breeze. If his dreams had been limited to his wartime compatriots he might have had a more restful sleep, but the face of the woman sleeping below had haunted him throughout the night. In his dreams they were once again riding down by the river, their differences overwhelmed by the pleasure of each other's company. But in his dream her horse kept leading her onto the far side of a slough, and try as he might, he couldn't get his animal to cross the water. She was calling to him, but though he struggled with his horse, cursing and spurring, the animal would only splash out into the water, then shy back to land, keeping Williamson from the other side.

From years of early morning rounds Williamson could tell by the smell of the morning air that it was near time to get up anyway. Dressing quickly, he secured his Henry and crept down the creaky staircase, careful not to wake Mrs. Routh. Emerging at the bottom of the stairs, he saw the faint glow of a light in the kitchen, where he found Abby sitting alone at the table, nursing a cup of coffee.

"I was just about to come up and wake you."

"Good morning."

"The coffee's hot on the stove, and there's biscuits from last night's supper if you want one. I wrapped up a couple for later. It'll be a long time until we eat again."

Williamson poured a cup of coffee and stood near the stove, sipping. Abby removed a revolver from a kit bag, where she stored the biscuits, and checked the weapon's load.

"Yesterday was the first time I ever saw you with a gun," Williamson said. "Are you figuring to use that today? Because if you are, I'd like to at least get a chance to talk to this Tallis before you shoot him."

Abby rotated the cylinder. "Not unless I have to." She eyed his rifle. "You're not exactly bringing a peace pipe, and you don't even know the man."

"I think I'm starting to," he said. "Besides, that bayou is probably full of varmints."

Abby replaced the weapon and, taking the kit bag in one hand, stood up. "Bring that cup with you if you want, but I think we'd best be getting down to the water. Demetrius is already there preparing the boat."

About four hundred yards from the house, Demetrius stood by the jonboat. He held it steady while they climbed inside, Williamson occupying the center seat between the oars and Abby the bow.

"I greased them oars real good, Miss Abby."

Williamson took one in each hand and rotated it, noting the free action. "You did good."

"Thank you, Demetrius," Abby said.

"You and the captain be real careful now. And watch for them stumps."

"We will. You keep an eye on Mother. And if anyone comes around here that you don't know, you shoot 'em on sight. Do you understand that?"

Demetrius patted a revolver tucked into his belt. "I'll watch out for your mamma real good."

CATFISH BAYOU RAN southwest, parallel to the Mississippi River, for almost a mile and a half before turning sharply west, then continued another mile until it emptied into Lake Bruin. It had been years since Williamson had rowed a boat, but the timing was something that a sailor never forgets, and after the first mile, though slightly winded, he was well enough into a rhythm that Abby had to ask him to slow down in a couple of spots. She offered to relieve him on the oars more than once, but each time he refused; given his unfamiliarity with the bayou, he figured he had rather be tired from rowing than soaked and snakebit from treading water after they gutted the jonboat on a stump he could not spot. The mosquitos were thick in places, and the bayou alive with wildlife. A largemouth bass jumped so near the boat Williamson almost struck it with an oar, and the constant call of the swamp birds played a background to the rhythmic strike of the oars as he rocked forward and drew back, driving the boat along the water.

They talked very little as they glided across the bayou, Williamson's thoughts lost in the wake of his boat as it disappeared into the early morning mist. Why would someone assume Claire's identity? To what extent had Hudson Van Geer made his suspicions known to the woman claiming to be Claire? Could he have confronted her? Would he have dared confront her until meeting with V. R. Sheldon and learning the whole story? If he had, why would that have given Stewart Van Geer cause to murder his father?

Lake Bruin was calm as their boat cleared Catfish Bayou, and Williamson kept rowing as they began crossing the thousand yards to the far side. Just after eight o'clock, Abby guided the jonboat alongside a dilapidated pier and tied off the bow. As they climbed out and began dodging the rotten boards to make their way to shore, Williamson rotated his shoulders and stretched his arms out behind him to forestall the stiffness he knew he would feel later that night. About a hundred feet inland, he saw smoke rising from the chimneys of perhaps a half-dozen shanties—low, narrow, deteriorating buildings with tin roofs. Two children chased each other around in front of the nearest shack, and a tall, overall-clad negro approached to meet them.

"Miss Routh? Is that you?"

"Yes, Thurl. It's me."

"Well, Lord a'mercy," he said, removing his hat. "We sho' ain't seen the likes of you in some time."

Abby introduced Williamson, explaining to him that Thurl had been a servant on the Boulet Plantation until the war, and he and several other negro families had remained as sharecroppers afterward.

Williamson wasted no time, immediately asking Thurl how well he had known Claire Boulet.

"I knowed her all her life, Cap'n," Thurl said. "My woman, Cleo, helped raise that girl until she died back in sixty-three. Yes sir, Miss Claire is a fine young woman. Shame how she went off like she did."

"When did Claire leave?"

Thurl scratched his head. "Well, sir, let me see. The fire will be two years come October." He pointed to a hill about a hundred yards away, where a charred foundation stood in outline against the morning sky. "Right yonder is where the house sat. I reckon the last time I saw Miss Claire was after she got out of the hospital. She come back to get what little of her belongings hadn't burned up."

"Abby tells me she was hurt in the fire," Williamson said.

"Yes sir, that girl near 'bout died trying to save her mamma and daddy." Williamson thought he detected a tear in the old negro's eye. "She'll probably be bad scarred on her hands and arms for the rest of her life."

"And Claire never returned?"

"No, sir. She left here with them two women, and I ain't never seen her again. Next we heard she had done sold the place, and then Mr. Tallis come."

"You say she left with two women? Who?"

"They was some white trash Mrs. Boulet hired right after the war."

"I met those two once," Abby said. "I don't recall their names, but I remember that I didn't care for them. They acted uppity just because they tended to Claire. Most of the coloreds had left, except for Thurl and about four others that stayed on to crop. That's when Mrs. Boulet hired these two white women to keep house for her."

"Do you remember their names?" Williamson asked.

"One was called Margaret, and the other one was Marie," Thurl said.

"Marie what?" Williamson asked. "Was her last name Trehan?"

"Could have been, I suppose. Don't recall ever knowing her last name. But she was one woman I didn't want to get to know."

"Why?" Williamson asked.

"I'd rather not say, if it's all the same to you, Cap'n."

"Thurl," Abby said, "whatever you can tell Luke might help. If you know something about Claire and these women, then please . . . tell him."

"Hoodoo," Thurl whispered, glancing around as though someone were watching him. "That Marie woman fancied herself a hoodooer."

Williamson nodded. Marie Trehan must be the connection with the mojo found in his cabin.

"Where were these women when the house burned?"

"They was stayin' in it. Or they was supposed to be," Thurl said, his face growing stern. "But they sho' wasn't no burns on *their* arms."

"Are you saying they didn't help Claire try to save her parents?"

"I ain't sayin' nothin', Cap'n. Some of us wondered about the whole thing, but the fact is, the house went up so fast there wasn't nothing anybody could have done. By the time we woke up and seen the flames, the place was mostly gone. Me and two other men ran up to the house, and that's when we found Miss Claire. She had done drug her mamma and daddy out of the building, but it was too late. They was burned something awful. Miss Claire was barely alive herself. We got her in a wagon and carried her to the doctor in St. Joseph. It's a pure miracle that she lived."

"And the two women in the house?"

Thurl looked away. "Wasn't a burn mark on 'em," he said bitterly.

"So after all that, why did you stay?" Abby asked.

"Wasn't really noplace else for us to go. Me and some of the other hands had hoped to buy us a little piece of this ground after the fire. We worked this land all our lives. Maybe we was wrong to feel this way, but we kind of figured we was owed it. We figured Miss Claire might sell the plantation, or maybe that she'd sell off a few little pieces to me and some of the other boys. But then we heard it had done been sold, and then Mr. Tallis come here to run the place. So now we just stay 'round here doing a little piddlin' work, since Mr. Tallis done got rid of most of the cattle and hogs." Thurl stepped closer to Abby and spoke in a low voice. "That man sho' don't know nothin' 'bout farming. He brought about a half-dozen white men down here with him, but they don't lift a hand at much of nothing. They spend most of their time up there in that far cabin drinkin' corn liquor."

"Is that where we can find Tallis?" Abby asked.

"Yes, ma'am." Thurl smiled knowingly. "I figured you'd be coming, all right. I heard tell he tried to buy Hardscrabble."

"We're not selling."

"Yes, ma'am. Heard that, too. Mr. Tallis, he already manages most of the land between your place and St. Joseph, so I hear."

Three riders approached from the far cabin and reined up some twenty feet from Williamson and the others. A heavyset, bearded man removed his hat and addressed Abby.

"Good morning, Miss Routh. I hope this visit is for you to tell me your mother's changed her mind."

"Then you're going to be very disappointed, Mr. Tallis. Nothing's changed since you came to the house last week. We're not selling Hardscrabble. Not to you, not to anyone."

Tallis sighed and leaned forward on the pommel of his saddle. "Now, the people I represent have offered you a fair price for your land," Tallis said. "It's folks like you that are holding up progress. You're going to give up that land one way or another." Abby offered no response, and Tallis eyed Williamson. "Then if you ain't here to sell your land, what are you doing here? Or did you just come to talk to the coloreds?" Before she could answer, Tallis snapped at Thurl. "You ain't getting paid to stand around, boy."

Thurl offered no reply, but gave Abby and Williamson an apologetic nod and walked away.

"Exactly what are *you* getting paid to do?" Williamson asked.

"Who are you?" Tallis replied. The riders on each side of him stared hard at Williamson.

"Luke Williamson. I run a packet company."

"Riverman, huh?"

"That's right. I understand you handled the purchase of the Boulet Plantation from Claire Boulet."

"That's a matter of record. Did you come all the way over here to ask me that?"

"Who did you buy it for?"

"Well, that, sir, would be none of your business."

"How well do you know Claire Boulet?"

"Well enough. What business is it of yours?"

"Well enough to describe her to me?"

"Describe her? What the hell for?"

"You bought this land to put a railroad across it, correct?"

"That's a definite possibility," Tallis grinned. "I suspect that don't make you rivermen none too happy."

"I could care less what you do with this land," Williamson replied. "As long as you obtained it legally."

"Well, you ain't the law *anyway*. Are you accusing me of something?"

"I believe the woman that corresponded with you on the sale of the Boulet Plantation wasn't Claire Boulet."

"That's crazy talk. Where did you ever get a notion like that?"

"Maybe I'm wrong. If I am, prove it. Describe Claire Boulet for me. And tell me who you bought this land for."

Tallis hesitated, and Williamson figured he suspected a trap. He wasn't surprised when the heavyset man replied, "I don't have to prove jack shit to you."

Williamson tried another approach. "How long have you been in the railroad business, Tallis?"

"I'm not. I'm a land speculator."

"I see. So you're not the person building the railroad."

"Never said I was."

"Then who is? Who are you buying the land for?"

"I've already told you, that's none of your damned business."

"I can ride into St. Joseph and find out from the parish court clerk."

"Maybe. Maybe not," Tallis replied. "Either way, I'm getting tired of listening to all these questions. So, unless you've got some serious business, you and Miss Routh can just get the hell out of here."

"Serious business? I'd say land fraud is pretty serious business. Let's see if I can figure out how it works." Williamson dug his toe in the dirt and glanced down as if in deep thought. "Mr. and Mrs. Pierre Boulet die in a sudden fire. Their daughter, Claire, leaves Tensas Parish for good with two attendants after recovering from the injuries sustained in the fire." He looked up at Tallis. "Now this is where I'm guessing, but you be sure and tell me how close I get to the truth. Something happens to Claire. Maybe she got sick, or just died from the complications of the fire. Or maybe someone killed her. Another woman steps forward and claims to be Claire Boulet. Away from north Louisiana, who would know? But it has to be someone who knew Claire and knew about her family and land. After a few months, the new Claire Boulet conveniently sells her property through correspondence to someone who just happens to need the land for a railroad."

"That's a hell of a story, mister."

"Yes, it is. And if it's true, that makes your deed to the Boulet Plantation worthless."

"You're hard to figure, Williamson. Why are you down here sticking your nose into my business."

"The Rouths are my friends."

"Well then, if you were really their friend, you'd quit spinning tales about the Boulets and talk to your good friends the Rouths before something unfortunate happens."

"And when I prove that the woman claiming to be Claire Boulet perpetrated a fraudulent land sale, that's going to make whoever hired you pretty mad, wouldn't you say?"

"I say you've worn out your welcome," Tallis said.

"You're probably right." He turned to Abby. "Abby, I think we can go now. You told Mr. Tallis what he needed to hear, and he told me what I needed." Not trusting the riders flanking Tallis, Williamson began backing along the pier toward the boat, his Henry rifle, though still pointed at the ground, gripped tightly in his right hand.

"You're making a big mistake, Miss Routh," Tallis shouted. "A real big mistake."

"Maybe," she said, reaching inside the kit bag and holding up her revolver. "But not as big a mistake as you'll make if you ever come around our place again." The sight of the revolver sent Tallis and his men reaching for their weapons, and Williamson, shocked by her brash display, quickly lifted his rifle to the ready.

"Put that away," he ordered Abby, never taking his eyes off the riders. "Put it away now!" He looked directly at Tallis. "Easy now. No need for gunplay. Miss Routh was just making a point. We'll be leaving now." He motioned toward the boat with his head. "Abby, step in the boat and secure the oars."

She gave him a puzzled look but complied, and Williamson pushed the boat away from the pier, leaping to a seat on the bow, never taking his eyes off Tallis and his men. As Abby rowed them away from the bank, Williamson wondered if he had made a mistake. Perhaps he'd said too much. Pressed too hard. What if he was completely wrong? What if Tallis was an unknowing victim of Claire Boulet? Possible, but not likely. Tallis was hiding something. Something big. He would have to get a telegram to Baldridge at the first opportunity. Nothing he had found out meant that Stewart Van Geer didn't kill his father, but he was more convinced than ever that the woman claiming to be Claire Boulet was the key to what happened to Hudson Van Geer.

Once a safe distance from shore, he offered to take over the oars, but Abby refused.

"Pulling out that gun back there wasn't very smart," Williamson said. "You could have gotten us both killed."

Abby kept up her steady, rhythmic rowing. "I'll have to fight them sooner or later."

"Maybe they'll back off now—now that they know I'm investigating Claire Boulet." Williamson realized that was the first time he had referred to what he was doing as "investigation," and he recognized equally well that he was far deeper into this business than he ever expected to get.

"You don't understand," Abby said, pulling back on the handles and driving the boat forward. "You just sealed our fate."

"Me?"

"Yes, you. The big riverboat captain come down here to save the lowly planter," she said. "You'll be lucky now to save yourself."

"What are you saying?"

"It's simple, Luke. First of all, time is up for Mother and me. I knew that when I came over here this morning and told him we wouldn't sell. Tallis gave us one week, and the week is up. I had hoped, however, that he might not go through with whatever he had planned for Hardscrabble. That is, until you just forced his hand."

"*I* forced his hand? You're the one that pulled a gun on him!"

"Listen, Luke, if what you charged about Claire Boulet is true, do you really think Tallis is going to let you leave Tensas Parish to tell anybody?"

"I'm sorry if I made things worse, Abby. I didn't mean to."

"Don't worry about it. It was coming anyway. Just be glad of one thing."

"What's that?"

"It takes three times as long to reach Hardscrabble by horseback. At least we can be ready for them when they do come."

"If they come," Williamson said, still clinging to hope.

"No, Luke. *When*."

———

BY MIDAFTERNOON WILLIAMSON and Abby had returned to Hardscrabble and informed Mrs. Routh of their confrontation with Tallis. At one point Williamson considered riding to St. Joseph to get help from the sheriff, but he feared not getting back before Tallis and his men reached the plantation. He might have sent Demetrius, but that would have meant one less hand in fight. Instead, he determined to prepare the house and grounds for the night just in case Abby's worst fears came true. Tomorrow, upon the arrival of the *Edward Smythe*, he would detail some armed crewmen to Hardscrabble until he could contact the law regarding Tallis's threats and pursue the connection with Claire Van Geer and the sale of the Boulet Plantation. The *Edward Smythe* could run shorthanded to Vicksburg, where he would hire replacements for the men he left at Hardscrabble. It was the right thing to do; he would have done the same thing for anyone in that situation.

But he knew better. He knew Abby had never forgiven him for disappearing after the war, and perhaps in some way he could atone for what he hadn't done in the past. Either way, they had to get through tonight before worrying about tomorrow. Williamson set about evaluating a defense he hoped he would never execute.

The cypress swamp ran in a rough semicircle behind the Routh home, effectively securing the rear from approach; negotiating that swamp at night was out of the question. Anyone approaching the house would have to come either up the road, where they would be clearly visible by moonlight across the unplanted cotton fields that spread across the front of the house, or through a grove of trees that shadowed the swamp for five or six hundred yards to the extreme right. Williamson had Demetrius meet him in the near end of the grove with some fence wire, which the two men strung neck-high over the cow path that led through the grove. In two other locations, both right and left of the path, they also strung wire. Next, they stacked hay bales and two-by-fours in the loft of the nearest of two barns, some hundred yards from the house. That would be Demetrius's position; he could get a clear shot at anyone moving between the barn and the house, or attempting to get into the rear.

Williamson planned to use two windows of a second-floor corner room, one on the front of the house overlooking the road and fields, the other, on the right side of the house, allowing a limited view of the grove. He placed an extra box of 44.40 Henry rifle cartridges on the floor in the corner between the two windows. Fearing that Tallis might make good on his threat to burn the house and barns, he, Abby, Demetrius, and Jewell filled every bucket on the plantation, as well as the bathtub in the house, with swamp water, and stationed the buckets within easy reach. He had noted a band of clouds rolling in from the northwest on their way back that afternoon, but though he hoped for rain, Williamson knew he couldn't count on it, given the dry spell the entire Mississippi River valley had been experiencing.

By dark the wind had picked up, swaying the trees in the grove, and the temperature had cooled down several degrees. If not for keeping vigil, this would have been a good night to sit outside on the front porch with Abby. Instead he sat alone in a rocking chair on the second floor, his rifle across his lap, watching alternately the woods and the road leading up to the house. He had sent Jewell on his horse to station herself about a quarter mile south, where the road leading up to the house joined the road leading from the direction of St. Joseph—the roundabout route Tallis would have to take to get to them. He planned to relieve her in a few hours with Abby, and he hoped that they would be able to give him early warning of any uninvited visitors. Abby was stationed downstairs also watching the front of the house. Demetrius was positioned in the barn, watching the fields and the back of the house, and Mrs. Routh, limited by her arthritis, watched the back door, holding Luke Williamson's revolver at the half-cock and ready.

Slightly more than an hour after dark, Abby entered Williamson's room to bring him a cup of coffee.

"Thank you," he said. "You must have been reading my mind."

"I just remember you and coffee," Abby said, moving to look out the side window. For just a moment Williamson thought he saw the hint of a smile. If it was, it would have been the first one he'd seen since arriving yesterday. "Did you warn Jewell not to ride through the grove?"

"Of course I did."

"I was just asking," she said. "Demetrius came back laughing and carrying on about the wire you two strung up."

Williamson sipped his coffee. "We put together a little welcome for them."

"Well, that's fine. But you just be sure you and Demetrius take those things down tomorrow. I'm liable to forget they're there and get knocked flat on my behind."

Williamson stole a glance at the same. Nice thought.

"What else do you remember?" he asked.

"What?" Abby moved across the room and lit a small lamp, as the darkness of the summer evening encroached quickly upon the fields and grove outside.

"You said you remembered about me and my coffee. What else do you remember?"

She replaced the lamp globe and cut her eyes at him. "I remember plenty."

"Most of it good?"

"Some of it." She returned to watch out the window overlooking the grove.

"How about the night we rode down by the river and built that campfire?"

Abby nodded slowly. "We talked for hours. You told me all

your plans that night. You said that after the war you'd own your own boat." She allowed herself a modest smile, her eyes meeting his gaze for longer than usual. "You did it, too. That must make you very proud."

In that moment, as he met her gaze, Williamson realized why she had haunted his mind all those years, and he wanted to tell her how much he had missed her, but the words would not come. He could manage only an awkward acknowledgment.

"We had a good time," he said, quickly glancing out the window.

"I remember how cold it turned and how I thought I would freeze," she said. "But you—"

"What?"

"Nothing."

"No, you were going to say something."

"Just how you put your arms around me and . . . it doesn't matter. That's all past."

"Is it?"

"It is for me," she said, her smile disappearing. "I'm going down to check on Mother."

Abby started past him. Williamson, realizing that he might not get another chance, reached out and grabbed her sleeve. She paused and looked down at him in the rocking chair, tears swelling in her eyes.

"Abby, I . . . I just wanted—"

The sound of a galloping horse stole Williamson's attention and brought him to his feet, peering out the front window. Abby moved close beside him.

Jewell reined up on Williamson's horse just below the window, calling up to where they stood. "Miss Abby! There's riders comin'. Five, maybe six."

"Are they coming up the road?" Williamson asked.

"Can't say for sure. I couldn't stay around to see. Figured I'd best get on back and warn you before they come upon me."

"You did good, Jewell," Abby called to her. "Now ride over to the barn and tell Demetrius, then hide yourself and the captain's horse in the barn."

"Yes, ma'am," she replied and hurried the animal away.

Although the moon had just begun to rise, the gathering clouds limited its help as Williamson searched the darkness for some sign of movement.

"Blow out that light behind us, then go downstairs and put on a lamp in the living room."

"Why?"

"To make the place look normal. If it's completely dark, they'll know we're lying in wait for them. Then hurry back up here and watch the grove." Abby thundered down the stairs, returning within two minutes. As she reached the top of the stairs Williamson called to her. "I think I see something."

She rushed to join him, revolver in hand. "Where?"

Williamson pointed out the side window. "Do you see a light through the trees?"

Abby peered into the darkness. "Yes. Looks like a campfire maybe."

Williamson worked the lever on his Henry rifle and chambered a round. "I wish it were." Abby looked at him, puzzled. "Torches," he said solemnly.

"Oh, no," she groaned.

"I'm afraid so. Switch windows with me. You watch the fields out front, and I'll try to get a shot at the first one that approaches the house."

Through the heavy leaves of the trees in the grove, Williamson watched the dull glow grow brighter as the riders moved toward the house. To try for a shot now would force the men with torches to take cover, making it more difficult to pick them off, so he decided to bide his time until he could get a reasonable shot. The glow closed within two hundred yards of the house, then one hundred, and he could make out what he guessed to be three separate torches. He knew immediately when the riders broke into a gallop because the glow of the torchlight bobbed from within the trees. Drawing aim just below the first flaming torch, he waited for the first rider to clear the grove, where he planned to pull the trigger. But the rider never emerged from the trees. The movement of the light halted abruptly, and the horse the man had been riding came dashing clear of the grove and past the rear of the house out of sight. The wire he and Demetrius had strung had taken a casualty, and now the torch the man had dropped set the dry grass around it ablaze, illuminating a second rider who had suddenly halted upon seeing his comrade so rudely unhorsed.

"Sheets," Williamson said.

"What?" Abby asked.

"Sheets. They're wearing goddamned sheets."

"Do they really think we won't know who they are?"

"I don't know what they think, but I know one that won't be thinking anything else." The burning grass gave Williamson just enough of an outline to squeeze off a round, which ripped the other rider from his saddle and sent him to the ground amid the blazing grass.

"Good shot!" Abby shouted, slapping Williamson on the back.

"You're supposed to be watching the front," he snapped.

"I am. But I sure enough saw that shot you just made."

Williamson smiled to himself but kept up the front. "I'm going to have to make some more before we're through."

The wounded man began to scream to his friends for help as the fire overtook him, and Williamson caught the shadows of two men struggling to pull the first one out of the burning grass, but he couldn't get a decent shot.

"Goddammit," he mumbled.

"Luke, someone's coming this way," Abby called out.

Williamson looked over her shoulder out the front window

and saw a torch-bearing rider moving across the field in front of the house, well out of range, and headed in the direction of the barn.

"That one's up to Demetrius," he said, returning to his watch on the grove. The fire started by the downing of the first man had spread to encompass some fifty or sixty feet of the grass and was climbing at least three trees in the grove. Williamson noted with some sense of relief that the wind was blowing away from the house and he hoped that the rain he had sensed earlier would soon arrive, else the blaze might consume the better part of the grove before choking out in the swamp. He watched as the attackers, stung by the loss of two men and apparently uncertain about further progress through the grove, began to move from left to right, out of the illumination of the fire in the general direction of the front of the house.

"More coming your way, Abby. Keep your eyes open." Williamson started for the stairs.

"Where are you going?"

"I've got to get to the ground. If they reach the edge of the trees and rush the house, I can't get a shot at them from up here."

"Luke!" she shouted at him, bringing him to a halt at the top of the steps. "Be careful."

"I will. You just shoot anything moving out of those woods, understand?"

"I understand."

Williamson's plan was simple. He would slip out the back door and drop to the ground under the house. Sitting as it did upon stone pillars that allowed high water to flow beneath it, the house offered some seven feet of clearance above the ground. He would station himself to watch any approach from the front and obtain a decent shot at anyone emerging from the woods.

A frightened Mrs. Routh heard him coming down the stairs, and with arthritic hands, brought a trembling weapon to bear in his general direction as he emerged from the hallway.

"Don't shoot, Mrs. Routh. It's me. Captain Williamson."

"My Lord, Captain," she said, her voice as shaky as her hand. "I heard you shoot, and I figured they were coming."

"They *are* coming, Mrs. Routh."

"Oh, my goodness."

"Now listen carefully," Williamson said. "I'm going out this back door and under the house. Once I leave, I want you to point your weapon at this door and shoot anybody that comes through it. Anybody. Understand?"

"I believe so."

"Good." Williamson left the building and made his way beneath the house, working from pillar to pillar, looking first right toward the grove, then straight ahead toward the fields, and glancing occasionally to his left toward the barn. From the direction of the barn he heard a shot, then a second, then a third. Soon a dull glow emerged from that direction and he realized that the far, rear corner of the barn was ablaze. From beneath the house he couldn't see the loft to tell what had become of Demetrius, but he assumed the worst. Abandoning momentarily his watch on the grove, he moved to a pillar on the left edge of the house, from where he observed a rider emerging from the glow of the spreading barn fire.

With only seconds to act, Williamson lifted his rifle to engage the horseman approaching, torch blazing, the sheet he wore lashing in the growing wind as he galloped toward the house. The rider swerved, causing Williamson to lose his aim and waste precious seconds repositioning on the other side of the support column. But as he emerged for what would be at best a momentary opportunity for one shot before the rider delivered his fiery assault, Williamson heard the crack of a rifle from the direction of the barn. The rider drew up sharply and slumped forward in the saddle, the torch he still held dangling beside his horse and terrifying the animal into a frenzy. The horse shed his wounded rider and his torch fell harmlessly away from the house, the horse disappearing into the darkness. Outlined by the blaze of the barn, Williamson saw Demetrius standing at ground level, rifle in hand, searching about for another target. But upon the report of a weapon from the front of the house, Demetrius dropped, prompting Williamson to fire in the direction of the large oak tree where Abby had only the day before driven him to cover upon his arrival at Hardscrabble. He fired twice more, his rounds chewing away bark from the old tree, before he rushed to a support pillar nearer his target. He could make out the edge of the sheet the man wore dancing in the wind from the other side of the tree, and though he could not get a clear shot, he could see the man was attempting to light another torch. He could hear Abby firing her revolver from the front window, but he doubted she could get much better shots from where she stood. Glancing through the pillars to assure himself that no one had gained the building from the rear, and that no one had emerged from the grove, Williamson maneuvered behind the pillar supporting the left front corner of the house and lifted his rifle to aim at the spot where he expected the man to emerge with a lighted torch. He might rush the house, but most likely, having gotten within fifty feet, he would be satisfied to throw the torch and hope it caught. If the torch reached the dry bushes that lined the porch—the same ones that had scratched him so badly the previous day—Williamson knew he would be powerless to stop the blaze. The house would be lost. He couldn't count on Abby to stop the man, and he figured he had one shot at best, so he steadied the rifle on an outcropping of stone in the pillar, cocked the weapon, and watched. From the spreading glow of the newly lit torch on the far side of the tree, he knew he would not have to wait long. His finger caressed the trigger as he firmed up the plant of the rifle butt in his shoulder, adjusted the weld of his check to the stock, and peered through the V-shaped sight. Suddenly the assailant stepped back from the oak tree, revealing only half his body for no more than two seconds as he drew back the torch and swung his arm forward in a throwing motion. But it was enough time for Williamson, and his Henry delivered a round that caught the man in his left shoulder and spun him to the ground, interrupting his throw and sending the torch bouncing across the brick walkway, where it came harmlessly to rest. Williamson rushed the oak tree and moved quickly upon the wounded man, delivering the butt of his rifle to the man's skull as he tried to scramble away. He looked at the blazing barn to his left, where he could make out Jewell attempting to drag Demetrius to safety. He should help her. But what of the house? Of the other attackers? And Abby? He hadn't considered it when he rushed the tree, but she might well have shot *him*. And when he realized that she hadn't and he could see nothing of her in the darkness of the second-floor window, he wondered what had become of her. He re-counted in his mind—two in the grove, one at the barn, the one lying in front of him. If Jewell was right, that left at least one or two more. But where were they? With the losses they had taken, they might have drawn off, but he doubted it. Williamson dashed across the open toward Jewell and Demetrius and had almost reached them when someone fired at him from behind the house, sending him diving into the dirt.

"Get down, Jewell," he shouted. She released Demetrius and lay over him, covering him with her body. With the blazing barn illuminating the side of the house, Williamson fired two shots in the direction of the rear steps, rolled over and fired two more, and rolled over again in the direction of Jewell and Demetrius. He was out of ammunition. From his pocket he produced a half-dozen 44.40 cartridges and quickly loaded them. Another shot came from behind the house, kicking up dirt near his left foot.

"Jewell," he called loud enough to be heard over the crackling blaze behind them. "Where's Demetrius' rifle?"

"Behind you," she replied. "Right near where you are."

Williamson felt around in the grass and eventually caught

the glint of the blazing barn on the chamber of Demetrius' rifle. He retrieved it, checked to find it loaded, and rushed in a crouch to Jewell and Demetrius. To his surprise, he drew no fire. A quick examination of Demetrius revealed that he had taken a round in the thigh and was bleeding severely. He handed the rifle to Jewell.

"Can you use this?"

"Yes, sir."

"Then fire a couple of shots at the base of the back steps."

"Now?"

"Right now."

Jewell fired and Williamson pulled Demetrius into a slight depression that took him out of the line of fire. He instructed Jewell to make her way back to him, then to tear off a piece of Demetrius' shirt and tie it tightly around his leg just above the wound. She tied the cloth while Williamson covered her, all the while searching the house for movement and worrying about Abby and Mrs. Routh. When Jewell had secured the makeshift bandage on Demetrius' leg, Williamson had her again cover him while he made a rush for the house. Again, he drew no fire as he reached the safety of the pillars and worked his way from one to the other until he reached the back steps. He found no sign of the man who had fired at him, but as he peered up at the back door, he realized his worst fears. He had closed the back door when he left, and now it stood open. Someone had gotten inside the house. From inside the house above him, he heard a shot, then a second, and a third. He ran for the back steps and rushed up them toward the back door, and as he approached the open door, two more shots rang out from inside, tearing away a piece of the doorjamb and backing him up against the outside wall.

"Abby!" he called out.

"Luke?"

"It's me. Abby, are you all right?" he asked, remaining backed against the wall.

"I'm all right."

"Your mother?"

"I'm right here, Captain," Mrs. Routh replied.

"Someone's in the house," Williamson said.

"Not anymore," Abby said. "Mother put a bullet through him."

Williamson smiled. Glancing around at the swamp to his rear and peering around the corner of the house toward the grass still ablaze in the grove, he sensed it was over. While he wouldn't be certain until daylight, he had been in enough fights to have a feel for such things, so he told the two women to hold their fire and made his way into the house.

"Did we get them, Captain?" Mrs. Routh asked.

"I think so. If there are any others out there, I believe they've given it up. We'll keep watch until morning to be sure."

With Abby keeping watch, Williamson helped Jewell bring Demetrius into the house, and he and the Rouths watched the remaining sections of the barn collapse into the fiery heap as Jewell cleaned her husband's wound.

"I got the bleeding stopped, but he needs to see a doctor, Mrs. Routh."

"I don't think we should move him tonight," Williamson said. "The *Edward Smythe* arrives tomorrow. I have a man on board that can see to him. We can take him to Vicksburg to get that bullet removed."

A gentle rain started about eleven o'clock, growing gradually more intense and reducing the threat of a fire spreading beyond the barn or jumping the trees in the grove. The rest of the night Williamson and Abby kept watch, while Jewell attended to Demetrius and Mrs. Routh tried to get some sleep. When Abby moved near him about three that morning and whispered to him how much she appreciated what he had done for them, he felt self-conscious. Part of him wanted to take her in his arms and hold her; yet he felt as though so much had come between them, and he dared not set her up to be disappointed yet again. He put his arm around her and told her to get some sleep so she could relieve him on watch in an hour. She was asleep in moments, and the hour came and went, but he did not wake her. He simply held her against his chest as he watched out the window, occasionally taking his eyes off the fields in front of the house long enough to admire her soft features, bathed in the light of a low burning lamp, as a steady rain pattered on the roof over the front porch of Hardscrabble.

14

Monday, June 23
Dearborn Hotel

THE SOFT TOUCH of a hand upon his forehead, a cool washcloth on his cheek. He wanted to respond, but he felt as though he had window weights on his eyelids, and his mouth felt sewn shut. For all his efforts, he couldn't seem to move his hands and feet. In his mind he was calling out, screaming, but no one could hear.

Hoofs thundering on the deck of the Paragon. Crazy. Nash-ville Harry pulling ahead. Got to get to shore. Got to beat . . . who? Who's the other rider? A woman with no face. Is it you, Sally? Is it you? No face. She's got no face. Wandering the alley, looking in windows. I can hear her calling me. Sally's calling me. Where are you? Searching. Searching the stable loft. Paus-ing for a game of pool. Crazy. Got to find her. She'll be mad. Searching for her everywhere. Sally? I hear you calling. Where are you? Stop hiding from me.

The hand was gone from his forehead, and he could feel his

skin cooling beneath the dampness of a cloth. *Sally? Where are you?* He tried again to speak, but the words would scarcely come. Nothing but darkness. He thought he saw Stewart Van Geer hanging in the gallows, eyes closed, chin on chest, dangling, twisting in the wind.

"Have you seen her? Have you seen her?" he mumbled. He heard Sally Tyner speaking to him, but he couldn't understand her. As she spoke, he saw Stewart Van Geer again, swinging on the hangman's rope, his eyes open and beseeching him. Baldridge was terrified.

Dead man eyes. Dead man talking. No words coming out.

Baldridge could sense a light on in the room and someone speaking to him.

"Masey? Masey?"

He felt the sheet against his body being pulled up over his chest and tucked in at his chin.

Am I dead? Can't be dead.

He heard footsteps on the hardwood floor, the sound of water pouring.

Water. So thirsty. His lips felt cracked and his tongue thick. Again he tried to speak, but the words came out jumbled.

"Masey?" a woman said.

Sally? Helen Van Geer? What's she doing here? Where? Where am I? Claire Van Geer? Not Claire. Tewley's afraid. I'm afraid.

He felt a cup at his lips and a few drops of water on his tongue, and though he tried to drink it down, he couldn't seem to swallow. And soon he was choking. Someone rolled him onto his side, and he felt a hand on his face.

Feet walking. Walking away. Why can't I open my eyes? Why can't I speak? I must. I must speak.

A few moments later Baldridge's eyes snapped open, as though something had startled him. But the room was a blur, and he could make out only the outline of a window in the lamplight.

Nighttime. What night? Where?

Silence. Gone was the touch of a hand, the cool cloth on his head. No one moved. He could smell his own sweat against the fragrance of freshly laundered sheets. Struggling to turn over, he managed to raise his shoulders and sit up on his elbows. He tried to gaze about the room, but his eyes wouldn't focus. Mouth open, he passed his tongue over dry, cracked lips as he tried to corral his thoughts.

St. Louis. Had a few drinks. Looking for Sally. Why? Looking where? Goddamned Williamson. Where is he? Where is he?

Voices outside the room, louder, nearer, as he began to lose consciousness. He slumped back onto the pillow, and though he struggled to remain lucid, he couldn't seem to fight off the approaching darkness.

Am I dying?

He heard footsteps outside the door. Someone entered.

"Masey?"

He wanted desperately to speak, but no words would come, and the voices became a dull, unintelligible rumble, then faded away into silence and darkness.

15

LATE TUESDAY NIGHT, under the watchful eye of its new captain, Martin Cummings—personally trained by Luke Williamson—the *Edward Smythe* made the bend near President's Island and sped the last few miles toward the landing at Memphis, Tennessee. Williamson had named the *Edward Smythe*, sister boat to the *Paragon*, after his late business partner who had gone down with his ship, the *Mary Justice*, in October 1872. A Federal troop transport during the war, the *Edward Smythe* had been converted to a passenger packet and placed into service only a few months earlier. Williamson knew his presence made Cummings nervous, so he tried to steer clear and stay out of his way in day-to-day operations, but the circumstances had already caused him to interfere more than he wanted.

When the *Edward Smythe* arrived Sunday morning at Hardscrabble Landing, Williamson had met Cummings with a host of instructions. He brought Demetrius and one of Tallis's men to the boat for transport to a hospital in Vicksburg, and was barely on deck before he promptly ordered Cummings's first mate, Davis, to send an armed six-man party, under the supervision of the second mate, to the Routh home. Giving orders was second nature, so Williamson thought nothing of it at the time, but upon confronting the fuming Cummings a few moments later, he realized he had made a mistake.

"These are *my* men, Captain Williamson. And I'm captain of the *Edward Smythe*. Nobody sends a party ashore unless I say so."

"Martin, I was just—"

"You may own the boat," Cummings said, "and you can fire me if you think I'm not running it right—"

Williamson tried to smile. "Nobody wants to fire—"

"But you're not going to order my men around."

Williamson noticed a vein in Cummings's neck popping out. He had never seen his new captain so angry, having always considered him a bit more timid in his presence than he ought to be.

"Martin, I—"

"When you come aboard the *Edward Smythe*, and God knows it's your boat and you can come aboard anytime you want, you're a passenger, Luke, unless it's got something to do with the business end of things."

Williamson's instinct was to challenge him, to back him off, but the words wouldn't come, and he allowed as how Cummings was right. He'd gone too far. A few months on his own running his own boat had given Cummings some of the swagger and spirit he had been lacking—an attitude necessary for survival in the steamboat business—and despite being chastised, Williamson was glad to see it.

"You're right, Martin. I was out of line. I should have come to you first."

"Damn straight."

"Won't happen again."

Williamson then explained his encounter with Tallis at

Hardscrabble. He told him briefly about the connection to Hudson Van Geer's murder and how Tallis and his men had tried to burn out the Rouths the night before. Upon hearing the cries for help from one of Tallis's wounded men, Williamson had dragged him into the house about four o'clock and awaited a renewal of the attack, but neither Tallis nor any of his men had returned. The rain had continued up until midmorning, putting out any remaining fire in the grove, and at first light Williamson had gathered the bodies of three of Tallis's men and placed them under a small shed. Jewell had stopped the bleeding in Demetrius's leg, but Tallis's man, suffering from a round that had passed through his upper left shoulder and a second, embarrassing shot that had torn away a piece of his ass, received from Williamson a simple choice: tell him everything he knew about Tallis, and be taken by steamboat to a hospital in Vicksburg, or keep his mouth shut and die. The man talked plenty. He and the others had been hired by Tallis almost eight months ago to help him convince the surrounding farmers to sell their land and, as the man put it, to "keep the niggers in check." While he claimed to know nothing about Claire Boulet, he did confirm that Tallis was working for some railroad man—a man he had met only once—based out of St. Louis. His description was vague and might have matched any of a hundred men, and Williamson hoped that if he received medical attention in Vicksburg, he might live and be able to identify the railroad man at some future date.

Upon hearing his story, Cummings readily agreed to leave a team of crewmen at Hardscrabble and even sent another man by horseback back to St. Joseph to bring the local law. Williamson had confidence that Cummings's second mate, a decorated Southern war veteran, would be able to handle anything Tallis might throw at the Rouths until the law could get involved. Even then, he had the only witness to Tallis's involvement with him on the *Edward Smythe*, so there would be little the sheriff could do until the man was returned to St. Joseph to give a statement. He could have left him at Hardscrabble, but the chance was good that without attention he might die before the sheriff could arrive. No, he had made the right decision to bring him along. Now he had to keep him alive.

Williamson had been on the ship less than an hour before he ran into Anabel McBree.

"What are you doing on board the *Edward Smythe*?"

"I needed to check on the cooks. They've been on their own almost a month now."

"I thought you were evaluating them every six weeks."

Anabel looked away from him, and Williamson knew she was hiding something. "What's going on, Anabel? It isn't like you to leave your work on the *Paragon* this way."

"To tell the truth, I'm worried about you, Captain. Been worried ever since Jacob found that mojo, and I'm sho' enough worried since I had a chance to talk with some folks down at a landing about fifty miles south of here."

"About what?"

"About who was a hoodoer in these parts," she explained. "I heard tell that about a year ago a conjure woman was staying up here around St. Joseph. Nobody gave me her name, but she's supposed to be something powerful."

"How about Marie Trehan?" he asked.

"Nobody said a name. Where did you hear about this Marie woman?"

"The colored folks working the old Boulet Plantation told me about her. She disappeared with Claire Boulet some months back."

"Could be the one, Captain."

Williamson was glad to see her on board, and while he was far from admitting to belief in mojos, he figured her expertise might come in handy when they got back to St. Louis.

At Vicksburg, while a doctor came aboard to examine Demetrius and Tallis's man, Williamson prepared a telegram to be sent to Baldridge and Tyner, outlining his suspicions about Claire Boulet's identity, the motive for Hudson Van Geer's murder, and the connection to the railroad. The doctor indicated that both Demetrius and Tallis's man should be hospitalized in Vicksburg; and after Williamson had explained the latter's role in the attack on Hardscrabble to the local law, the *Edward Smythe* steamed out of Vicksburg in the wee hours of Monday morning, June 23.

In Memphis, Williamson was met with a telegram from Salina Tyner.

JUNE 24, 1873
ST. LOUIS, MISSOURI

CAPTAIN LUKE WILLIAMSON
C/O THE EDWARD SMYTHE, MEMPHIS WHARF

STEWART VAN GEER FOUND GUILTY STOP
SENTENCED TO HANG ON SATURDAY STOP
MASEY BALDRIDGE SERIOUSLY ILL STOP
RETURN AS SOON AS POSSIBLE STOP

SALINA TYNER
DEARBORN HOTEL
ST. LOUIS, MISSOURI

Williamson wasn't surprised that Stewart had been found guilty, or that he would be sentenced to hang, but he knew Claire Van Geer was somehow involved, and he couldn't let the investigation end without finding out how. He drafted a telegram to Tyner: he expected to arrive in St. Louis on Wednesday evening, and he would come immediately to the Dearborn Hotel. Not wanting to spell out too much over the telegraph wire, he simply indicated that he believed others were involved. Perhaps if he could find out who and in what way they were connected, the information might mitigate against a hangman's noose for Stewart Van Geer. Perhaps he deserved it. Perhaps he didn't. Either way, Williamson figured the Big River Detective Agency was getting paid to find out the truth. Sparing no speed, the *Edward Smythe* left Memphis at 1:00 A.M. on Wednesday morning.

"HE'S BEEN LIKE that for four days now," Tyner explained to Williamson as he made his way to Baldridge's bedside. She stood near Dr. Hollister, her dress uncharacteristically wrinkled, looking as if she hadn't slept in some time. "Once, maybe twice, he's come to, but he's rambling and disoriented when he does. Then he lapses back again and you can't roust him. He dreams a lot. He seems delirious most of the time."

"It's not inconsistent with alcohol poisoning," the doctor said, standing at the foot of the bed. Williamson glanced at him as if demanding an introduction. "Doctor Ned Hollister," the doctor said, leaning over the bed to shake Williamson's hand.

"Luke Williamson," he replied. "You think that's what it is?"

"From what Miss Tyner has told me about Mr. Baldridge's habits, it would be my best guess."

"Guess?"

"Frankly, Captain, I've never seen anything quite like this. I would have thought he'd have come around by now. I hoped I wouldn't have to give him nikethamide, but I don't see much way around it. He'll just have to take his chances."

"Is this stuff, this—"

"Nikethamide."

"Yeah. Is it dangerous?"

"It can be. But we've got to bring your friend around, else he's going to dehydrate. Miss Tyner informs me that she has been able to get only a little water in him. With no food or water in his system, he can't fight the fever much longer."

"The fever comes and goes," Tyner explained to Williamson. "Nights seem to be the worst. He's been talking out of his head whenever he's clear enough to be understood. Last Monday night I came back in the room and the bedcovers were messed up and Masey was laying across the bed as if he'd been up. He'd been thrashing around, but I'm not sure he was ever conscious. When I came back in the room he was mumbling something about murder. I guess he's having dreams about the case."

"If you give him this medicine," Williamson said, "what can happen to him?"

"We've got to bring him around. To shock him back to consciousness. We've tried cold water, warm water, massage, nothing seems to work. Nikethamide into his bloodstream acts like a stimulant, like the caffeine in coffee, only a lot stronger."

"So what's the problem?"

"Sometimes it can be too much for the heart. I've heard of patients whose hearts stopped."

"Heard? You mean you haven't ever tried this?"

"Not personally. But I've communicated with doctors who have. It's a relatively new treatment for alcohol stupor."

"But you're not even sure that's what's wrong with him," Williamson said.

Hollister nodded. "True. But I don't know anything else to do."

When Williamson first considered bringing up the question, he wondered what Tyner and the doctor would think of him. He had no hard evidence that such a thing could be possible, or even that it could have been done to Baldridge, yet the doctor was clearly out of answers. "Dr. Hollister, do you believe in hoodoo?" Williamson asked.

Hollister appeared disturbed. "You mean voodoo?"

"Yeah. Putting curses on people and what the coloreds refer to as herb doctoring."

"There's absolutely no basis for such claims," Hollister said. "Sure, I've heard of it." He glanced in the direction of Jacob Lusk and Anabel McBree, who were standing near the door. "Some ignorant people even believe in such things. They go to their root doctors and pay for all manner of worthless potions and mixtures." Hollister shook his head. "You know what happens to most of them?"

"What?"

"They die. That's what happens to them. But what's this got to do with Mr. Baldridge?"

"Maybe Masey's been cursed with this sickness," Williamson said.

Tyner chuckled. "Luke, you can't be serious."

"About a week ago someone tried to put a curse on me," he continued, lifting his hands before him. "Now before you say I'm crazy, hear me out. Jacob found what he called a mojo, under my mattress on board the *Paragon*."

"You look perfectly healthy to me, Captain," Hollister said.

"That may be because we found the mojo and threw it overboard."

"Captain," Hollister began, "I'm surprised that a man of your position would actually lend belief to—"

"I'm not saying I believe it, Doctor. I'm just asking you if you have ever encountered such a thing."

"Never. Not in twenty years of practicing medicine."

"But you also admit you've never seen anyone in Masey's condition," Williamson added.

"Well, not exactly. I mean, I've seen alcohol stupor, but—"

"But not like this."

"No, not this bad."

"Then is it *possible* Masey could be suffering from something else?" Williamson could not believe he was actually saying this. "Like some kind of curse?"

"What's gotten into you, Luke?" Tyner asked.

Williamson explained that Marie Trehan was involved in voodoo. Since she and Claire Van Geer may have had a reason to keep Baldridge from finding out the truth, he insisted that it was at the very least possible that Trehan put some kind of curse on Baldridge. Until the past week, he had never given a moment's thought to such matters, preferring to believe they were the product of superstition and ignorance. But now, faced with what he knew about Trehan and the fact that even the doctor couldn't figure out what was wrong with Masey, he had to at least explore the possibility. He fully expected Tyner to light into him for such foolishness, but instead she grew pensive as he spoke.

"She had candles," Tyner said.

"Who?"

"Claire Van Geer. When I went to see Claire, there were candles in her room. Mounted on a coconut, of all things."

From the spot in the back of the room where Anabel McBree stood, quietly listening to the exchange, she suddenly spoke. "What color candles?"

Tyner turned to her. "I believe they were lavender."

"Three of 'em?" Anabel asked.

"Yes. There were three."

"Was there a piece of paper under the coconut?"

"There was paper underneath," Tyner said, "but I didn't get close enough to see what was written on it."

Jacob Lusk whispered something to Anabel, then slipped out the door as she spoke. "Sounds like a hoodooer to me. Whenever they want to make some bad work—"

Hollister leaned back and tugged on his vest. "This seems to me to be getting a bit out of hand."

"Let her finish," Williamson said. "Go ahead, Anabel."

"When a hoodooer wants someone dead, they write the name of the person and put it under a coconut. Then they pour beef gall and vinegar inside and set lavender candles on it. It puts out a powerful smell."

"Claire's room had a strange smell," Tyner said.

"They won't never let those candles go out. They'll keep puttin' new ones on the stub of the old ones, marking every day until the person is dead."

"Anabel, are you saying it's possible that's what wrong with Masey?"

"I don't know, Miss Tyner. I'd have to take a look at him."

"So, are you one of these conjuring women?" Hollister asked, a wry smile on his face.

"I ain't no hoodooer, but my grandfather doctored folks with roots and herbs for years. He told me some about it."

Williamson and Tyner both looked at Baldridge at the same time, then at each other, prompting Hollister to angrily declare, "Surely you two don't believe in this nonsense. It's completely unscientific."

"I think Anabel should take a look," Williamson told him.

"I agree," Tyner said.

"This is preposterous," Hollister said. "Your friend is in an alcoholic stupor."

"You *think* he is," Tyner corrected.

"Yes, Miss Tyner. I *think* so. But I *know* what he's *not* suffering from, and that's some ridiculous curse."

"Three days you've come to see him, and still he's no better. In fact, he's worse."

"These things take time."

Williamson motioned Anabel to come to the bedside, informing the doctor, "Then it won't hurt to have Anabel take a look, now will it?"

Hollister angrily closed his bag and tucked it under his arm. "I'll not be a party to this. I'm prepared to treat your friend according to accepted medical practice—"

"With a drug that may kill him," Williamson said.

"He'll die anyway without something to bring him around."

"Then why not let Anabel have a look?"

Furious, Hollister stamped across the room and into the hall. "Miss Tyner, you called me to help your friend. But it looks to me like you and the captain have chosen superstition over substance. You know where to find me if you decide against this madness. I only hope it won't be too late." Hollister closed the door and stormed down the hall.

After a few minutes of examining Baldridge, Anabel stepped back and crossed her arms, her eyes still studying his pale body. As he watched her, Williamson almost determined to go after Dr. Hollister. Was he out of his mind? How could he give credence to a myth like this? Yet he hesitated long enough to give Anabel a chance to answer. When she had not spoken after almost a minute, he turned to Tyner.

"What should we do, Sally? Do you want me to go after Hollister? Let him try this drug?"

"I don't know, Luke. I can't—"

The door to Masey's room burst open, and Jacob Lusk rushed in.

"Cap'n!" he shouted. "Look here what I found on Mr. Baldridge's horse." He held up a flannel bag similar to the one he had found under Williamson's bed. "Somebody had tied it underneath his saddlebag. Wasn't no way he would have seen it unless he was lookin' for it."

Anabel took the bag from Jacob and examined its contents under the lamplight on the dresser. "It's a mojo, Captain," she said, speaking almost to herself. "Looks like somebody has throwed down on Mr. Baldridge the way they tried to put the mojo on you." She looked at Williamson, her voice growing louder. "Captain, I saw a man that looked the way Mr. Baldridge does when I was just a child—not more than ten years old. He had the drinelin' sickness. Just drineled away to nothin' over about a week. When they called my granddaddy it was too late. He brought in some herbs and tried doctorin' him, but he said he got to him too late."

"Then what can we do for him?" Tyner asked.

"Ain't nothin' none of *us* can do," she replied. "If this conjure woman throwed down on him like you suspect, it's gonna take a powerful root doctor to cure him."

Williamson questioned her. "Where can we find somebody like that? We can't very well get to Louisiana—"

"Captain, hoodooers and root doctors ain't just in Louisiana. They're pretty much everywhere, if you knows where to look. They keep to themselves and don't talk much about what they do, but folks know where to find them when they need a potion."

"Do you know of anybody around St. Louis?" Tyner asked.

"One man. Bo Lawrence."

"Where is this Lawrence?"

"Toombs is his last name. Bo Lawrence Toombs. But people just call him Bo Lawrence. I ain't never met him myself, 'cause I don't mess with hoodooers, but I hear tell he keeps a place down by the river somewhere on the south end of the city."

"Would he treat Masey?" Tyner asked.

"Can't say for sure. Root doctors are funny 'bout their patients. But we can ask him. Mr. Baldridge needs help, and that doctor is right about one thing—he ain't got too long to get it. Me and Jacob can go after Bo Lawrence at first light tomorrow if you want us to, Captain."

"You might as well," Williamson said. "Nothing else seems to be working."

Until well past midnight, Williamson told Tyner of his experiences in Louisiana, and he resolved to try to talk with Robert Van Geer on Thursday morning. It was almost 2:30 A.M. when he returned to the *Edward Smythe*, and by the time he had caught up on his paperwork, it was after four. He stretched out on his bed, but before putting out the light, he leaned over and took a quick look under his mattress—just to be sure. Then he blew out the lamp and settled back to sleep the remaining two hours until daylight.

16

BEFORE RETURNING TO the *Edward Smythe* with Jacob Lusk and Anabel McBree, Luke Williamson had promised to send someone to relieve Tyner for Baldridge's care the next morning. After they left, Tyner nursed Baldridge until well past three o'clock—seeing him through the sweats, delirium, and a strange, sudden thrashing about, followed just as quickly by almost deathlike stillness, a stillness that compelled her to press her cheek close to his mouth to be sure he was still breathing. Through his restless periods he mumbled and sometimes spoke out loud. She was sure from some of the things he said that Baldridge was back in the war, for he would contort his face into the most painful expression, and he seemed to be perpetually in fear or dread. If this was alcohol and Baldridge could have seen himself, Tyner knew he would never drink again. Unfortunately, he couldn't, and with all that had transpired the night before, even Tyner wasn't discounting the possibility that, as crazy as it sounded, Baldridge might be suffering from some kind of curse. Through it all, the one thing he kept repeating was the word "Tewley." She recalled that as the name of the Van

Geers' stableboy and resolved to at least talk to him the following day.

About an hour past daylight, after Baldridge had calmed down enough for Tyner to grab a few hours of sleep, her relief arrived from the *Edward Smythe*. The two women that showed up informed her that Jacob and Anabel had gone in search of the Toombs man they had talked about last night, and they planned to bring him to the hotel by evening. They also passed word from Captain Williamson that he was going to try and talk first with Robert and later with Stewart Van Geer. He asked for her to join him at the jail later that morning if she could, but if he didn't see her, he would meet her here at the hotel to check on Baldridge around suppertime. Tyner left some instructions regarding Baldridge's care and took a carriage to the Van Geer home. Once there, she discovered that Helen Van Geer had gone to the jail to spend time with Stewart, but the attendant that answered the front door also told her that Tewley had been missing since Friday.

"He wasn't at the table for supper that night," the attendant explained, "and he wasn't to be found around the grounds. One of the stablehands looked for him all day Saturday, but couldn't find a trace. When he checked his room above the stable, he found what little belongings the boy had were still there. He just disappeared."

Tyner asked if Mrs. Van Geer had been informed of the boy's disappearance.

"Mrs. Van Geer was sad to hear Tewley left," the attendant told her. "She's the one that set us to looking for him. But when he didn't show back up by Sunday evening, Mrs. Helen figured he was just upset about Mr. Hudson's death. Mr. Hudson took a special liking to that boy, though I couldn't ever see why myself."

When Tyner asked if the woman could think of any place she might look for Tewley, she had offered no suggestions. The remainder of the help was off—Mrs. Van Geer still honoring her husband's Thursday-off policy—so they would not be able to assist her in her search for the young man.

"We figure he's just skedaddled," she told her. "An orphan will do that, you know. Especially with Mr. Hudson dead and all."

It had been over two weeks since Van Geer was murdered, and the notion that Tewley would choose now to disappear did not ring true. Tyner suspected that Baldridge had discovered something, perhaps something the boy knew. That a boy with no family and no one else to turn to would suddenly leave the Van Geer home meant that something, or someone, must have frightened him. She paused to consider where an orphan might go in a city the size of St. Louis. Perhaps a church might take in a boy like that. He might even find work on the docks or in a rail yard. But where would he go at night? Where would he sleep? To whom would he turn? Then she got an idea. If he was half as close to Hudson Van Geer as everyone claimed he was, there was one place she might find him.

JUST BEFORE NOON the driver eased the carriage inside the low brick wall that surrounded St. Vincent Cemetery and, following Tyner's instructions, stopped in the shade of a cedar grove. They waited over an hour, positioned so they could keep an eye on Hudson Van Geer's grave, the brown mound of fresh dirt still rising above the surrounding plots. From what Luke and others had told her, Tyner couldn't help but think how Van Geer would have liked that—towering above his peers, calling attention to himself—at least for a while. Eventually the dirt would settle, the grass would grow, and unless you sought out the marker, ol' Hudson would look just like everyone else. A half-dozen people, most bearing flowers for the grave of some loved one, came and went while they waited in the growing heat of the day.

The driver returned from a stream about two hundred yards away with a bucket of water for his horse, placed the bucket on the ground, walked back to where Tyner sat in her carriage, and propped his foot in the front spokes.

"Any sign of the young 'un, ma'am?"

"Not yet."

The driver pulled out a handkerchief and wiped his brow. "Are you sure you're gonna find him in a cemetery?"

Tyner fanned herself. "No, I'm not sure. But I don't know where else to look."

"I used to play in a cemetery when I was a boy," the driver said, pressing a conversation that Tyner didn't desire.

"Is that so?"

"Yes, ma'am. Played there most every day—at least until my uncle scared me off."

"I see." She leaned forward to see around him.

"Don't you want to know what scared me?" he said with a wry grin.

"Not particularly," she said, still struggling to see around him.

"Loggin' chain." She could tell he was waiting for her to ask him what he meant, and if she were honest, she did wonder about it, but she knew to answer him would just urge him to continue, which he did anyway. "He said that if I kept running across them people's graves, the devil would throw a big ol' loggin' chain around my ankles and drag me down to perdition."

"Is that right?" She motioned for him to step back.

"Yes, ma'am." He took his foot down from the wheel and began folding his sweaty handkerchief as neatly as a table napkin. "That's why I don't believe you're going to find no youngster in a cemetery."

Tyner leaned forward and squinted. "Is that so?"

"Yes, ma'am, I just don't—"

"Well, I guess you're wrong. Because I think that's Tewley

coming from the far side of the cemetery." She pointed out the window. "See that boy walking over there?" The driver acknowledged that he did. "I want you to walk around to the left. Act like you're looking for a gravestone. He'll start watching you, and I'll come up from the right."

"What you gonna do to that boy, ma'am?"

His tone offended her. "Just talk to him. But he may try to run, and if he does, he'll probably go your way, and I want you to stop him."

"Ma'am, I didn't hire on to go chasing nobody through no cemetery," he argued. "I'm a carriage driver. I don't like walking around them graves. I don't—"

"You're a grown man, for God's sake," Tyner said. "Why don't you act like it?"

"Ma'am, I don't—"

"Now go on like I told you. I'll pay you double your carriage rate."

"Double?"

"That's what I said. Now go on. He's heading toward that new grave." The man started making his way through the cemetery, walking rather as if he was afraid he would step on something fragile.

She couldn't resist calling to him. "You didn't hear chains clanking together, did you?" The look on his face told her he didn't find any humor in her remark, but he complied with her instructions. As she had suspected, Tewley proceeded directly to Hudson Van Geer's grave and took a seat in the sun at the foot. He noticed the driver walking around three or four rows away, but he never spotted Tyner coming up behind him.

"You loved him, didn't you?" she whispered, startling the boy. He jumped to his feet, and in a moment of indecision, before he recognized her from her visit to the Van Geer home, she had time to grasp his arm.

"Tewley, I want to talk to you."

"No!" he shouted, struggling to pull free.

"Tewley, I'm not going to hurt you. I swear it. I just want to talk to you."

"Let me go!"

"Not until you talk to me!" she shouted, then called out even louder, "Calm down. And sit down! If you cared anything about Hudson Van Geer, if what he did for you meant anything at all to you, then you'll sit still and talk to me. Right now."

The boy stared at her as his mind wrestled with her demands, then he ceased trying to pull away.

"Are you going to talk to me?" she asked.

"Yes."

"And you won't run away?"

The boy shook his head.

"Promise?"

"Yes."

"Promise for Mr. Van Geer?"

"Yes."

Tyner let go of his sleeve, but the boy tensed up as the driver approached, calling to Tyner, "Is that the youngster?"

"Who's he?" the boy said, clearly frightened.

"He's my carriage driver." She motioned him away. "He's going to wait in the carriage while we talk."

The driver walked away, and Tyner lifted the edge of her dress and sat down on the ground beside the boy.

"Tewley, I know you ran away from the Van Geer home," she began. "I don't know why, but I'm sure you had a good reason."

"Are they mad at me?"

"No, Tewley, they're not mad. Mrs. Van Geer misses you. She's just confused, that's all. She doesn't know what she did to make you run off."

"She didn't do nothing."

"All right." Tyner nodded. "Did somebody else do something? Did somebody else make you run away?"

The boy looked at Van Geer's tombstone. Tyner sensed that he wanted to talk, but his fear hindered him.

"Tewley, I realize that you don't know me, but I want to help you. I'm trying to help Mrs. Van Geer, too."

"Are you with that other man?"

"What other man?"

"The one that came to the house with you to see Mrs. Van Geer that night? The one that came to see me."

"Masey? You're talking about Masey Baldridge. Did he come to see you at the Van Geer house?"

"Yes. On Friday."

"Tewley, is that why you ran away? Because of Masey?"

"He scared me. They told me you and him was evil. That you wanted to hurt Mr. Hudson. I didn't want to believe them, but that's what they told me. I was afraid if I talked to that man they'd do something awful to me. So I ran off."

"Who, Tewley? Who is it you're scared of? Who told you that Masey and I were out to harm the Van Geers?"

"Miss Claire. And Marie. They said I shouldn't talk to you. I even did something bad for her."

"What are you talking about?"

"Marie has been teaching me to read for almost a year now. But sometimes she shows me her magic stuff, too. She told me not to tell Mrs. Helen. It was fun at first, but then I got scared. I know I shouldn't have been listening to her. My mamma wouldn't have liked it. But Marie kind of makes you listen to her. It's like you can't help it. Then when Mr. Hudson got killed, and when you and that man came along, Marie got real mad. She said you was evil. So I did what her and Miss Claire told me."

"And what was that?"

"I put one of her mojos on that Baldridge man. And another one on that riverboat captain."

"Why did you do it, Tewley?"

"I was afraid. Marie can hurt people. I was afraid she'd curse me too if I didn't."

"Do you still think Mr. Baldridge and I are out to harm the Van Geers?"

Tewley shook his head, a tear creeping down his cheek. "No. I been thinking about it ever since that Baldridge man came to see me." He looked up at Tyner as though a great realization had come to him, then began to cry as he spoke. "It's Miss Claire and Marie. They're the bad ones. But I'm still scared of them. They'll curse me for sure, especially if she ever found out what I saw."

Tyner put her arms around the young man and pulled him close to her. "It's all right, Tewley. Nobody's going to put any ol' curse on you. I promise you that." She wiped his eyes with the cuff of her sleeve. "Now, what exactly did you see, Tewley, that makes you think Miss Claire and Marie would want to hurt you?"

"It was the day Mr. Van Geer died. I saw Mr. Robert at the house."

"Stewart Van Geer's brother Robert?"

"Yes. He never comes to the house. Never. I'd only seen him once before, a long time ago. I had gone with Mr. Stewart down to one of the boats. That's where I saw him."

"And you're saying he was at the Van Geer home the day Hudson was murdered?"

"Yes. Him and Mr. Hudson was arguing."

"Did any of the other help see him there?"

Tewley shook his head. "No one was there but me. It was the help's day off."

"What time of day was it?"

"I don't remember. But it was a little while before Mr. Hudson was killed."

"How long before? Fifteen minutes? An hour? Longer?"

Tewley's troubled face indicated he was at least trying to remember. "About an hour, I guess."

"How is it you came to see them?"

"Mr. Hudson usually let me be off the same day as the rest of the help, except that week. He had me grooming one of his horses. I came in the house to ask him if he was going to be riding the next morning. That's when I saw him and Mr. Robert."

"And they were arguing?"

"Yes."

"You mean, shouting at each other?"

"Yes, ma'am. Mr. Robert was mad about something his daddy said."

"Do you know what it was?"

"No, ma'am. I didn't hear that part. But it had something to do with Miss Claire."

"Did Robert see you?"

"No, ma'am. I was gonna ask Mr. Hudson about his horse, but when I heard them fighting, I just stayed out in the hall."

"How long?"

"Until Mr. Robert left."

"How long was that?" Tyner inquired.

"He didn't stay too long."

"Do you remember anything he said?"

"Only when he was leaving. Mr. Hudson said he wasn't gonna stop until he knew the truth. That's when Mr. Robert called him a 'crazy old fool.' Mr. Hudson got real mad and fussed at him about the railroad and everything."

"And then Robert left?"

"Yes."

"Did you see Stewart Van Geer come to the house?"

"No, ma'am. I didn't even say nothing to Mr. Hudson. I figured he was real mad, so I just went on back to my room over the stable."

"Did you tell any of this to the police?"

"The policemen never asked me."

"What about to Claire or Marie Trehan? Did you tell any of this to them?"

Tewley shook his head. "No." He looked at Tyner. "I'm sorry about putting that mojo thing on your friend. It's just that Marie said that Mr. Hudson purged, so I figured—"

"Purged? What are you talking about?"

"He had foam coming out of his mouth when he died."

"I thought you didn't see his body?" Tyner said.

"I didn't. Like I said, Marie told me."

"What does 'purged' mean?"

"Something I learned from Marie. If somebody dies without speakin' their mind, they'll foam at the mouth for sure. Mr. Hudson purged."

"And you believed that?"

"Marie knows a lot about them kind of things."

"I understand, Tewley." Tyner wondered when Marie Trehan would have seen Hudson Van Geer's body to know whether or not he "purged." Helen Van Geer had told her the body was covered with a sheet when she and Marie arrived home, and she even mentioned that some of the police had wiped the blood away from his face.

"Do you believe in them curses?" he asked.

"Not really."

"I think sometimes they work."

"Tewley, a young boy was seen jumping out of the back of the hearse that was carrying Hudson Van Geer's body to the cemetery. Was that you?"

The boy looked down at the ground. "Yes, ma'am."

"What were you doing in there?"

The tears began to swell again in his eyes. "Mr. Hudson was real good to me. When my daddy died he took me in." Tewley looked again at Tyner. "I didn't have no one to look after me, you know."

"What were you doing in the hearse?"

"I was just trying to make sure whoever killed Mr. Hudson didn't get away."

"How's that?" Tyner asked.

"Marie told me one time how to do it. You get a fresh egg," he explained, "and you put it in the hand of the person that was killed, and the person that done the killing can't get away. He'll get what's coming to him."

Tyner got to her feet and pulled the boy close to her side. "Tewley, that's what Mr. Baldridge and the captain and I are trying to do, too. We want to see the man that killed Hudson Van Geer punished."

"Do you think Mr. Stewart killed his daddy?"

"I don't know," she replied, "but I believe that Claire Van Geer and Marie Trehan may have been involved. And from what you've told me, I'd say Robert Van Geer may have been too. Although I don't know why."

"All those people?"

"It's possible."

"How can you find out for sure?"

Tyner brushed the boy's hair back and knelt down beside him. "That may be where you can help me, Tewley. That is, if you want to. If you want to see everybody punished that had anything to do with Hudson Van Geer's murder."

Tewley nodded slowly. "I'll help, ma'am."

"Good," Tyner said, leading him toward the carriage, where the driver stood whittling on a piece of wood. "Now I've just got to figure out what to do."

WHEN TYNER RETURNED to Masey Baldridge's hotel room that afternoon, Tewley was with her, and the two of them entered the room to find Jacob Lusk and Anabel McBree watching a frail-looking old white man who stood beside Baldridge's bed, holding some dried roots in his left hand and a ceramic crucible in his right. The curtains to the room were pulled shut, and a large red candle burned on the dresser beside the bed.

"Who's that?" Tyner asked.

"Bo Lawrence," Lusk replied. "It took us a while, but we found him."

"Toombs? Your root doctor?"

"Yes 'm," Lusk replied.

Tyner's instincts kept telling her how ridiculous this whole business was, and momentarily she considered intervening. She should clear the room right now and get the regular doctor back in here. That is, if he'd even come after last night. What if that old man hurt Masey? How could she ever forgive herself for letting this go on? But the more she watched Toombs, the more fascinated she became by his calm, deliberate demeanor. The light from the candle cast ominous shadows over Toombs's wrinkled face as he stared down at Baldridge, who showed no signs of the restlessness of the night before. Yet he seemed as deeply trapped in unconsciousness as ever. Placing the roots beside the candle, Toombs drew from his pocket a small pouch, opened it, and emptied some tiny seeds into his hand.

"What's that?" Tyner whispered.

Anabel McBree answered her. "Mustard seeds."

Tyner watched Toombs extend his arm over Baldridge's face and roll a few seeds between his fingers. "Does he know what he's doing?"

"He's a seventh son," Anabel said reverently. "And born with a veil."

"So?"

"That means he's gonna have a strong mojo hand. Strong enough to stop whoever throwed down on Mr. Baldridge, I hope."

The sound of the door opening behind her revealed Luke Williamson. He took in the scene in the room.

"What the hell's going on in here?" he said, loudly enough

to draw a disapproving stare from Toombs, who now stood crushing some dried roots in his crucible. When he saw Toombs looking at him, he said, "Who the hell are you?"

"Cap'n," Lusk said, trying to calm him, "that's the man we told you about last night. Bo Lawrence. He's come to doctor Mr. Baldridge."

Williamson tossed a disbelieving glance at Tyner.

"Luke, I just got here," she said. "Anyway, last night we told Jacob and Anabel they could try."

"Yes, but I didn't think they'd really come up with the fellow."

"Well, they did." Tyner took him by the arm and whispered in his ear. "I've got my doubts too, but from what I learned from Tewley," she said, pointing out the boy, who now stood solemnly watching the affair from the corner of the room, "I'm willing to give it a chance."

"What are you talking about? And why didn't you come to the jail and see Stewart Van Geer with me?" Williamson asked.

Pulling Williamson off to the far corner, Tyner began to speak in a low voice. Meanwhile, Toombs continued to mix crushed herbs and roots into his crucible, with Anabel, Jacob, and Tewley all silently watching.

Momentarily, Toombs held up to the light of the candle a small plant with yellow petals. The light fell upon the plant's translucent, reddish spots, prompting Tewley to speak out loud. "That's John the Conker root!" he said, eliciting from Toombs a nod of acknowledgment.

"How did he know that?" Williamson asked.

"That's what I'm trying to tell you, if you'll listen," Tyner replied.

"I'm listening. What's John the Conker?"

Anabel moved over to where Tyner and Williamson stood, speaking softly. "He's talking about John the Conqueror root. The red spots is the blood from John the Baptist, what lost his head. Bo Lawrence says it's especially powerful since yesterday was the birthday of John the Baptist."

"What's he going to do with it?" Williamson asked, frustrating Tyner; he wouldn't let her finish telling him about Tewley.

"Make a potion, I believe, Captain," Anabel said. "I told him about Mr. Baldridge on the ride here to the hotel. He said he would put valerian root on his pillow and mix guinea pepper with High John and a little wine to make up his potion."

"He's actually going to feed that to Baldridge?"

"Yes, sir. That's what he's gonna do," Anabel said.

For a moment Tyner thought that Williamson would intercede. Eventually, his attention regained, Williamson listened as she told him the rest of her story.

"So Masey told you that Robert Van Geer said he hadn't seen his father in a year?" Williamson asked.

"That's right."

"And the boy over there said he saw him with Van Geer the day of the murder?"

"Right," Tyner said.

Williamson took a seat in a high-backed chair, trying to sort out the information. "So we know Robert Van Geer lied about seeing his father. But why?"

"So no one would know he was at the house that day?"

"Maybe. And we know Claire Van Geer is an impostor, and that Hudson Van Geer was suspicious of her."

"So who is she?"

"I don't know for sure, but I'd be willing to bet she's the second woman that the negroes at Boulet Plantation said left Tensas Parish with the real Claire Van Geer."

"Then where's the real Claire?" Tyner asked. Williamson looked at her as though expecting her to answer her own question. "All right," she continued, "maybe she's dead. But why? Let's say this woman and Marie killed the real Claire Boulet. Let's even say she married Stewart Van Geer and that Hudson got suspicious. That still doesn't mean that Stewart didn't kill his father. Maybe he didn't care. Maybe he loved this woman and didn't want his father to reveal the truth."

"I don't think so," Williamson said. "I had a long talk with Stewart Van Geer today. His mother was there too, and frankly, Sally, it's the first straight talk anybody has heard from the man since the murder. Helen Van Geer even said so. It was like he'd been walking in a daze and suddenly woke up. At least that's the way he described it."

"What kind of daze? What do you mean?"

"Remember how Masey told you he acted the day we first went to see him?"

"Like he was drunk or something."

"Yes. His mother even said he was sick."

"I know. A doctor looked at him. He testified at the trial that Stewart was depressed. Suffering from malaise, I believe."

"Well, whatever it was, he seems to be coming out of it."

"That's just great. Just in time to hang," Tyner said.

"Sally, Stewart Van Geer says he doesn't remember committing the murder."

"But he confessed."

Williamson shook his head. "He says that on the day of the murder, the last thing he remembers was sitting on the front porch. He said Claire brought him a glass of lemonade. He drank it. A few minutes later he remembers getting a headache, and the next thing he remembered was standing in the police station, gun in his hand, telling the police he killed his father. Sally, he barely even remembers when Masey and I came to see him."

"So why now? Why does he suddenly get clearheaded now?"

"I don't know. That's what I can't figure. But today he talked as straight as you and I. Even his mother was amazed. Of course, it just hurt her all the more that he says he doesn't remember the killing. She still wants to believe he's innocent."

"Do you think she could be right?"

"I don't know. But he's scared. The realization has hit him that he's going to hang day after tomorrow. And he's sharp enough to realize that his wife has quit coming to see him."

"Claire's not visiting him?"

"Not in three days. The police say she brought him a meal and visited him every day until Sunday."

"Sounds as though she stopped caring about him when he was sentenced to hang."

"If she ever did."

Tyner watched Toombs mixing a potion in a teacup. The old man took a sip of it himself, then lifted Baldridge's head and placed the cup against his lips. She wasn't sure whether any of the substance was actually going down, but she wouldn't have been surprised if he had started choking. He didn't, however, and Toombs continued his ritual. Something about watching Toombs force-feed his potion to Baldridge gave Tyner an idea. She turned to face Williamson and asked him a question.

"When did you say Stewart Van Geer started to straighten up?"

"Two, maybe three days ago, according to his mother."

"And Claire and Marie stopped coming on Sunday."

Williamson met her gaze. "Are you saying—"

"She brought him food."

"And drink. Lemonade."

"You don't suppose that—"

"You're not going to start talking about mojos and curses, are you?"

Tyner shook her head. "No. But Stewart said he blacked out before the murder after drinking lemonade that Claire brought him."

"You think she put something in the lemonade."

"Could be. If she kept bringing it to him during the week after the murder, and suddenly stopped, and he cleared up over the next two or three days—"

"Makes sense," Williamson said, pointing toward Bo Lawrence Toombs. "At least twice as much sense as any of this."

"A man as dazed as Stewart Van Geer might say anything."

"You mean the confession?"

"Particularly if he came around with a gun in his hand and his father lying in a pool of blood at his feet."

"So who killed Van Geer?" Williamson asked.

"Robert? Claire?"

"Maybe both of them. Masey said that Robert admitted to introducing Claire to Stewart over a year ago."

"He introduced *somebody*," Tyner said.

"Do you think he knew who Claire really was?"

"I'd almost bet on it," she said. "But if he did, what are they up to? And what's the connection between Claire and Robert?"

"Let's say that Robert Van Geer is out of his father's will."

"Do you *know* that?"

"No. I'm guessing. But go along with me on this."

"All right."

"Sally, if Hudson Van Geer is dead, who stands to control the Van Geer fortune?"

"Helen Van Geer . . . or maybe Stewart."

"Right. Unless Stewart is hanged."

"Then it would go to Helen," Tyner said.

"Unless something happens to Helen."

"Are you saying that Robert would—"

"According to Missouri law, he would be the only surviving child, and unless Hudson Van Geer specifically said he *couldn't* receive the business, it would go to him."

"But Helen is still alive," Tyner said.

"*Right now* she is."

"Wait a minute. Claire is pregnant. Her child would stand to inherit if anything happened to Helen."

"That it would, and Claire would be a winner either way," Williamson said.

"So do you think Helen Van Geer's in danger?"

"Maybe."

"From whom? Claire? Robert? Her own son?"

"Could be. If they would kill Hudson Van Geer, why would they stop there?"

"All that for money?

"Money, power, influence . . . who knows? Railroad building is expensive. Robert had tried to convince his father to bankroll him, but Van Geer refused. Maybe Robert wouldn't take no for an answer." Williamson smiled, and Tyner could tell he had made a connection. "The railroad," he said quietly. "The damned railroad."

Williamson went on to theorize that there must be a connection between Claire Van Geer's sale of the Boulet Plantation to Tallis, and Robert Van Geer's speculation in the railroad. If they had known each other before Robert introduced her to his brother, it was the only link between the two that made any sense. Perhaps Robert Van Geer saw a way to get control of some of the Tensas Parish property critical to the railroad venture. The woman claiming to be Claire could never return to Tensas Parish, lest she be recognized. But if she conducted a distant sale of the land to an intermediary, who would control the property on behalf of Robert Van Geer, he could gain control yet remain in the shadows. But why? If he was such a staunch railroad man, why would he want to remain behind the scenes? Williamson resolved to find Robert Van Geer and question him that afternoon.

"Do you think we should go to the police with this?" Tyner asked.

"I'll talk with Detective Kenton after I find Robert Van Geer. I think we can prove Claire Van Geer is an impostor. At the very least, that amounts to fraud in both the marriage and the land deal with Tallis."

17

Thursday, June 26

LUKE WILLIAMSON WATCHED out the window of the Fieldhurst Freight office as a thin, spectacled, middle-aged man, dressed in a blue suit and carrying a valise under his arm, stepped carefully across the tracks and hurried toward the building. As soon as he entered, a young clerk rose from his desk to meet him.

"Mr. Fieldhurst, this gentleman is here to see you," the clerk said, speaking softly, yet loud enough that Williamson could make out his words. "He's been here over an hour. I told him you might be late returning, but he insisted on waiting."

Fieldhurst extended a hand. "Gerald Fieldhurst, at your service . . . uh, Captain, is it?"

Williamson shook his hand. "Yes. Luke Williamson."

Though he had never seen Fieldhurst, the man now shook his hand as though he was an old acquaintance. "My, my. You're quite a famous riverman around here." Fieldhurst showed him to his office and offered him a chair. Williamson stood. "What brings a steamboat man to the land of the locomotive?"

"I'm looking for Robert Van Geer," Williamson said. "I understand he works for you, but your man outside says he's not around."

Fieldhurst shook his head and adjusted his necktie. "That's correct. Robert hasn't come to work."

"You mean you haven't seen him today?"

"No. Not since Monday. And I must say it's quite unlike Robert."

"Do you have any idea where I might find him?"

"No, Captain, I don't. I sent one of my men to check the house he rents on Lucas Street, but his neighbors haven't seen him in two or three days. That worries me. It's not at all like Robert to disappear this way." Fieldhurst took a seat in the overstuffed chair behind his desk. "Why are *you* looking for him?"

"I want to talk to him about a family matter." The minute he said it, he wished he could take it back, for Fieldhurst clearly wasn't fooled.

"You're not a very good liar, Captain. I do follow the newspapers, you know. I read how you had formed some sort of detective business." Fieldhurst shook his head. "Bad business decision, Captain. You've got no experience. You should have stuck to riverboats. I give your little detective endeavor six months. Not a day more."

"We'll see."

"I suppose this visit has something to do with Hudson Van Geer's death?"

"It might. But I'd rather discuss it with Robert."

"You're the second man that's been here to see Robert in the last two weeks."

"I believe the other man was an associate of mine. Mr. Baldridge."

"Fellow with a bad leg?" Fieldhurst asked.

"That's right."

"Yes, I saw him talking with Robert one day. I don't know what your man said, but it certainly upset him. Robert wasn't worth a dime the rest of the day, as I recall. I just attributed it to the mess about his father. I read where they're going to hang that other Van Geer boy."

"What kind of work does Robert Van Geer do for you?"

Fieldhurst smiled. "Robert is looking ahead, to the future, Captain. He knows where the money is to be made."

"You mean the railroad?"

"With all due respect, Captain Williamson, the steamboat industry is dying."

"That's not what my ledger sheet shows."

"Well, perhaps not now. But over time—"

"Over time, we'll compete."

"You're the exception, Captain. You run a good packet line. You may last a few more years, but the railroad is the future. Robert Van Geer understands that."

"And that's why he left Hudson Van Geer and the family's packet business?"

"Perhaps. I don't know. I don't get into other people's family squabbles. Hudson Van Geer had a chance to go into business with me, but he was too narrow-minded to take it. Thank goodness his son wasn't."

"What does Robert do for you?"

"Quite a number of things, actually. When he came on with me about two years ago, I put him in charge of freight handling. His experience with his father's steamboats came in handy." Fieldhurst lifted an eyebrow. "And quite frankly, having the Van Geer name in the railroad business didn't hurt any either."

"And now? What does he do now?"

"I made Robert a vice president almost a year ago. Now he handles acquisitions almost exclusively."

"Acquisitions of what?"

"Railroads," he said proudly. "I kept the company name as

Fieldhurst Freight, but the fact is, my company owns a part of at least a dozen different railroad lines all over the Southeast. And more popping up all the time. Are you sure you wouldn't like to diversify yourself, Captain? We're always on the lookout for new investors."

"No, thank you. So . . . Robert Van Geer buys railroads?"

"No, Captain. That would be much too expensive," Fieldhurst replied. "You don't know much about the railroad business, do you?"

"It's not a subject I care to study."

"No. I guess it's not. We don't buy entire companies. We look for bond issues—either government or private—where someone is selling bonds to establish a new rail line. Like the stock being sold to build the line from Joplin to St. Louis. Maybe you've heard?"

"No."

"As soon as we learn of a bond issue, we buy a piece of the company early, and as more stock is sold, and the price per share goes up, we sell the stock for a profit."

"What about land for the railroad?"

"Land? Oh, you mean right-of-way? Don't deal in land speculation. Too chancy for me. We're interested strictly in the partial shares."

"So Fieldhurst Freight has no interest in buying land and selling it back as right-of-way for a railroad?"

"None whatsoever, Captain. Where did you get such an idea?"

"Do you have anything to do with a rail line that's supposed to be built through Tensas Parish, Louisiana?"

"Tensas Parish? Where exactly is that?"

As Williamson explained the location, Fieldhurst produced a map from a drawer and laid it out on his desk. Leaning over the table on both arms, he squinted through his gold spectacles. "You're talking about the Northeast Louisiana Overland Railroad."

"Am I?"

"From the place you described, that would have to be it."

"How are you involved?"

"Just as an initial investor," Fieldhurst said. "Like I said before, we bought some of their initial offering, and—"

"Who bought it?"

"Well, Robert Van Geer bought it on behalf of my company."

"And you didn't buy any land?"

"Of course not. I told you, Captain, that's just too chancy."

"But people do it, right?"

"I'm sure they do. It's a free country. People can buy whatever they want. But Fieldhurst Freight doesn't speculate in land. Why do you keep asking me that?"

"If a man knew where a railroad would be laid, and he bought the property, wouldn't he stand to make a lot of money selling it to the railroad?"

"If he knew for sure where it would be laid," Fieldhurst replied. "But that would be a rather unethical—"

"Would Robert Van Geer know that kind of information about this Northeast Louisiana outfit?"

A concerned look came over Fieldhurst's face. "I'm not quite sure I know what you're driving at, Captain."

"I'm asking you if it's possible that Robert Van Geer was not only handling your stock purchases but running some land speculation on the side."

"Captain, Robert Van Geer is a dedicated member of Fieldhurst Freight, and I don't think—"

"Is that possible, Mr. Fieldhurst?"

"Well, I suppose anything is possible, but—"

"Suppose I told you that someone was buying up property in Tensas Parish with the sole purpose of inflating the price and selling it back to the Northeast Louisiana Overland?"

"I'd say that was a pretty foolish fellow," Fieldhurst said with a smile. "If somebody tried to fleece Northeast, they'd simply reroute the track around such a landowner. Then the speculator would be out of luck."

"What if they couldn't reroute the track? What if no bypass existed?" Williamson asked.

Fieldhurst glanced down at the map as Williamson moved next to him and pointed to the vicinity of Hardscrabble Landing. "The only high ground that would support a railroad from Vicksburg and into central Louisiana is located right here. Now, I'm no railroad man, but even I can figure out that to be forced to bypass that neck of land between the swamps and the Mississippi River would require a company to build track all the way around Lake Bruin. That would be twenty or thirty miles of track. How much would a company be willing to pay to keep from having to do that much extra work?"

Fieldhurst studied the map. "I see what you mean."

"Mr. Fieldhurst, someone is systematically buying up property all along the route of this Northeast Louisiana Railroad. A man named Tallis, under this individual's employment, has even resorted to attempted murder to get a key piece of this land."

"What's that got to do with me? Or with Robert Van Geer?"

"This Tallis isn't smart enough and doesn't have the capital to pull off something like this. I think Robert Van Geer may be the money behind him."

Fieldhurst removed his spectacles and buried his face in his hands. "This could explain the discrepancy," he mumbled through his hands.

"Do you know something about this?"

"I probably shouldn't show this to you, but what you told me about the Northeast Louisiana bothers me." From a bookcase Fieldhurst drew a ledger and opened it, thumbing over several pages until he stopped and showed an entry to Williamson. "About six months ago, Robert came to me indicating that we should increase our buy of Northeast Louisiana. We owned 8 percent, and my personal rule is to diversify our holdings and never own more than 10 percent of any new railroad."

"I see."

"But Robert had been down there on a visit and came back quite excited about the freight potential once they actually finished the land purchases and started laying track."

"So did you buy more?"

"Against my better judgment, I authorized Robert to buy up to 15 percent of the company. That amounted to $25,000. I wouldn't have noticed any problem if my decision hadn't started bothering me. I had violated my own policy, Captain, and it ate at me for months. One day, while Robert was away, I asked one of my clerks to pull the Northeast file so I could examine this purchase again. I thought it would make me feel better about the whole thing. It didn't. When I went over the file, I couldn't find the certificates for the additional 7 percent of the company. I asked Robert about it, and he said that he had bought the stock, and everything was all right, but that Northeast had been delayed in sending the certificates. I had no reason to doubt his word, Captain. Robert has handled dozens of these transactions for me."

"So you believed him?"

"Yes. He told me he'd get everything straightened out in two to three weeks. That was the end of May. Now he's disappeared," Fieldhurst said, folding the map and looking at Williamson.

"Is it possible that Robert used your company's money to buy land that he intends to resell to the railroad?"

"But he would have to know we'd eventually figure it out when the stock wasn't there."

"Unless he took his profit from the land sale, and then put either the money or the stock back in your account."

"I confess that I haven't kept a close eye on Robert's accounts over the past six months. He's always been so good at his purchases that—"

"I'd say there's a real good chance this isn't the first time he's used Fieldhurst Freight's money. This Tallis fellow in Louisiana has been buying land for months now."

"I'm almost afraid to examine the certificates of the other purchases Robert handled."

"But you will check them, won't you?"

"Of course I'll check. If someone is using my company's money to make illegal deals, I want to know about it."

"And you'll let me know as soon as you find something out?"

Fieldhurst nodded. "Yes, Captain, I will. Although I fail to see what any of this has to do with Hudson Van Geer's death."

"It's a long story, Mr. Fieldhurst. I'd love to tell you about it, but I haven't figured it all out myself just yet."

"Just exactly how did you find out about Robert's dealings in Louisiana?"

"Investigation," Williamson said proudly. "Just plain old detective work." With the promise that he would inform Fieldhurst if he located Robert Van Geer, Williamson thanked him for his cooperation and indicated that he would look forward to hearing from him soon about his examination of the company's records.

Williamson was almost out the door when Fieldhurst called to him. "And, Captain—"

"Yes?"

"Make that a year."

"Beg your pardon?"

"What I said about your detective business. Make it a year."

"THE HUDSON VAN GEER murder case is closed, Captain. Mr. Van Geer's murderer has been found guilty and sentenced to hang on Saturday," Detective Kenton said. He sat at his desk, patiently listening to Williamson's story about Claire Van Geer, Tallis, and Robert Van Geer, occasionally scribbling some notes on a piece of paper but allowing Williamson to do most of the talking. *After about twenty minutes, he spoke.*

"Let me be brutally honest with you, Captain. So far, all you *may* be able to prove is that this woman who says she's Stewart Van Geer's wife is a liar. You've got no evidence that either she, or this Marie Trehan, had anything to do with the Boulet family's fire, much less Hudson Van Geer's death."

"Don't you see?" Williamson said. "Claire couldn't allow Hudson Van Geer to find out about her past."

"Why not? So the marriage would be annulled? So what?"

"So no Van Geer fortune. And what would become of the child she's carrying? And then there's Robert Van Geer—"

"Yes, yes. Robert. Whom you claim has disappeared."

"He *has* disappeared. Just as we were getting somewhere investigating Claire."

"But he has no connection to Claire."

"He knew her before. He introduced her to Stewart."

"Captain, you still can't prove he had anything to do with his father's death. Stewart Van Geer confessed to the crime, or have you forgotten?"

"I don't believe he did it. I think—"

"I know. I know. You think he was under some kind of curse," Detective Kenton said with a chuckle. "Captain, I can't very well go to Judge Grove and tell him that. He'd have my badge."

"What about the stableboy, Tewley? He says that Robert was at the Van Geer home, arguing with his father, the day of the murder."

Detective Kenton nodded. "I'll admit that's new information."

"So he had a chance to kill Hudson Van Geer. And he had a reason to do it."

"But so did Stewart Van Geer!"

"But why? No one ever has been able to give a reason for Stewart killing his father that makes any sense."

"He and Hudson Van Geer had an argument."

"About what?" Detective Kenton didn't answer. "Stewart got along well with his father. If anybody was on the outs with Hudson Van Geer, it was Robert."

"But other than the fact that they didn't get along, you've established no good reason," Detective Kenton said. "What does Robert have to gain by his father's death?"

"The Hudson Van Geer fortune, for starters," Williamson said.

"I considered that in my initial investigation," Detective Kenton said confidently. "With his mother and brother alive, Van Geer's will offers Robert no access to Van Geer's money. The old man specifically made it that way."

"Exactly. Because of his involvement with the railroad. But with Stewart, and eventually Helen Van Geer, out of the way—"

Something in Kenton's face told Williamson that for the first time since he started talking, the man was giving serious consideration to his theory. But Kenton clearly did not want to admit he could be wrong.

"We investigated this case, you know," Kenton said. "We talked to the servants at the home, to Mrs. Van Geer, and this Claire woman, and even Robert Van Geer."

"I know you did."

"And Stewart Van Geer confessed."

"Maybe that's why you didn't look any further," Williamson suggested.

"But we had a confessed killer!"

"Everybody says that Stewart hasn't been himself for weeks. Not since the shooting. Only over the last couple of days had he started making any sense. I know. I talked to him."

"He was dazed. Depressed. Who wouldn't be? But we had a doctor look at him on Judge Grove's order."

"I'm not sure it was something a doctor would find. Like I told you, I think Claire and Marie were somehow controlling him."

Williamson could tell that the detective was thoroughly frustrated. He let out a long sigh, and spoke in measured tones. "Maybe there is more to this murder than we know," Kenton finally conceded. He pointed his finger at Williamson. "But I'm not buying this voodoo thing."

"I'm not saying that I do, either. But something has been going on. Something that involves Claire and Marie Trehan. And you've got to find out what it is before Stewart Van Geer hangs."

Grudgingly, Kenton agreed to accompany Williamson to speak with Claire Van Geer, and he ordered some officers to work on locating Robert for more questioning. Williamson and the detective went to the Dearborn Hotel first so that Kenton could speak with Tyner and get Tewley's full story, and Williamson could check in on Baldridge. Immediately upon entering, Williamson knew from the glow on Tyner's face that Baldridge was better, and when he saw him sitting up in bed, eating a bowl of soup, he could hardly believe his eyes.

"When did this happen?" he asked.

"About two hours ago. I'd been watching him, sitting with him all morning. He was still completely out. The restlessness has been stopped ever since that old man was here."

"Are you saying—"

"I'm not saying anything, except about two hours ago I'm sitting in the chair and Masey turns and asks me what day it is. Right out of the blue, he came to."

"That's amazing."

"It sure is. Of course, he's been asking for whiskey ever since. But I haven't given him any. He drank some water, and this soup is the first thing he's had to eat since Saturday. He's even been up on his feet some."

Williamson introduced Detective Kenton, then stepped over to see Baldridge, whose grip was weak when he shook his hand and patted him on the shoulder.

"You had us pretty worried, Masey."

Baldridge moved slowly as he placed his soup bowl on the table beside the bed. "I still feel kind of light-headed, and I ain't got much strength just yet." He leaned over and whispered to Williamson, "You wouldn't have anything to drink on you, would you? My flask is plumb empty, and Sally won't bring me any whiskey."

Tyner overheard his comment as she spoke with Detective Kenton. "He's *definitely* better," she called to Williamson.

"What the hell happened to me, anyway, Luke?"

Williamson considered telling about the mojo and the root doctor that had come to treat him, but he saw Tyner shaking her head, so he figured that would raise more questions than he could answer.

"I think you had too much to drink."

"That's what Sally told me. Apparently I passed out sometime on Saturday at the courthouse, but I swear, the last thing I remember is talking to that young boy over there." Baldridge pointed to the corner where Tewley sat quietly in a chair, wide-eyed but silent. "The boy knows something, Luke, and I was this close to getting him to tell me when he took off on me. I don't remember much after that, except some pretty wild nightmares. Somebody was trying to kill me," Baldridge said. "Sally says I was delirious, wrestlin' and talking out of my head most of the time." He took another spoonful of soup, then looked up at Williamson. "Sally told me about Stewart Van Geer getting sentenced, and about what you found out on Claire." Baldridge looked chastened. "I'm sorry I let you and Sally down, Luke. I guess I just—"

"Don't worry about that now. Just get well. I've got Detective Kenton to agree to question Claire Van Geer again, and his men are looking for Robert."

"Yeah, Sally said he cut and ran on you. Any idea where he might be?" Baldridge asked.

"No, but something tells me he'll turn up." Williamson explained a plan he'd hatched with Kenton to confront Claire Van Geer with the captain's information and see how she responded. Baldridge wanted to accompany them, and even made motions to get out of bed, but Williamson halted him.

"You're in no shape to be going anywhere."

"But you might need some help—"

"You wouldn't help us. Right now, you'd just be in the way." The hurt look on Baldridge's face made Williamson regret he'd chosen those particular words.

"This is my case, too," Baldridge protested.

"Not today it isn't."

"Luke's right," Tyner added. "You'll be better tomorrow. I don't want you out of that bed except to go to the bathroom. Is that clear?"

"You sound like my mother," Baldridge said, managing a smile.

"Most of the time you *need* a mother."

An attendant Williamson had sent for from the *Edward Smythe* arrived as they were talking. Urging Baldridge to rest and recuperate, Williamson, Tyner, Tewley, and Kenton left the hotel.

Almost an hour before dark, Williamson and the others arrived at Stewart and Claire Van Geer's home. Tewley was told to remain in the carriage and out of sight until someone signaled for him to come inside. Tyner tried to calm the frightened boy, assuring him that no harm would come to him as long as he told the truth. When she opened the front door and saw Tyner, Marie Trehan's black eyes flashed with anger.

"What do you want here?"

Tyner stepped forward to push her inside, but Marie held the door. "We're going to have a little talk with you and Claire."

"Claire is not here. No. You're not to come inside."

Kenton showed his badge. "Miss Trehan, I'm with the St. Louis police."

"I know who you are. I already talked to you. Now you leave."

Tyner forced open the door, sending Marie stumbling backward. Kenton, clearly disturbed by her approach, looked at Williamson, but the captain only shrugged and followed Tyner inside.

"Where's Claire Van Geer?" Tyner demanded.

"I've got a better question," Williamson said. "*Who's* Claire Van Geer?"

Trehan, obviously startled by the remark, stumbled over her words as she tried to answer. "I . . . I don't know—I don't know what you mean."

"I believe you do," Williamson said, "and this detective wants to hear about it."

"Hear about what?"

"Let's start with you and the woman pretending to be Claire Boulet. I know what the real Claire Boulet looked like. She was seriously scarred on her arms by the fire at the Boulet Plantation. The woman that lives in this house is an impostor, and you know it."

Trehan was visibly shaken. "Miss Claire isn't here. You must leave the house now."

"Where is she?" Tyner asked.

"She's out."

"Where?" Tyner persisted.

"To see her mother-in-law."

Kenton stepped forward, beginning a series of questions aimed at establishing Trehan's whereabouts on the night of Hudson Van Geer's murder. She claimed to have gone to bring Helen Van Geer to the house, since Claire was feeling ill from her pregnancy. Then she claimed to have been at the house for the next two hours, "attending to chores."

"Were you with those two women?"

"I was here at the house."

Tyner interrupted. "Helen Van Geer never saw you. She told me she stayed with Claire in her room the entire time she was here. She never mentioned seeing you once."

"I was right here," Trehan protested, looking at Kenton and trying desperately to change the subject. "Officer, this woman is a trespasser. She sneaked into our house last week and crept up to Miss Claire's—"

Kenton motioned for Tyner to bring in Tewley.

"How do you know Robert Van Geer?" Kenton continued.

"He's Helen Van Geer's son," Trehan replied. "What kind of question is that?"

"When's the last time you saw Robert Van Geer?"

"At his father's funeral."

"And before that?" Kenton asked.

"Months. I hadn't seen him in months."

"You're a liar," Williamson said.

Trehan looked as if she were ready to rip into the captain but managed to contain herself.

"Suppose I told you someone saw you at the Van Geer home within minutes of the murder?" Kenton said.

"That would be a lie."

"Miss Trehan," Kenton said, "if you're lying to protect Claire Van Geer, you're guilty of fraud. If you're lying to protect Robert Van Geer, you may be involved in murder. Now, I'm going to ask you one more time. Were you with Robert Van Geer at Hudson Van Geer's home on the night he was murdered?" Trehan stood silent, the rage in her eyes aimed equally at Kenton and Williamson. Tyner's footsteps sounded on the front porch.

"Very well, then," Kenton said, calling outside to Tyner. "Bring him in." Tyner and the boy entered the front door and stood in the hall, her arm around his shoulder, the boy's hand shaking as Marie Trehan eyed him in disgust.

"What's *he* doing here?" Trehan said.

"He saw you and Robert Van Geer at the Hudson Van Geer

home the night of the murder," Kenton said calmly. Williamson was surprised at Kenton's approach. Tewley had seen only Robert Van Geer that night.

"That's impossible," Trehan snapped. "None of the servants were there." She quickly amended her remark. "And neither was I."

"One was there," Tyner said, running her hand gently through the young man's hair to calm him. "The one that's *always* there. The one that's got no place else to go."

Trehan looked at the boy, and asked, "Tewley, why are you saying these things?" It amounted more to a threat than a question. She forced a smile empty of sincerity. "There are forces that punish people who—"

"Is that how you terrorized the boy, with all this voodoo business?" Tyner said.

"I know nothing about any voodoo. Over the past few months, when he would come here to do chores and study reading, Miss Helen asked me to teach him. I may have shown Tewley how to do some healing with herbs. That's all. The boy seemed interested. I just—"

"Oh, he's interested, all right," Tyner continued. "Terrified is more like it—at having to run your little mojo errands. And I've seen some of your 'healing' firsthand."

Trehan exploded. "Oh, you haven't seen anything yet, you bitch." Her eyes were wild as her gaze moved between Williamson, Kenton, and Tyner. "You people have no power over me! I have the power," she said, backing away toward the stairs. "I've always had the power. Even Margaret would be nothing without me. Nothing. Do you understand? Just a housegirl like me."

"Who's Margaret?" Williamson asked, recalling the name the negro Thurl had mentioned at the Boulet Plantation.

"Don't you have all the answers, *Captain*?" Trehan snapped.

"The woman claiming to be Claire Boulet."

Trehan continued backing up the stairs. "You know she would have never gotten this far without me. Not without my power."

"Who killed Hudson Van Geer?" Kenton demanded, stepping slowly toward the stairs. When Trehan thrust her hand into her dress pocket, Kenton reached instinctively for his pistol, but he did not clear his holster, for she produced only a handful of dried chicken bones.

"It wasn't poor, pregnant Claire, I'll tell that much."

"Then who?" Kenton said.

"Figure it out yourself!" she shouted, and with a maniacal smile she tossed the bones to the floor at the bottom of the steps, and ran madly up the stairs.

Detective Kenton and the captain pursued, overtaking her in one of the far bedrooms. The room was lit with more than two dozen candles, and Trehan leaned over a bureau where she had scribbled something on a piece of paper and was attempting to stuff the paper into a coconut resting on a dresser. Kenton took the defiant woman into custody with surprisingly little struggle and led her downstairs. Williamson moved around the room, blowing out the candles, until he came across a small black bottle resting beside the pitcher he had seen Marie and Claire bring to Stewart in jail. The bottle had no label, and when he opened it and took a whiff, the strong medicinal odor sent him stumbling backward. He wasn't sure what it was, but he put the lid back on and slipped the bottle into his coat pocket.

Downstairs, Detective Kenton asked them all to come along to the police station to provide statements against Trehan; he would send some officers to the Van Geer home to bring in Claire for questioning once he had Trehan in jail and the statements from everyone. But with Robert Van Geer still unaccounted for, and Claire, or Margaret, or whatever her name was, supposedly with Helen Van Geer, Williamson feared Helen was in danger. He convinced Kenton it would be best for him to go directly to the Van Geer home and at the least be sure that Claire, if she was there, remained so until the police could question her.

As Kenton led Marie Trehan out the door ahead of them, she stopped and viciously glared at Williamson, Tyner, and the boy. "You will rue the day you challenged me!" Then she walked out with Kenton.

"What was she doing upstairs?" Tyner asked as she took Tewley's hand to follow the detective.

Williamson unfolded the paper he had found and showed it to Tyner. "Looks like your name and the first part of mine written here," he said.

Tewley began to cry, and Tyner produced a handkerchief and wiped his eyes. "Don't worry, Tewley. She's not going to hurt anyone now." She looked up at Williamson. "Is she?"

"Let's hope not," he said.

"Good luck with Claire," Tyner said.

"I'll need it," he said, and the three of them walked outside.

18

W H E N L U K E W I L L I A M S O N reached the Hudson Van Geer home, the front rooms were dark, and momentarily he thought the place deserted. He guided his mount to the right and scanned the servant quarters toward the rear of the property, where he saw light in the distant cabins. Then he noticed the glow of lamplight from one of the side rear windows of the main house, so he tied his horse, stepped up on the porch, and tapped the thick oak door with the door knocker. He waited a bit more than a minute and, getting no response, again pounded the knocker. Eventually the door opened about six inches, the light from a handheld lamp penetrating the dark summer night.

"Who's there?"

Williamson recognized Claire Van Geer's voice from the day he met her at the jail.

"I want to see Mrs. Van Geer," he said.

"Go away. Mrs. Van Geer wishes to see no one. She is in seclusion."

Claire tried to close the door, but Williamson jammed it with his foot. "I demand to see Mrs. Van Geer." He could hear Helen

Van Geer calling through the house to her daughter-in-law, asking as to the visitor.

"It's Captain Williamson," he shouted. "I need to speak with you, Mrs. Van Geer!"

"Claire?" Helen Van Geer called as she walked down the dimly lit hallway. "Claire, aren't you going to let him in?"

"Mrs. Van Geer, this man has no business here," Claire protested as Williamson squeezed inside. "Hasn't he done enough to—"

"It's important that you and I talk," Williamson shouted to Helen over Claire's protest.

"Have you some news about Stewart? Oh, I pray you do. I pray it's not too late."

"Mother Helen, really! I must insist—"

Williamson cut her off. "And I think Claire will be very interested in hearing this, too. After all, it is her husband's life that's at stake."

"Claire was kind enough to come over this evening and sit with me," Helen said, leading Williamson down the hall and into the billiards room. Claire followed close behind with the awkward gait of a pregnant woman as her mother-in-law continued. "You cannot imagine what horror this is, Captain, waiting around helplessly for the authorities to hang Stewart. Perhaps I'm foolish but I still believe my son to be innocent." Helen put her hand on Claire's. "Claire was so good to come so I wouldn't be alone."

"How kind of her," Williamson said, his comment met with only Claire's stern countenance.

Helen lit a wall-mounted lamp. "Tell me, Captain. What word do you have for me about my son?"

"Mrs. Van Geer, I want you to sit down," Williamson said, removing his hat and placing it on the billiard table. "You may want to have a seat, too," he told Claire.

"I'll stand," Claire countered. "I don't expect you'll be staying long."

"Very well, have it your way."

"I shall."

"Mrs. Van Geer, someone else was at this house the night your husband was killed. Someone other than Stewart." He glanced at Claire, who fiddled nervously with the lamp she held. "Someone who did not want Hudson Van Geer to ever tell anyone what he was about to find out."

"Find out? About what?" Helen Van Geer asked.

Williamson turned to Claire. "Why don't we ask Margaret?"

"Margaret? Who's Margaret?" Helen Van Geer asked. "Captain, you're not making any sense. I don't—"

"He hasn't made any sense since the day you hired him," Claire said. "All he's done is drag the Van Geer name through the mud with his snooping around and his—"

"Shall you tell her, or shall I?" Williamson interrupted.

"Tell me what?" Helen said impatiently.

"Your daughter-in-law's real name."

"Claire, what's the captain talking about?" Helen asked, her eyes beseeching the young woman.

"Mother Helen, I have no idea." Claire ran her hand over her extended abdomen. "But all this is upsetting me. I'm not feeling well. I think the captain should leave now."

Williamson ignored her. "Mrs. Van Geer, right now Marie Trehan is with the police."

"Marie? What for?"

He pointed at Claire. "She and this woman have conspired to defraud Stewart, and you, and your late husband."

"I don't understand."

"The *real* Claire Boulet was badly burned in the fire that took her parents' life almost two years ago. Both of Claire Boulet's arms were permanently scarred from the hands to the elbows."

"How do you know this?" Helen asked.

"I went to Louisiana—where this woman claims to be from—and talked to people who knew Claire Boulet."

"Mother Helen, really!"

"But why?" Helen asked. "How did you come to—"

"Hudson Van Geer suspected Claire to be an impostor. I don't know how he knew. Perhaps in his river travels he met someone, or knew someone, or somehow came across information that didn't match with what this woman was telling him. Anyway, my colleague Masey Baldridge found a letter in your husband's desk; in it, your husband sought information on Claire Boulet. I suspect that he found out what he wanted to know, or was about to find out. And that is why he was killed."

"That's preposterous," Claire said, taking Helen's hand and attempting to bring her to her feet. "That Baldridge man is a drunk. You can't believe anything he says. Please, Mother Helen, make this man leave before—"

"Before I get to the truth? Not a chance, Margaret," Williamson said. "That *is* your name, isn't it? Margaret? That's what Marie Trehan said, anyway."

"Marie wouldn't—"

"Claire?" Helen finally stood up, and Williamson could see her glancing at the woman's arms. "Claire, your arms aren't scarred. You don't—"

"My name is Margaret Doyle," she told Helen coolly, then turned to Williamson. "You sorry bastard. You've ruined everything! If I had a gun, I'd kill you myself!"

"Claire!" Helen's hand rose to her lips, her face reflecting all her doubts.

Williamson pressed her. "Is that what you did to the real Claire Boulet? Did you shoot her? You and Marie?"

"No, they didn't," a man's voice called out from the hallway behind him. Williamson heard a weapon being cocked as Robert Van Geer stepped into the light.

"Robert!" Helen Van Geer said, clearly taken aback. "Son, what are you—where have you—what are you doing with that gun?"

"The good captain here is explaining that to you, Mother, if you'd just listen. But then . . . you never did listen much, did you?"

"Son, I don't—"

"Keep your hands clear of your waist, Captain," Robert ordered, keeping his gun pointed at his chest. "Margaret, check him for a gun." As Margaret lifted a Navy Colt from Williamson's belt, Robert continued. "All those times I tried to get you to talk with father. All those lost opportunities because he was so stubborn and narrow-minded. You could have helped. You could have prevented all this."

"Prevented what?"

"I'd say he's talking about your husband's murder," Williamson said.

"Oh, my God," Helen groaned, staggering back onto the sofa.

"He was here that night," Williamson continued. "He and Marie Trehan. Maybe he was with Stewart, maybe not. I'm not sure. Stewart was probably in no shape to know, either way." Williamson focused on Robert. "How did you do it? What did you use to get Stewart here? Was it the stuff in that little black bottle on the dresser in Claire's—excuse me, Margaret's—bedroom?"

Margaret gave Robert a frightened look, but he seemed quite calm. "Marie has her ways," Robert said with a smile.

"Shut your mouth, Robert. You've said enough already."

"Robert—son—please tell me what's going on here," Helen pleaded, tears streaming down her cheeks. "Tell me—"

"Don't say another word," Margaret ordered.

"What difference does it make now?" Robert replied.

"So who pulled the trigger?" Williamson asked. "Was it you? Marie? Did you somehow make Stewart do it?"

"Not Stewart," Robert said with a nervous laugh. "He was Daddy's little boy. Did whatever Daddy asked him to. He wasn't even conscious when we got him here."

"You and Marie?"

"That's right. Margaret stayed with Mother."

"Robert, shut the hell up!" Margaret shouted.

"I'm not going to shut up. Mother's got a right to know. Don't you, Mother?" The sobbing woman offered no response. "You never knew anything else going on in this house. So you might as well know this." He moved to stand directly in front of his mother, keeping the gun pointed squarely at Williamson, and explained how he had met Margaret in the ship's bar on one of the Van Geer boats when she was traveling with Marie Trehan and the real Claire Boulet well over a year earlier. When he learned where the Boulet Plantation was located, he realized immediately that the land was critical to the Northeast Louisiana Railroad. He and the two women had hatched a plan to get rid of the real Claire Boulet and have Margaret assume her identity. He would introduce her to Stewart, and the two would get married.

"But why have her marry Stewart?" Williamson asked.

"I needed access to the money. With Margaret in the family, I knew I could get to enough to make some deals."

"Land deals," Williamson said.

"You've certainly been thorough, Captain."

"Your mother paid me to be thorough."

"Too bad. That conscientiousness is going to get you killed."

"Stewart," Helen sobbed, "please, son. I had no idea—"

"You *never* had any idea, Mother. You never paid any attention to the way Father treated me."

"But why kill him, son?" asked a near-hysterical Helen Van Geer. "Why kill him? And Stewart? Look what you've done to your brother! Have you no remorse?"

"For what? For giving that selfish bastard what he's deserved for years? For trying to take this company in a new direction? For trying to make something of this family's money?" Robert showed no emotion as he looked squarely in his distraught mother's eyes. "I only regret that I didn't do it years ago."

"Van Geer, you must know you can't possibly get away with this now," Williamson said. "The police have Marie Trehan. They'll be coming after you, too. This whole fraud will be uncovered, and you—"

"It doesn't matter anymore," Robert said. "Oh, I wanted to build the Van Geer empire into something tremendous. That was my dream. But my meddling father threatened to cut that short."

"He found out about Claire, and your involvement in the railroad—"

"I still could have handled that," Robert said. "Father was kind enough to tell me of his suspicions before anyone else, so with him dead . . . but then you and your detectives came along. So now Claire and I will just have to settle for the money we can get."

"But you can't get to Hudson Van Geer's business accounts," Williamson said.

"No, I can't. My father saw to that. Diligent man, Hudson Van Geer. Paid close attention to the details. That's probably how he found out about Claire. But Claire and me got even. She's been making withdrawals on the Van Geer account for the past two weeks. My father may have been careful, but my brother wasn't. Stewart was stupid enough to give her access to the company funds. And the people at the bank were more than sympathetic to the financial and legal needs of a sickly, pregnant woman whose husband was on trial for murder. Besides, I forged Mother's signature on a number of the documents. As I suspected, no one bothered to check."

"Tell me, Van Geer," Williamson asked. "How much was your father's life worth? A hundred thousand? More?"

"Enough to get a long way away from here and disappear forever," Van Geer said with a smile. He turned to Claire. "What about the jewelry?"

"It's in this bag," Margaret said, producing a heavily loaded cloth sack from behind a chair in the corner. "I got it while she was resting." As she handed it to Robert, Helen stared at him in disbelief.

"Don't be so upset, Mother. We'll need the money. After all, *we've* got a baby on the way."

"Robert! Son, no! No!"

Robert nodded. "Yes, it's mine. I don't think she believes me, Margaret. Tell her."

Margaret smiled. "I tried to be with Stewart as little as possible. He was such a weak little man."

"You see, Mother, I'm better than Stewart at *everything*."

"What do you intend to do with us, son?"

"Don't worry, Mother. I'm not going to hurt *you*." Robert leaned over and kissed her on the cheek, whispering, "But just so you'll know, it would have been your turn after Stewart hanged. Not much use in it now." He pointed the cocked weapon at his mother's head. "Unless you just want to be with Father." Williamson entertained the notion of jumping him, but he feared the man might get off a shot before he could grab the gun. Robert must have sensed his intention, for he quickly aimed the weapon back at Williamson. "No," Robert said. "Wouldn't be good business. And after all, that's what this is. Just good business. Like father, like son. Right, Mother?" Helen Van Geer was too shaken to reply, but Robert kept on. "And I'm not going to kill the captain, either. At least not here in this house. Claire and I have horses waiting on us out back. When I arrived, I took the liberty of moving the captain's to join ours behind the house. Captain Williamson will be coming along with us. That way I can be sure we're not followed."

"What about Marie Trehan?" Williamson asked.

"Too bad about Marie. Guess she'll be left behind to answer questions. But with Claire and me gone, the police will have no proof of the murder, so she'll be free before long." Robert slung the bag of jewelry over his left shoulder, motioned with the weapon for Williamson to precede him out into the hall, and told Claire, "Bring Mother to the back porch. She can see us off."

"Anybody home?" someone called from the direction of the front door.

Robert froze in his steps, then pulled Williamson back into the billiards room by his collar. He looked around nervously and ordered Margaret to take the captain into Hudson Van Geer's office and keep him quiet. Grasping his mother by the arm, he moved her back to the sofa and made her sit down, placing the barrel of his revolver behind her neck.

"Invite him in," he told her.

"Please, son, don't—"

"Do as I tell you, Mother," he said, then rushed to join Margaret and Williamson in the darkened office.

"Come in," Helen said weakly. "We're back here."

19

WALKING WAS HARD enough, given that he had been off his feet for so many days, but riding wasn't much easier. The .45 Colt revolver he had strapped on in the hotel felt as if it weighed a hundred pounds, and without the hotel's stable man to saddle Nashville Harry, he wouldn't have been able to get here at all. As it was, every step the horse took seemed to jar his entire body, and he had leaned against the animal's neck to steady himself in the saddle. Maybe Luke and Sally were right. Maybe he had no business being out of bed. But the thought of them working the case without him made him restless, and not a little envious, so he decided to make the effort. Williamson thought he was a lazy drunk—he'd said as much when they first took this case—but Baldridge was determined to pull his weight. The only place he knew to look for them was the Van Geer house; besides, there was a good chance Helen Van Geer would have some whiskey, and right now, he could use a drink. Sure, Tyner had told him not to get up unless he went to the bathroom. He just figured he'd tell her that he went to the bathroom at the Van Geer home.

The front door stood partially open, and he could see a light down the hallway and on the left, so Baldridge, weak and groggy, slowly limped up the steps and began feeling his way down the dark hallway. He thought he saw shadows on the floor, cast from the billiards room where he and Tyner had talked with Mrs. Van Geer.

"Anybody home?" he called out in a weak voice. He heard someone moving about, and then Mrs. Van Geer replied.

"Come in. We're back here."

Entering the billiards room, Baldridge, though his vision remained somewhat cloudy, recognized Helen seated on the sofa.

"Mrs. Van Geer," he said, studying her momentarily as he supported himself against the wall. "The . . . uh . . . front door was open."

"What do you want, Mr. Baldridge?" she asked stiffly.

"I was looking for the captain and Sally Tyner. I thought they might be—"

"I haven't seen them," she said, but even in his weakened state, Baldridge could tell something was wrong. Perhaps all the horror of the murder and her son's sentencing was taking its toll. Perhaps it was something else.

"It's—it's rather late, Mr. Baldridge. I'd rather talk with you some other time. If you'd be kind enough—"

Baldridge moved closer to her. "Mrs. Van Geer, are you all right? You don't look too good."

"Please, Mr. Baldridge. I'm just fine. Now if you'd be kind enough to leave—"

"All right," he said, quickly surveying the room. On his way toward the door he saw Williamson's hat on the billiard table. He hesitated momentarily and, minding his precarious balance, walked into the hall. "I'll just let myself out, Mrs. Van Geer. I'll come back tomorrow."

"That will be fine, Mr. Baldridge," she said, not bothering to rise from the sofa.

Baldridge limped to the front door, opened it, and slammed it shut, remaining inside the dark corner of the hallway. He drew his revolver and began inching along the wall. He heard voices in the billiards room and, noticing the shadow of someone moving toward the hallway, backed against the wall, as much to steady himself as to remain unseen. A man looked out the doorway and toward the front door, and Baldridge froze in the darkness.

"He's gone. Let's go. Move quickly," the man said.

Even in the poor light, Baldridge recognized Robert Van Geer, so he brought his weapon to shoulder height and cocked it. "Hold it right there, Van Geer."

Robert stopped and looked over his shoulder into the dark hallway as Baldridge gradually emerged into the light. Horribly weak, Baldridge approached Robert. "Lower that weapon to your side and then drop it to the ground."

Robert said nothing, but complied with the order. Baldridge closed the distance to three or four feet. "Move slowly around the corner and into the room. Keep your hands where I can see them."

With his hands held over his head, Robert entered the billiards room, and Baldridge moved carefully behind him. "Now where's Luke Williamson?"

"He's right here," Margaret said, forcing Williamson at gunpoint from behind a tall cabinet. "With a gun in his back."

Robert Van Geer lowered his hands and turned to face Baldridge, despite Baldridge's order to the contrary.

"We've got ourselves a little problem here," Robert told him. "Margaret and I were just about to leave, and then you came along. You should have left like Mother told you."

Baldridge was weakening fast, and the weapon in his hand grew heavier, so he joined his grip with his left, struggling to keep his weapon sighted on Van Geer. Who was Margaret? Claire Van Geer stood behind Williamson. Helen Van Geer was the only other person in the room.

"Luke, what's going on here?" Baldridge asked.

"Keep the gun on him, Masey," Williamson replied.

"You'd better drop your weapon, Baldridge," Robert declared, "else Margaret is going to blow a hole in your captain."

"Don't do it, Masey. He'll kill us all for sure," Williamson said.

"Your friend doesn't have to die, Baldridge," Robert said. "All you have to do is drop your gun and let us walk out of here. Nobody has to die."

"Don't believe him. He killed his own father. He won't hesitate to kill us."

"Keep quiet, Captain," Robert said.

"I'll kill him," Margaret declared. "Baldridge, I swear, I'll kill him."

Baldridge had a standoff on his hands. He summoned all his strength to stay on his feet, yet he knew it was only a matter of time before he collapsed. Williamson must have sensed it, too, for he kept encouraging him.

"Hold on, Masey. The police will be here. Hold on," the captain said.

Baldridge could see Williamson's words had brought desperation to Robert Van Geer's eyes, so he tried to hold his hand still, but the weapon began to waver, and his legs felt weak and quavery. He was going down . . . and he knew it. Baldridge hit the floor like a sack of wheat, and his revolver, jarred from his hand by the impact, slid across the floor in the direction of the sofa. But he did not lose consciousness, and he caught a glimpse of Van Geer retrieving his own weapon from the hallway and pointing the pistol at him. "Stop!" Van Geer shouted. "Stop right there!" Baldridge tried to get to his feet, perhaps foolishly under the circumstance, but he was too weak and slumped back onto the floor. "I should have put an end to this a long time ago," Robert said, then cocked the weapon, pointed it at Baldridge's head, and called over to Margaret. "Kill the captain, and let's get out of here."

Baldridge was desperate to stop him, but he could only manage a slow crawl toward Robert, and he prayed that Williamson would make a move, though he knew it might cost him his life. If he didn't, they were dead anyway.

"Luke!" he shouted, but his voice was overwhelmed by that of Helen Van Geer.

"Robert!" she shouted, causing him to stop abruptly as he lowered the weapon toward Baldridge's head.

"Mother?" With shaky hands, Helen stood in front of the sofa, pointing Baldridge's weapon at her son. Robert Van Geer seemed incredulous. "Mother, what are you doing?"

"You are not going to kill these people, son," she said. "You've killed enough." She cocked Baldridge's .45 Long Colt.

Robert grinned. "Mother, put that down. You have no intention of shooting your own son." He called to Margaret. "Let's finish this."

As he turned to regain his aim at Baldridge, Helen Van Geer fired, the round striking her son squarely in the chest and driving him to the floor beneath the table where his father's wooden steamboat models were displayed.

"Robert!" Margaret shouted as she watched him tumble to the floor, clutching his bloody chest. Williamson used the distraction to close the distance to Margaret and wrestle the weapon free from her hand. He grabbed her by her hair and pushed her to the floor, next walking over to Helen Van Geer to take Baldridge's revolver.

Baldridge, still down on the floor himself, watched as Robert tried to drag himself across the floor toward Helen, the smell of fresh blood filling the room and the lamplight illuminating a dark, damp stain in his wake.

"Mother," he mumbled, spittle and blood oozing from his mouth.

She knelt in front of him, her hands cradling his face.

"My son," she said softly. "My poor, poor son."

Fumbling erratically with one hand, Robert grasped the leg of the table holding his father's display and tried one last time to pull himself to his feet; but the table toppled, and the display tumbled down, sending the wooden steamboats crashing to the floor, shattering into pieces that landed all around his body. With Helen sobbing and sitting on the floor, cradling Robert's head in her hands, he tried once more to speak, but instead slumped into death, the paddle wheel from one of his father's wooden models clutched tightly in his hand.

20

Saturday, June 28

THE *PARAGON* HAD arrived in St. Louis late Friday night, docking next to the *Edward Smythe* until the latter departed for New Orleans on Saturday evening. Once the police had arrived at the Hudson Van Geer home Friday night and taken Margaret Doyle into custody, Williamson, Tyner, and Baldridge all returned to the *Paragon*. Before the *Edward Smythe* departed, Williamson asked Captain Martin Cummings to stop at Hardscrabble Landing and replace the detail he had left behind to guard the plantation. Tyner overheard him sending word to Abigail Routh through Cummings that he hoped to follow along in a few days on the *Paragon* to help the Rouths pursue legal action against Tallis, whose role in the fraud at the Boulet Plantation had been made clear to the police by Margaret Doyle. Despite Tyner's good-natured inquiries about his relationship with Abby, Williamson had offered no details, frustrating Tyner considerably.

Tallis's role had become clear after Margaret Doyle was

arrested Friday night. Her pregnancy had been difficult enough, but being pregnant in jail was more than she cared to contemplate. Faced with the choice of spending the rest of her life behind bars for conspiracy to commit murder or telling the truth about Hudson Van Geer's death, Margaret spent the better part of Saturday detailing the plan that she, Robert, and Marie had hatched to kill Van Geer and get control of the family's fortune. When Marie heard that Margaret was talking, she couldn't wait to trade her side of the tale for what leniency the court might offer, so she, too, outlined the conspiracy. After taking their statements on Saturday afternoon, Detective Kenton sat down with Baldridge and Tyner at the Washington Square police station to brief them on the details. He seemed disappointed that Williamson wasn't able to attend his briefing.

"He's got both his boats at the wharf," Tyner said, "so he's got his hands full today."

"And he's as happy as a pig in slop," Baldridge added.

"But Luke sends his regrets, and he says he'll get the full story from us tonight," Tyner said.

Kenton seemed disappointed. "That's too bad. I wish he could have joined us. You know, he did a hell of a job investigating this case. He sure as hell showed me up. And that's doing something, because I'm not often showed up."

"The captain's a good man," Baldridge said. "And for all his complaining about our detective business, I think he gets a kick out of working with us. Don't you think so, Sally?"

"I don't know that I would go that far. But I think this case was important to Luke because of who Hudson Van Geer was."

"What do you mean?" Kenton asked.

"A riverman. I think the captain felt like he owed him something."

"Well, if he did, he's paid in full," Kenton said. "Both women's stories were essentially the same. Your Captain Williamson thought they may have had something to do with the death of Pierre and Anna Boulet, but I don't think so. Both insisted it was simply an accident of which they took advantage. I tend to believe them. No charges there."

"What about Claire Boulet? The *real* Claire Boulet?"

"Both of them claimed, as I suspected they would, that Robert Van Geer was the author of the entire plan to kill Claire and have Margaret assume her identity. They both said that Robert pushed the real Claire Boulet overboard from the *City of Quincy* late one night on the way to to Vicksburg; however, Marie claimed that Margaret drugged her first, and Margaret claimed it had been Marie."

"My money's on this Marie," Baldridge said, rotating his neck. "I *still* ain't feeling a hundred percent yet."

"Both admitted to helping him carry her weighted body down to the deck rail," Kenton added, "but each charged that Robert actually threw her overboard. Can't charge them with murder. I got no body, and both say the other was involved. No witnesses."

"But they helped carry her to the rail," Tyner said.

"Accessory would be all I could charge them with," Kenton said, "and I doubt I could make that stick."

"So far, I haven't heard you charge them with anything," Tyner complained.

"Just bear with me, Miss Tyner. Margaret said that Robert came up with the idea of her assuming Claire's identity and marrying Stewart to eventually get control of his father's fortune, but she denied any hand in the voodoo, citing Marie as the instigator. But it doesn't matter, because you can't charge anyone with putting a curse on somebody."

"There ought to be a law against it," Baldridge declared.

"So are you a believer in all this voodoo business now, Mr. Baldridge?"

"I ain't sayin' I am, and I ain't sayin' I ain't. But something sure kicked the shit out of me, and Stewart Van Geer too. Whatever it was, I don't ever want to face it again."

"It's really quite simple what happened to Stewart Van Geer," Detective Kenton said. "He was drugged."

"Drugged with what?" Baldridge asked.

"The black bottle that Captain Williamson turned over to us—the one he found at Stewart Van Geer's home—contained paregoric. Marie Trehan told us about it, and we had a doctor check it for us. It's true."

"But how?" Baldridge asked.

"The lemonade," Kenton said. "Marie told us that Margaret put it in the lemonade she gave to Stewart the day of the murder."

"Do you believe her?"

"Maybe. Of course, Margaret claims it was Marie. Either way, it explains how they got Stewart Van Geer to the Van Geer home, and why he remembered so little about the killing."

"So Stewart never pulled the trigger?" Baldridge asked.

"No. Marie admits to taking him there, but she says he was pretty well addled from the opium in the paregoric," Kenton explained. "She confirms that Robert killed his father, then they brought Stewart around and placed the gun in his hand. I'm not exactly sure what they said to him, but somehow they convinced him, in his weakened state, that he had pulled the trigger. He made his way to the station, and you two know the rest."

"But Stewart was still out of his head when we interviewed him the first time," Baldridge said.

"Luke thought it had something to do with the lemonade," Tyner said.

"The captain's right again," Kenton agreed. "Margaret and Marie brought the man supper and a pitcher of lemonade every night up until about a week ago—once the verdict was in and they knew Stewart would hang, they stopped coming."

"So they kept him drugged with the lemonade?" Tyner asked.

"That's what Margaret says."

"I told Luke he was drunk," Baldridge said, quite satisfied

with himself. "I told him so." Suddenly puzzled, he added, "But I smelled that lemonade, Kenton. Even tried to get her to give me some. I would have known if anything as strong as paregoric had been added."

"I'm sure you would," Tyner chided.

"That's not what the doctors tell me," Kenton said. "The citrus base of the lemonade cuts the heavy narcotic smell. If the lemonade is strong enough, they say no one would notice the paregoric."

"All right," Tyner said. "That would make sense about Stewart. But what about Masey? Masey never drank any of that concoction. He was never around either of those women long enough for them to drug him."

Kenton shrugged. "I can't explain it. I don't believe in this voodoo business, but . . . the simple truth is that I don't know what made Mr. Baldridge sick. Then again, I'm not a doctor."

"Sally says the doctor didn't know either," Baldridge added.

"Then your guess is as good as mine."

"So what *do* you intend to charge Marie Trehan and Margaret Doyle with?" Tyner asked.

"Conspiracy to commit the murder of Hudson Van Geer, and the attempted murder of your Captain Williamson."

"What about me?" Baldridge asked indignantly. "I had a gun held to my head, too."

"Yes, you did, Mr. Baldridge. But technically, neither of these women did it. And I'm not about to try and charge anybody with assault with a mojo."

Kenton chuckled at his little joke, but Baldridge clearly did not think it funny.

"So, what happens to Stewart?"

"Mr. Stewart Van Geer was released today shortly before noon, just as soon as we had enough information from these two women to clear him of his father's murder."

"And Helen? Masey told me how she shot Robert," Tyner said.

"There will be no charges filed against Mrs. Van Geer."

"What about the man in Louisiana? Tallis?" Tyner asked.

"As to this man Tallis, we have already contacted the authorities by telegraph in Tensas Parish with what information we've been able to develop about Robert Van Geer's land dealings. We're bringing Robert's employer, Mr. Fieldhurst, in to ask him some questions. I think it's fair to say that within a few weeks, perhaps a month, we'll get to the bottom of the fraud case. Then I'm sure there will be other charges against Trehan and Doyle."

SATISFIED THAT THEY had enough information to update Luke Williamson, Tyner and Baldridge returned to the *Paragon* about four Saturday afternoon. As soon as they came on board, and Baldridge had passed Nashville Harry to one of the deckhands, they were met by Jacob Lusk, decked out in his dress uniform.

"The cap'n wants us up in the new office," Lusk told them. "Right away."

They followed Lusk upstairs and found Williamson smoking his pipe and sitting in one of the new chairs recently arrived to furnish the expanded office. Anabel McBree was sitting opposite him, wearing the most elegant dress that Tyner had ever seen on her. Though she was visibly uncomfortable out of her ship's uniform, Tyner walked over to her and complimented her on her clothes.

"Cap'n bought it for me," Anabel said proudly. "He insisted I wear it for the celebration."

"Celebration? What celebration?" Tyner asked.

"Our first real case as the Big River Detective Agency . . . *solved*," Williamson declared. "Now, you two sit down and tell us everything you learned at the police station."

The entire group offered rapt attention as Tyner and

Baldridge filled them in on Kenton's briefing. When they came to the part about Stewart Van Geer being released, Williamson interrupted.

"I already knew he was free."

"How did you know that?" Baldridge asked.

"Because he came by to see me this afternoon," he said. "He said he wanted to thank us for saving his life, and his mother's as well. He is absolutely convinced that his brother would have killed her as he had planned. And—" Williamson said, dragging out his words, "he also . . . left us . . . *this*." He retrieved a small pouch from the drawer of the new lamp table beside his chair.

"What's that?" Baldridge said.

Williamson opened the pouch and fanned out greenback after greenback. "One thousand dollars," he announced, drawing a gasp from Tyner.

"What?" she said, moving to put her hand on the bills. "Luke, are you serious?"

"Stewart Van Geer is one grateful man."

"It's really ours? He really gave it to us?" Tyner said.

"For services rendered," Williamson proudly declared. "He said we should consider it a bonus, but in his opinion, we had more than earned it." A knock at the door preceded two stewards with a rolling cart containing wine and cheese. "Bring it in," Williamson ordered.

Tyner noticed that Anabel stood up instinctively to supervise the service, but Williamson gently put his hand on her shoulder. "Have a seat, Anabel. You and Jacob will be getting served today. It's our way of thanking you for everything you did."

As the stewards uncorked the wine bottles and began moving around the room filling glasses, Baldridge walked over to Anabel.

"I don't know . . . I don't know that I believe in this mojo stuff," Baldridge said. "But Sally and Luke told me what you did for me while I was sick. And whether it was or it wasn't . . . you know, this curse business . . . either way, I want to thank you."

Anabel smiled and shook his hand, as did Jacob, and Baldridge, anxious to change the subject, turned to Williamson.

"I was just wondering, Luke. What do you suppose will happen to that woman's baby?" Baldridge asked. "I mean, if they put her in jail."

"She'll have it in jail."

"Won't the state take custody?" Tyner asked.

"Normally they would. But Stewart Van Geer told me this afternoon that he and his mother have agreed to raise the child."

"Are you sure?" Tyner asked.

"That's what he said."

"That's awfully decent of him," Baldridge said, "given all that's happened."

"That's exactly what I told him. He said it was time a Van Geer did something decent for a change. He's agreed to look after Tewley as well."

"Will Tewley want to go back, though?" Tyner asked.

"Where else would he go?"

"That's a point."

Williamson stood up and invited everyone to bring their wine glasses and file out onto the deck, where he had something to show them. Lining the deck rail, they turned to face him as he stood in the doorway of the new office. Above him was a piece of tarpaulin stretched out to cover a two-by-four-foot area above the door.

Lifting his glass, Williamson proposed a toast. "To the Big River Detective Agency."

Williamson pulled a rope, dropping the tarpaulin to reveal an attractive sign, etched in mahogany, trimmed in silver, and mounted above the door.

Big River Detective Agency
M. Baldridge; S. Tyner; L. Williamson
Detectives

"Welcome to our new office," Williamson added. Tyner gazed at the sign in amazement. Williamson had been the one partner least enthused about forming the business in the first place. All along, she had figured him to pull out first if things didn't go well. He was a man used to success, and she knew he would not long tolerate mediocrity. Apparently, he had tasted enough success to whet his appetite for the business.

"My name's first," Baldridge proudly pointed out.

"Alphabetical," Williamson replied. "Don't get too big for your britches. It's still my boat."

They all laughed.

"It's wonderful, Luke. The office, the sign, everything. It's just wonderful."

"I'm glad you think so. Now if we can just make it work."

"Oh, it's gonna work, Luke," Baldridge said. He extended his glass for a toast. "Because we're gonna be the best."

The celebration continued for another half hour, with Baldridge imbibing with uncharacteristic restraint, and with Williamson sharing his concern that the law follow up on Tallis and the fraudulent purchase of Boulet Plantation. He told Tyner that if the land had been sold illegally, it might well go into receivership, making it possible for some of the negro share-croppers to buy a piece of it after all. When he told her he planned to go back to Hardscrabble and personally see to the matter, Tyner challenged him.

"Why is it that I get the distinct impression that land fraud isn't the only reason you want to return to Hardscrabble?"

"Well, there's the Rouths. I want to be sure they're out of danger."

"But if Tallis is arrested, they should be safe."

"Well—"

She could tell the conversation made Williamson nervous, and she was loving every moment of it.

"Come on, Luke. Why don't you just admit it? You're going back to see that Abby woman."

"You never know, Sally. You just never know."